Jenni Fletcher was born in the north of Scotland and now lives in Yorkshire, with her husband and two children. She wanted to be a writer as a child, but got distracted by reading instead, finally getting past her first paragraph thirty years later. She's had more jobs than she can remember, but has finally found one she loves. She can be contacted on Twitter @JenniAuthor or via her Facebook Author page.

A MARRIAGE MADE IN SECRET

Jenni Fletcher

MILLS & BOON

First Published in Great Britain 2021
by Mills & Boon, an imprint of HarperCollins*Publishers* Ltd,
1 London Bridge Street, London, SE1 9GF

www.harpercollins.co.uk

HarperCollins*Publishers*
1st Floor, Watermarque Building,
Ringsend Road, Dublin 4, Ireland

A Marriage Made in Secret © 2021 Jenni Fletcher

ISBN: 978-0-263-28407-2

06/21

MIX
Paper from
responsible sources
FSC® C007454

To the best trio of lockdown buddies
I could ever have wanted.

Chapter One

Palace of Vincennes, France
—summer 1325

'Your Grace!'

Mathilde jumped to her feet in alarm as a boy burst like a small, grinning assassin into the Queen's withdrawing chamber, provoking a chorus of muffled screams from the gathered ladies. If they'd been in London, she thought, he would have been dragged straight to the Tower for causing such a commotion, but fortunately for him, they were a long way from England, in a palace to the east of Paris on a rainy and uneventful afternoon.

The boy's cheeks were red and he was panting, but his face was alive with excitement, as if he knew that his intrusion would be a welcome one. To the surprise of almost everyone in the room, he was right. He didn't say another word, simply dropped down on to one knee, yet Queen Isabella lifted her gaze from the gilt-edged book of Arthurian tales she was reading and smiled.

Isabella, born a Princess of France and now the crowned Queen of England, smiled. Not a slight regal curve of her lips for once either, but a real, rare smile that transformed her whole face and sparked a fiery light in her usually impenetrable blue eyes.

Mathilde watched, enthralled. The first time she'd set eyes on the Queen, she'd thought her the most beautiful woman in the world, but at that moment she surpassed even herself, like a lily opening its petals in sunshine, emerging from a bud of passive prettiness into confident, blazing beauty. As Isabella rose imperiously to her feet, the effect seemed to become even more pronounced, the folds of her pale yellow surcoat catching the light from the dozens of candles around her so that they shone like molten gold. It was impossible *not* to stare at someone so dazzling.

'Madame Baudin has arrived?' Isabella arched one slender eyebrow and the messenger nodded, still panting from his exertions. 'Good.'

She waved her fingers in a gesture of dismissal. 'You may wait outside.'

The boy backed out of the room and the Queen's eyes turned speculatively in Mathilde's direction, narrowing slightly. 'You. Your name is Mathilde, is it not?'

'Yes, Your Grace.' Nervously, she dipped into a curtsy, dropping her embroidery in the process. In two months, the Queen had barely acknowledged her presence, let alone used her name, treating her with the same resentful disdain she reserved for all her newer attendants. Mathilde couldn't entirely blame her. They were only there because the King had locked up her loyal French ladies-in-waiting and replaced them with his English spies, but *she* at least wasn't a spy. She was a nobody, the daughter of a man to whom the King had owed a favour, that was all, a last-minute addition to Isabella's retinue before she'd embarked upon her diplomatic mission to France. *She* was new and young, as the other ladies never ceased to remind her. Obscure and impoverished, too, their tone suggested, which was true even if she couldn't help it. Her family weren't important or rich or even particularly noble, but her father's past loyalty had been enough to secure her a position at court. It was a great honour, one she wished every day had been bestowed upon somebody else.

'Come closer.' The Queen lifted one elegantly manicured hand, beckoning her forward, and she obeyed at once. Out of the corner of her eye, she saw Lady Berthe, chief of the spies, move as if to join them, before Isabella stilled her with a sharp look.

'Cecily?' The sharpness softened as the Queen called out to one of her older English attendants, the ones who'd joined her household when she'd first arrived in London as a young bride seventeen years earlier. There were only two of them remaining, Lady Cecily d'Abernon and Katharine Sykes, and both were fiercely protective.

'Yes, Your Grace?' Lady Cecily bobbed into a curtsy.

'I want to wear my lilac gown tonight, the one with the silver trim, but I'm afraid there's a tear in one of the sleeves.'

'I believe you are right, Your Grace.' Whether it was right or wrong, Lady Cecily's face was a picture of innocence. 'In fact, there are several items in your wardrobe that require attention. We have time to do some mending now, if Your Grace would excuse us?'

'Of course.' Isabella inclined her head as

if she were conferring some great favour.
'Mathilde here will stay and keep me company.
Kat, too.'

Lady Cecily curtsied again, bustling the spies
out of the chamber before they had a chance to
think up excuses to stay.

'That's better.' The Queen waited until the
door was completely closed before letting out
a long sigh, as if she'd been holding her breath.
'How old are you, Mathilde?'

'Seventeen, Your Grace.'

'So old? And with such pretty eyes. Yet still
unmarried?'

'Yes, Your Grace.' She blushed, pleased with
the compliment despite the sting in its tail. Her
sister Hawise had always said that her eyes
were her best feature, a deep, dark brown like
their mother's had been, though as for the rest
of her, she knew that she was ordinary. Pretty
enough, but no great beauty and without any
dowry. *That* was why she remained unmarried.
Why she'd been sent to court, too, or one of the
reasons anyway. At home she'd been surplus to
requirements whereas here she could earn her
own keep.

'You need not look so embarrassed. There
are worse things than remaining unmarried, is
that not so, Kat?' Isabella exchanged a know-

ing look with the widowed Katharine, who only grunted. 'Tell me, which would you prefer, a bad husband or no husband at all?'

Mathilde hesitated, baulking at the question. It wasn't one she'd ever had cause to consider before, but the Queen was waiting expectantly, the full penetrating force of her blue gaze focused upon her. 'I think no husband at all, Your Grace.'

'Then you may be just the girl I'm looking for.' Isabella's expression warmed. 'You hail from the north of England, as I recall?'

'Yes, Your Grace. From Rudstone Manor near Scarborough.'

'Ah, now I remember. Your father helped my husband during the rebellion.'

'He did.' She nodded eagerly. After fourteen years, her father still seized any opportunity to talk about the day the second King Edward had ridden into their courtyard, fleeing from Thomas of Lancaster's forces. 'He gave him food and fresh horses and then rode to York beside him. He always says it was the greatest honour of his life.'

'As it was…at the time.' A shadow of some emotion crossed the Queen's face, so fleetingly it was impossible to identify. Impatience? Annoyance? Mathilde dropped her gaze to the rug, afraid that she'd said something displeasing. 'So now my husband has repaid him by giving you a place in my household?'

'Yes, Your Grace. My father brought me to London to ask it.' And then abandoned her there, she thought bitterly, biting her tongue to stop herself from saying the words out loud.

'So you have no other connection to the King…or his friends?'

'None, Your Grace,' she answered with complete honesty. She'd only glimpsed the King from a distance and she knew nothing of his friends.

'Good. What do you think, Kat? Is she trustworthy?'

'If she's not, then she'll answer to me.'

'I am, Your Grace,' Mathilde countered at once, indignant at any suggestion otherwise.

'I believe you, girl.'

Isabella's tone was soothing and for the first time since leaving her family, Mathilde felt a sense of kinship with someone. No, she corrected herself quickly, that was the wrong word. She could never be kin with the Queen, but somehow the words made her feel less isolated.

'Come over here.' Isabella sat down in a window seat, as far away from the door as possible, laying a hand on the maroon velvet cushion beside her.

'Thank you, Your Grace.' Mathilde threw a quick glance at Katharine, who had her arms folded across her chest like a sentinel, before obeying, her heart thumping with excitement even as her knees shook with nerves. She was glad to sit down before they gave way altogether, although it felt strange to sit so close to someone as extraordinary as the Queen. As women, they were only thirteen years apart, but Isabella was everything she knew that she would never, *could never*, be.

'I have a request to make of you, Mathilde, one that must remain a secret between us.' Isabella paused significantly. 'I need someone like you to carry messages for me. Cecily has been unwell of late and Kat cannot walk as far or fast as she once did.' She pressed her lips together as Katharine made a loud tsking sound from across the room. 'Do you think you could help me, Mathilde?'

'I would be honoured, Your Grace.'

'I thought so.' Isabella pulled a ruby and gold ring from her finger. 'I knew that you weren't like the rest of them. Here, hold out your hand.'

Mathilde gasped as the Queen placed the sparkling band in the centre of her palm. It looked valuable, probably equivalent to several years' worth of harvests at home.

'Now, the boy will take you to someone, a guest. Show him this ring and tell him to meet me in the French King's private apartments at once.'

'Yes, Your Grace, but...' Mathilde drew her brows together. The boy had spoken of a Madame Baudin...

'A necessary deception.' Isabella seemed to understand her confusion, throwing a telling glance in the direction of her dressing chamber. 'When the others ask, which they will, tell them that an old nurse from my childhood has come to visit me. It doesn't matter whether or not they believe it. All that matters is that they do not discover the truth. This must be *our* secret, do you understand?'

'Yes, Your Grace.'

'Thank you.' The Queen touched a hand to her cheek. There was something almost maternal about the gesture, Mathilde thought, a tenderness that made her heart glow. 'Remember to trust no one except myself, Katharine or Lady Cecily.'

Mathilde nodded and stood, dipping into another curtsy without asking for any more details. The identity of the guest was none of her business and the dour expression on Katharine's face warned her not to pry. In truth, she didn't care who it was. Isabella, her Queen, had touched her cheek and asked for her help. That was all that mattered now.

Chapter Two

'Show him this ring...' Mathilde repeated the instructions under her breath as she followed the boy down a winding staircase and along a series of dimly lit corridors, then through a courtyard and along even more corridors. They were almost running, but her feet still felt too slow, unable to keep up with her whirling emotions. She had a suspicion that something important was happening, something momentous and clandestine. She had no idea what it was, but more than anything at that moment she wanted the Queen to approve of her. If she couldn't prove her worth through beauty or fortune, then she would prove it through steadfastness and loyalty instead.

The spies would pay her a fortune to tell them about this, she thought with a twinge of smugness. Not that she intended to. She wasn't included in their hushed conversations, but she knew they sent regular letters back to England, reporting on all of the Queen's dealings: whom she met, whom she spent time with, what they talked about and for how long. Personally, she couldn't see what her mistress had done to deserve such treatment, but they seemed to take pride in being thorough. It wasn't something that she wanted to be a part of.

Her steps slowed as they ventured into an area of the castle she'd never visited before, part of the original building judging by the aged look of the stone, far away from the splendour of the great hall and royal apartments. Whoever the Queen's guest was, it was becoming increasingly obvious that they wished to remain unnoticed. It was quieter and darker here, too, with few windows and fewer attendants, none at all after a few minutes, so that, despite her resolve, Mathilde couldn't repress a shiver of unease.

The boy passed her a lantern he must have put aside ready and she gripped the handle tightly, her anxiety growing the further along the corridor they went, as if she'd started along a dangerous road and had no idea how to find her way back. For a moment, her nerves faltered and she wished herself back in the safety of the Queen's rooms and beneath her notice again, but it was only briefly before she berated her-

self for cowardice. She wasn't going to fail in
her mission when it had barely begun.

At last they stopped outside an oak door so
thick and solid looking she thought it might require a battering ram to open. It would certainly
be impossible to hear through it if anyone were
tempted to eavesdrop. The boy knocked and
then, before she could tell him to wait, before
she even had a moment to gather her wits, he
scampered off, running back the way that they'd
come. Panicking, Mathilde opened her mouth
to recall him, but it was already too late. There
was a harsh, scraping sound as a bolt was drawn
back and the door swung halfway open.

'Yes?' The shadowy outline of a man appeared in the doorway.

'I…' She faltered, the strangeness of the situation making her tongue-tied as she lifted her lantern to get a better look at the speaker. He was
tall and lean and appeared to be no more than a
couple of years older than she was, but the se-
verity of his expression made her feel younger
and more insignificant than ever. Even frowning, however, he was arrestingly handsome, with
sharp cheekbones, a square jaw covered in bris-
tles, and features that appeared to have been
chiselled out of granite. He held himself with an
air of confidence, too, though his clothes were

crumpled and mud-spattered as if he'd been travelling, and his hair was ruffled, tumbling over his forehead in dark curls. It was almost black, she noticed, a deeper shade of brown than her own, but whereas her eyes were a similar colour, his were a glacial shade of blue, pale and piercing even in the gloom of the corridor.

'Can I help you, lady?' He sounded suspicious as if he, like Katharine, thought that she couldn't be trusted, blocking the half-open doorway with his body so that she couldn't see past.

'Sir.' She didn't know whether or not to curtsy so she dipped halfway down as a compromise, licking her lips to loosen them as she held up the ring. 'The Queen bid me show you this and to request that you meet her in the French King's private chambers.'

'Not me, I think.'

The frown fell away, his mouth quirking as he turned his head to speak to someone else in the room, presenting her with a clear view of his back. Mathilde glared at it, resenting the amusement at her expense. She might be a nobody, but she'd been sent by the Queen and he ought to show some respect.

At last he finished speaking and opened the door wider, as if deciding to trust her, after all, propping one shoulder against the stone archway as his gaze dropped down to her feet and then meandered slowly upwards again.

'We haven't met before, lady.'

A roguish half-smile played about his mouth and Mathilde's resentment increased tenfold. It was a statement, not a question, and she didn't know how to respond. The way he spoke implied that he ought to have met her, as if he were familiar with all of the ladies in the Queen's household, but his scrutiny made her uncomfortable. She wasn't used to being looked at in such a manner. She simply wasn't used to being looked at. Most men's gazes passed over her and moved on. *His* suggested that he was committing every inch of her body to memory.

'No.' She tossed her head to hide her embarrassment, but his smile only grew wider. It made the ice in his eyes melt a little, drawing attention to the long curly black lashes around them. She resented those, too.

'I didn't think so. I would have remembered.' A single dark brow rose upwards. 'You needn't look so nervous. I don't bite.'

'I'm not nervous,' she retorted, irritated that he could read her so easily. She needed to learn how to guard her expression, but such a thing was easier said than done. There were so many aspects of court life that she hadn't yet mastered, deceiving others chief among them. It was a skill that she needed to learn, and quickly!

'Ah, my mistake.' His voice was laced with scepticism. 'Then tell me your name.'

'My name?' She tensed, pressing her lips together in a thin line. The Queen had told her not to trust anyone and even if she hadn't, Mathilde didn't want to tell this man anything. She didn't want to be there at all, having this conversation. His pale gaze seemed to be having a strange, disruptive effect on her breathing, making her chest feel constricted and her heart thud in a way she'd never felt before, as if it were actually pressing against her ribs. 'I hardly know you well enough to share it, sir.' She gave him a haughty look, mimicking Katharine's disdainful tone whenever she spoke to the spies.

'Very wise.' He leaned forward slightly, his voice deepening. 'But then how are we to become friends?'

'Why would I want to become friends?' She took a hasty step backwards. 'I ought to go.'

'Then we can walk together.'

'*No!* That is, we probably shouldn't be seen together.'

'But then who will lead the way to the French King's chambers?'

He pushed himself upright, looking very tall and broad-shouldered suddenly, and she felt a fresh jolt of panic. She was anxious enough about finding her own way back through the maze of corridors, but she didn't want to start leading the Queen's guest in circles as well. Was she supposed to accompany him? *Them?* Isabella hadn't said either way. She had the vague suspicion that she was being toyed with on purpose, but before she could challenge him the door was pulled wide and another, older man appeared on the threshold.

This, she presumed, was the Queen's real guest, though she still had no idea who he was. He carried himself like a lord, but his clothes were plain, without any crest or insignia, nothing to make his identity obvious. He had a hood pulled over his head, too, though in the glow of the lamplight she spied thick brows, a neatly trimmed beard, and the same black and blue colouring as her tormentor. This man's features, however, were marred by an expression of arrogance. He gave a tight smile when he spied the ring in her hand and she stepped aside quickly, losing her voice all over again.

'Now you'll *have* to come with us.' Her young tormentor leaned close to murmur in her ear and her stomach jumped and immediately started tying itself in knots. It wasn't that she'd never been whispered to before. With three brothers and one sister she was accustomed to childish confidences, but this felt different. She'd never stood so close to a man who wasn't a relation before and the sudden warmth of his breath on her neck, exposed by her long braid, made her feel strangely dizzy, as if she'd been dancing for too long. The sensation wasn't entirely unpleasant, but she didn't want it, not here, not now and definitely not in front of these men, whoever they were. She only hoped that it passed before they reached the Queen. There was something about Isabella that made Mathilde think she could see everything.

'Allow me.' He reached a hand out for the lantern and she almost dropped it, letting go of the handle as his fingers brushed against hers. Fortunately he was quick, catching it in midair so smoothly that the tallow candle inside barely flickered.

She twisted her face away, enraged by the sight of his silent laughter. If he'd been one of her younger brothers, Laurent or Dicun or even Aland, she would have kicked him in the shins in retaliation, but common sense prevailed over temper. Tempted though she was to inflict some kind of painful injury, for all she knew he might be a baron.

Thankfully, she wasn't needed as a guide, after all. Despite his earlier taunt, her tormentor clearly knew his way around the castle, leading them in tense-sounding silence towards the royal apartments. Two others accompanied them, guards if their fearsome appearance was anything to judge by, although as far as she could see, they didn't carry weapons. To do so inside the King's palace would have been an unpardonable insult and these men obviously knew better.

Mathilde kept pace uncertainly, half of her wondering whether she ought to excuse herself and make her way back to the Queen's rooms, the other half too curious to break away. She had a feeling that she was heading even further down the dangerous path, but she still couldn't turn back, as if she were being pulled by some invisible but compelling force. Not for the first time, she wished that her father had better prepared her for life at court, but then he'd never been at court himself to learn the rules. All he'd ever told her was to be modest and respectful and dutiful, all of which she was, but she still felt hopelessly out of her depth. Time and again, she overheard whispers and hints of scandal, along with a name, Despenser, and understood none of it. Maybe this was finally her chance to learn...

A page opened the door as they approached the French King's apartments and Mathilde peered through, surprised to catch a glimpse of Isabella standing inside. She hadn't expected to see her there so soon, not to mention so close to the entrance after all her insistence on secrecy, but the Queen's expression was eager, excited almost. As her eyes fell on her guest she smiled the same breathtaking smile from earlier, but this time, Mathilde wasn't dazzled. This time there was something unsettling about it. It seemed too personal, too intimate, too triumphant almost, not the kind of smile a woman ought to give to a man who wasn't her husband.

Mathilde stopped just outside the door, seized with the sudden instinct to retreat as the Queen's guest pulled his hood back and strode purposefully into the apartment. The younger man followed, glancing over his shoulder as if to weigh her reaction, but there was no mockery in his eyes now. On the contrary, he looked almost sympathetic, his pale gaze darker and full of shadows, as if he regretted making her accompany them, after all. His expression told her that he'd seen the Queen's smile, too, only perhaps, unlike her, he knew what it meant.

'My thanks for the escort.' He spoke as if he'd really needed her help to find the way, holding the lantern out in such a manner that there was no risk of their fingers touching again. 'Don't get lost on the way back.'

She nodded, although she didn't answer. Instead she turned on her heel and walked away, resolving to forget that the last few moments had ever happened. As for her handsome tormentor, she never wanted to see him again in her life.

Henry watched as the girl retreated along the corridor, the lantern in her hand casting a faint glow of light around her slender figure and adding fiery red lights to her long, chestnut-coloured hair. He'd been suspicious of her at first—it was his job to be wary—but he'd swiftly concluded that those beautiful brown eyes—surely the biggest he'd ever seen?—were incapable of duplicity. In a court full of intrigue and ambition, there was something refreshingly clear and honest about them. They were luminous, without any hint of cynicism or calculation. He'd liked them. He'd liked her. It wasn't often that he trusted people, and never at first acquaintance, but if she'd been putting on an air of innocence then it was the best act he'd ever seen.

He'd been unable to resist teasing her, although in his defence he hadn't expected her to take his words so seriously. Most ladies of the court wouldn't have. Most would have teased him back, fluttering their eyelashes and sliding their hands to their hips for good measure. But then most wouldn't have been dressed in such old-fashioned garments either, looking as if they'd just emerged from some country backwater instead of the Queen's household. Who was she? And why would Isabella trust someone so young and obviously inexperienced? The girl had looked genuinely shocked by the sight of the Queen's smile for his master, as if she hadn't known what to make of it. As if she wished she hadn't seen it at all. Which she wouldn't have if *he* hadn't cajoled her into accompanying them.

Still, he was being punished for that mistake now. He could have stayed behind in their rooms, enjoying a well-earned nap after the long ride from Hainault, but instead he'd seized the opportunity of walking alongside the girl and now he was stuck here, discreetly trying to ignore the reunion taking place behind him.

He went to stand by a window, grimacing at the sight of sunshine illuminating the tops of the lime trees outside. *Of course* it would stop raining now that they'd finally arrived, after eight long hours in the saddle feeling like drowned rats.

'No sign of the Queen's brother.' Fitz, one of the Flemish bodyguards, came to stand beside him, speaking in an undertone. 'Our French King has made himself scarce, eh?'

'Perhaps he's been delayed.' Henry murmured noncommittally.

'Or perhaps he didn't want to interrupt a tryst?' Fitz smirked. 'How long will we be staying this time?'

'Not long. A day at the most.'

'You know there are still rumours despite all this secrecy.' Fitz jerked his head as a door closed on the other side of the room. 'She plays a dangerous game, your Queen. The English King will hear of his wife's behaviour sooner or later.'

'Probably.' Henry turned his face back to the window with a shrug. No doubt Edward *would* hear, but he still wouldn't believe it. That was his problem, never believing that anyone would dare to disobey him. Despite an almost successful rebellion against him, despite years of disquiet and unrest, despite all of the evidence staring him in the face, he would never believe it, expecting everyone to obey his rule no matter how badly he treated them, nor how greedily he behaved or how many promises he broke.

It was a kind of blindness, that lack of imagination. It would be his downfall. Sooner rather than later if his own master, not to mention the Queen, had their way. Then perhaps England would be a fairer country, a place where a man—*any man*—could earn position and fortune through ability and hard work instead of simply birthright, where even an illegitimate bastard like him could become someone of consequence.

A small brown-feathered dunnock landed on the ledge outside the window, its neat, unobtrusive appearance reminding him of the girl. His life was far too hectic and unsettled for him to spare much thought for women in general, but something about *her* intrigued him. Her face was perfectly clear in his memory. A pleasing one, round and lightly sun-bronzed, with a faint scattering of freckles across the bridge of her nose, but far too open, as if her eyes truly were the window into her soul. He wondered if she knew what she was involved in. He strongly suspected not. For her sake, he hoped the Queen didn't use her as an intermediary again. For his own, he willed their paths to cross a second time and then…well then, at the very least, he'd find out her name.

Chapter Three

Autumn 1325

Mathilde was in the palace kitchens before Prime, collecting a bowl of stewed fruit for the Queen to break her fast. The task meant that she was up earlier than the other attendants, but she didn't mind. The French palace was a busy place, filled with bustle and noise most of the time, but at dawn she could wander quietly through the courtyards, enjoying the scent of the herb gardens and the sweet, clean taste of the air. It was one of the few times in the day when she could enjoy a few moments of peace.

She stopped in the middle of one courtyard and drew in a deep breath, letting the scents of lavender, thyme and rosemary fill her nostrils and transport her back to her home in Yorkshire. Such moments were bittersweet, though her life at court had improved immeasurably over the past few months. Isabella wasn't cold and remote any longer, but treated her like a trusted, even valued, member of her inner circle. Homesick and heartsore though she still was on occasion, Mathilde no longer felt so alone.

Alone. The word sent a prickle of awareness down her spine. She hadn't noticed it at first, but now she could sense a pair of eyes watching her, though it took her a few moments to actually locate the source, standing only a few feet ahead, half-hidden behind one of the courtyard pillars, twining a stem of lavender idly between his fingertips.

Her breath hitched in surprise. She recognised him immediately although four months had passed since their first and last meeting and there had been no sign of him and thankfully no more subterfuge since. She'd assumed that he'd left the French court, so what was he doing here again now? He looked almost exactly the same as she remembered, dressed in a plain dark tunic as if he were still trying to attract as little attention as possible, with his curly hair hanging in the same careless way over his forehead. Only his eyes were different. Warmer and less wintry, although it might have been—it surely *was*—a trick of the light.

'I thought it was you.' He smiled and advanced towards her with the slow yet deliberate steps of a cat. 'The Queen's mysterious ring bearer. Can we be friends yet, lady, or are you still afraid I might bite?'

'No!' She turned sharply towards a door on a different side of the courtyard. If she'd been remotely pleased to see him, to find that he remembered her, too, then she wasn't any more. She certainly wasn't going to stand there and let him mock her again.

'Forgive me.' His teasing tone dropped away as he fell into step alongside her. 'We got off to a bad start. I was tired that day and my behaviour wasn't what it ought to have been. I apologise.'

'Very well.' Her steps didn't falter.

'Very well?' he echoed. 'Does that mean you forgive me?'

'We are instructed to forgive and so I do.' She threw him a swift sideways look. 'That doesn't mean we can be friends.'

'Just tell me your name, then.' He put a hand out to slow her down, but she veered away, curving her footsteps around him. 'Mine's Henry.'

'I didn't ask.' She was as severe as she knew how to be, but he only laughed.

'You're finally learning court ways then?

Good. I was afraid there was too much of the country in you when we last met.'

She ignored everything her father had ever told her about manners and modest behaviour and glared over her shoulder, barely resisting the urge to make one of the unladylike gestures her brothers had taught her for good measure. His words were less an expression of concern than an insult, a way of saying that he'd found her ignorant and naive that day. Both of those things might have been true—they probably still were—but she preferred not to be reminded of the fact. She already stood out too much among the Queen's more sophisticated ladies, like a goose in a flock of elegant swans.

'Henry Wright!' he called after her. 'Of Ludlow!'

She kept walking despite her surprise. *Just* Henry Wright, without any title? Perhaps he wasn't of particularly noble birth then, perhaps even less than she was, though she refused to gratify him by showing an interest. She didn't want to be seen talking to him alone either, especially when the castle was so quiet. To a stray observer it might look like a tryst and she knew that the Queen would be displeased if she heard of it.

She hurried back to Isabella's rooms, almost spilling the fruit in her haste, to find her mistress already sitting up against her pillows, her golden hair tumbling in lustrous, shining waves about her shoulders.

'Ah, there you are.' Isabella smiled a welcome and Mathilde felt her spirits lift immediately. She was no longer taken aback by the Queen's smiles. Over the past few months they'd become more and more frequent, so that now the only surprise was that she bestowed them on someone like her. The Queen didn't seem to care where she came from, nor that her accent, according to Lady Berthe, was that of a northern peasant. No matter what she herself might have witnessed, or what the spies said—and they muttered more and more the longer they stayed in France—Mathilde refused to think any ill of her.

'It's a beautiful morning, is it not?' Isabella gestured towards her open window shutters.

'It is, Your Grace.' She passed her the bowl on a tray. 'Mild, too. I forgot to take my mantle, but I hardly felt any chill.'

She clamped her mouth shut abruptly, realising that a simple yes would have sufficed, but Isabella only heaved a satisfied-sounding sigh.

'A propitious day, then. My son will be preparing to sail from England and I must make ready to meet him.' Her expression turned thoughtful. 'Perhaps you need a new mantle? Something special so that you will not forget it again.'

Mathilde dropped her gaze quickly. Being scrutinised by someone so beautiful was hard, making her feel even more ordinary.

'Red will become you, I think.' Isabella nodded with conviction before waving a hand at Lady Berthe. 'Give her my red cloak with the velvet hood.'

'Your Grace?' Mathilde lifted her hands in protest. 'I could not...'

'You can when your Queen commands it.' Isabella's tone wasn't threatening, but her words were final none the less. 'Berthe will have to remove the ermine, of course, but it should suit you very well. You deserve a gift and I need all of my ladies to look their best.'

'Thank you, Your Grace.' Mathilde bowed her head, suspecting that her cheeks were already a similar colour to the cloak, recognising the words as a veiled reference to her wardrobe, to the old linen kirtles and woollen gowns that had once belonged to her mother. They were the best that her father had been able to provide, but they were hopelessly old-fashioned by now and threadbare in places despite all her mending.

'I shall wear red this morning, too, for good

fortune.' Isabella's perfect cheekbones rounded with a smile that made her more impossibly beautiful than ever. 'This is an important time for me, Mathilde. We all need to make ready.'

Lady Cecily gave her the cloak later that afternoon, presumably because Lady Berthe couldn't bring herself to hand over something so fine to a person like her, Mathilde thought, although she was too pleased with the gift to care. She could have spent hours simply rubbing her cheek lovingly against the fabric. The woollen exterior was lined with velvet, ten times more luxurious than anything she'd ever worn before in her life.

'I have a green surcoat you can borrow this evening, too, if you like?' Cecily offered, leading her into a side chamber away from the spies. Her manner had also thawed considerably over the summer months, so much so that now Mathilde regarded both her and Katharine as friends. Family even, like a pair of older aunts. 'We're of a similar height so it should only need a few adjustments and the Queen has put aside some linen for you to make a few new dresses, too.' She squeezed her arm sympathetically. 'She does not mean it as an insult, rather as a gift for your service.'

'Thank you.' Mathilde smiled, torn between gratitude and embarrassment.

'Was this your mother's?' Cecily gestured at the gown she was currently wearing. 'I remember the style.'

'Yes. It was one of her favourites, but she has no more use for it.' She coughed and smoothed her hand awkwardly over the skirts. That was all she could say, all she could ever say about her mother. Sometimes she wished that she could speak about her more, but even after six years her feelings were too raw, like a festering wound that refused to heal. Sometimes she thought it had scabbed over, but then the scar came away and the pain and guilt were still as fresh and searing as ever.

'I see.' Cecily nodded with a look of understanding. 'Well, perhaps I can do your hair tonight, too?'

'I'm not sure...' Mathilde touched a hand to her head self-consciously. She'd worn her hair in the same style every day for the past five years, in a single braid over one shoulder. 'My father said that I ought to be modest.'

'As you shall be, but modest does not mean always looking the same. You can wear ribbons at least. Green ones to match the gown—'

'Red,' Katharine interrupted from where she

was sitting beside the fireplace sewing pearls on to a bodice. 'The Queen's right, she'll suit red. It will make a nice contrast with the green.'

'Maybe both?' Cecily walked across to a small chest and started rummaging inside.

Mathilde sat down on a coffer, excited by the idea of a new surcoat that evening, even a borrowed one. At home they'd never been able to afford pretty things and it was rumoured that the feast planned to celebrate the Queen's departure for Boulogne, where she was travelling to greet her eldest son Edward, was going to be more spectacular than ever. Hopefully it would also signal the beginning of the end of their stay in France. Isabella had said that the Prince was coming to pay homage to Gascony on her husband's behalf, but she'd still made no mention of returning to England afterwards and the uncertainty was making Mathilde even more homesick.

'Lady Cecily…' She took advantage of the relaxed mood to ask, 'Do you think we'll be going back to England again soon?'

'Going back?' Cecily's hand wavered as she drew a length of ribbon from the chest. 'I don't know.'

'But we've been here for six months now.

Surely the Queen wishes to return to her husband?'

'Some questions are better left unasked.' Cecily closed the lid softly. 'And some answers are better left unspoken.'

Mathilde sighed inwardly. She'd turned eighteen over the summer, but everyone here still treated her like a child.

'We should tell her.' To her surprise, it was Katharine who interceded on her behalf. 'Since she's caught in this web with us now, too.'

Web? Mathilde looked around the room, struck with a sudden image of the three of them all wrapped up together in silken spider's threads.

'We shouldn't involve her.'

Cecily's voice was firm, but Katharine ignored her, putting her sewing aside and rising ominously to her feet. She was a proud-looking woman, grey-haired, gaunt and unswervingly severe.

'Maybe we should let her decide whether or not she wants to know the truth?'

Katharine fixed her with a hard stare and Mathilde hesitated, wondering if perhaps Cecily was right and she'd rather *not* know. The dangerous path she'd envisaged four months ago loomed before her again, dark and forbidding, only this time with a fork in it, a route of escape if she chose to take it.

'Kat...' Cecily attempted another warning, but Katharine only jerked her head in the direction of the Queen's withdrawing chamber where the spies were all gathered.

'Why not? We know that she isn't one of them. She's proved that she can keep her mouth shut. Now, which do you prefer, girl, truth or ignorance?'

Mathilde straightened her spine. Put like that, there was only one answer. 'I want the truth.'

'Good. Then tell me, what do you think of a husband, a king, who delights in humiliating his wife, who gives away her fortune to his favourites, who ignores her wishes and threatens her very safety?'

'Kat!' Cecily's tone was admonishing. 'Stop it.'

'Stop what? She said she wanted to know.'

'I do.' Mathilde swallowed, determined to prove her worldliness, no matter how shocked she was by the words.

'What Kat's trying to say is that the King made the Queen's life in England a misery,' Cecily explained in a softer voice. 'While she remains in France, she's safe and treated with respect, even if we have to live with his spies.'

'You mean the Queen doesn't *want* to go back to England?' Now she felt truly shocked. Frightened, too. England was her home, her country, but if Isabella didn't go back then neither would she.

'Not unless he changes his behaviour towards her, no.' Cecily seemed to be avoiding her gaze.

'Pah!' Katharine gave a snort of contempt. 'How many opportunities does the fool need?'

Mathilde sucked in a breath. To call the King a fool was treason, but Katharine looked unrepentant.

'Tell me, girl, what do you know about Roger Mortimer? Do you know who he is?'

Mortimer? She searched her memory, surprised by the apparent change of subject. There was something familiar about the name. She'd heard her father speak of him once…

'Yes!' She sat up straighter, pleased to find something she *did* know. 'Roger Mortimer of Wigmore! He was imprisoned for rebelling against the King when—'

She stopped mid-sentence. If she remembered correctly, Mortimer was one of the Marcher lords and the stronghold of the Mortimer family was Ludlow Castle and…

Henry Wright of Ludlow.

The truth dawned as if a candle had suddenly

flared to life in front of her eyes. 'He was the man who visited the Queen in secret!'

'Very good.'

'But I thought he was sentenced to execution. Did the King pardon him?'

'Ha!' Katharine threw her head back scornfully. 'He escaped. He found himself an accomplice, drugged his guards, climbed a chimney, scaled a rope ladder and then rowed away to safety. Mortimer escaped from the Tower, the very bastion of royal power, humiliating the King in the process. Believe me, he'll never be pardoned now. That's why he's in exile.'

'But then why did he come here?' Mathilde drew her brows together, feeling hopelessly confused all over again. Why would the Queen meet secretly with a traitor? And what did that make Henry Wright, the man she'd been talking to, who she'd *almost* been excited to see, just that morning?

'Can't you guess?' Katharine leaned closer as if she were trying to gauge her every reaction.

Mathilde shook her head, unwilling to try. Any answer seemed tantamount to treason, but the intensity of Katharine's expression demanded one. A memory of the way Isabella had smiled at Mortimer flitted into her mind before she pushed it quickly away again. 'I don't know.'

'Good!' Cecily placed an arm around her shoulders. 'Our place is to serve the Queen, not to question her behaviour. We ought not to have opinions about it.'

'But we *do*, don't we?' Katharine's eyes flashed belligerently.

Cecily squeezed Mathilde tighter as if she still wished to protect her, though she didn't interrupt as Katharine started speaking again.

'The Queen believes that the time has come for her to make a stand.'

'Against the King?' Mathilde was so shocked that for a moment she thought she must have misheard. 'With a traitor?'

'Mortimer's only a traitor because he stood up against Hugh le Despenser, the King's favourite.' Katharine's tone made it clear where her own sympathies lay. 'In most English eyes, that makes him a hero.'

'But what kind of stand? What does she plan to do?'

'Nothing's certain yet, but once her son lands on French soil, Isabella has a weapon.'

'A weapon?' Mathilde heard the tremor in her own voice. 'How can a twelve-year-old boy be used as a weapon?'

'Because Prince Edward is the heir to the English throne, someone she can use as a figurehead to challenge her husband and reclaim her rightful position.' Katharine laughed, though it sounded more like a cackle. 'The King has agreed to send her exactly what she needs to defy him and he has no idea. Oh, we'll be going home eventually, but as for the manner of it, *that* remains to be seen.'

Chapter Four

'Keep moving!' Lady Berthe whispered viciously into Mathilde's ear, making her wince, though it still didn't help. She couldn't help but falter at the sight of the immense crowd gathered in the great hall that evening, like a brightly coloured, swarming hive of bees, more people than she'd seen gathered together in one place in her life. She had a sudden fear of being crushed, but fortunately the Master of Ceremonies announced the Queen at that moment and the mass of people fell away, opening a path up between them. It was no wonder. Isabella was resplendent, dressed in a pale silver-blue gown with a pearl-encrusted headdress and a long, shimmering silk train, looking like a mermaid or some other mythical creature.

Mathilde followed behind, for the first time not feeling utterly out of place in the Queen's retinue. As promised, Lady Cecily had adjusted one of her own surcoats to fit and the open sides, revealing the tightly cinched waist of her kirtle beneath, encircled by a red girdle, made her feel older and more sophisticated. She was even aware of a few admiring male glances as she walked, though she had no inclination, or any idea how, to respond.

The French King stepped forward as his sister Isabella approached the dais, his golden hair and bejewelled tunic making the resemblance between them more striking than ever. They were truly a gilded pair, these heirs of Philip the Fair and Joan of Navarre, Mathilde thought, allowing her gaze to wander past them and along the high table, past a row of elaborately dressed French nobles and courtiers before settling finally upon Henry Wright.

She felt a jolt as if Lady Berthe had just jabbed a malicious elbow into her ribs, her body turning hot and cold at the same moment. That is, her skin felt too hot, but her limbs appeared to have frozen. He was standing beside the chair of one of the nobles, as if he'd just been engaged in conversation, but what was he doing there, mingling with the court so openly? If what Katharine had told her earlier was true, then he was one of Mortimer's men and a traitor, too, or as good as, but unlike the first or even second time they'd met he was making no attempt to conceal himself now. There was nothing remotely secret about his position just a few feet from the French King and English Queen, looking dark and inscrutable and alert, as if he were noticing every detail of the scene before him.

No sooner had the thought entered her head than his eyes locked with hers, a lightning flash of blue darting across the room and making the air between them seem to pulse and crackle with tension. She caught her breath as one of his eyebrows lifted, but she refused to look away. She had the strange impression that if she looked for long enough then she would be able to tell whether he was friend or foe. She wasn't sure which she preferred, or what those definitions even meant any more, but she held on to his gaze without blinking, determined to get to the truth, until his lips curved suddenly and he winked.

Quickly, she twisted her face to the side, as he'd surely known that she would, her cheeks aflame with mortification. She didn't like what his wink implied and she was afraid that someone else might have noticed and got the wrong impression. To her relief, however, the Master of Ceremonies saved her again, announcing the meal and allowing her to take a seat along one of the six rows of trestle tables, thankfully on the opposite side of the room to Henry Wright. From there, she made a point of not looking in his direction again, focusing all of her attention on the entertainers who played lutes and harps and sang tunes while they ate.

It was a lengthy meal, as befitted the occasion. Mathilde counted off each of the twenty-four courses in turn, thinking that she would never get used to the way they ate at court. At home, three courses was a great feast. Here, it would have been considered an outrage. If only she could have saved some of the food and sent it home to her family. Dicun in particular ate like a horse and yet was *still* never full after a meal…

She paused with a piece of marchpane halfway to her lips, the thought bringing with it a rush of homesickness so strong that she felt almost winded, her heart hammering hard against her ribcage and her breath emerging in short, erratic bursts, ones that made it impossible to speak, yet she seemed powerless to do anything about it. There were actual tears welling in her eyes and, to her horror, she felt one start to roll down her cheek. Suddenly, in the midst of hundreds of faces, she felt utterly lost and alone, as if she were watching the banquet from inside a bubble, there and not there, a living phantom at the feast.

Chest heaving, she stood up and made her way around the edge of the hall. She knew that she ought not to leave, not without the Queen's permission, and that Lady Berthe would scold her for it later, but she had to get away before she did something even more embarrassing.

Mercifully, nobody stopped her as she rushed out into a stairwell away from prying eyes. There was a small window there, the shutters open to let cooling air into the hall, and she pushed her face up towards it, drawing in deep lungfuls until her heartbeat gradually returned to normal. Then she turned around, sagging back against the cold stone of the wall and chiding herself for ingratitude. She ought to feel honoured to be there, not as if she wanted to collapse in a heap and start sobbing.

'Are you following me now, lady?'

She jumped, knowing the identity of the speaker even before she lifted her head, though she still hoped she was mistaken. She wasn't. Henry Wright was sitting on one of the steps before her, half hidden in the shadows, one arm draped casually over a knee as if he hadn't a care in the world. She hadn't noticed him there when she'd entered, although she hadn't heard footsteps behind her either. In truth, she didn't know which one of them had followed the other, but either way she didn't want to see him. She wanted to be alone.

'Of course not!' She thrust her jaw out, blinking rapidly to clear the moisture from her eyes.

'What's the matter?' His tone shifted, turning to one of concern as he stood up and moved closer.

'Nothing.' She brushed a hand over her face. 'What are you doing here?'

'The same as you, I imagine. Enjoying a respite from the festivities.'

'I didn't mean that.' She scowled, vaguely surprised by her own rudeness. She was never rude to anyone, but he seemed to bring out the worst in her. 'What are you doing back at court?'

'Does that mean you're not pleased to see me?' His gaze travelled over her face. 'No, don't answer that. I can see that you're not.' He placed a hand over his heart as if he were genuinely hurt. 'You wound me, lady. I was only going to offer an ear. I'm happy to listen if you need to talk?'

Mathilde stared at him incredulously. How could he think that she'd trust *him*, a stranger, not to mention a possible, *probable*, traitor, with her innermost thoughts and feelings? And yet, for some inexplicable reason, she did, the words bursting from her lips before she could stop them.

'I miss my home.'

'You don't like the French court?'

'It's not that. It's a beautiful place and I know that I'm lucky to be here. I never expected to see London, let alone Paris, but...' She felt tears prick her eyes again. 'I still miss my home. It's getting easier, but I don't belong here.'

'True.' He nodded and she bristled, instantly and unreasonably offended. It was one thing for her to say it, but he didn't need to agree quite so readily. She didn't feel older or sophisticated any more. She felt foolish and naive and too far from home.

'I didn't say that it was a bad thing,' he added, correctly interpreting her expression.

'It feels like one.' She drew herself upwards, smoothing a hand over her stomach and then pulling it away again when she saw his eyes follow the movement. 'You didn't answer my question. Why are you back at court?'

'Because I was sent here.'

'Who by?'

He laughed softly, his teeth flashing white in the half-darkness. 'I don't even know your name, lady. If you expect me to trust you with such details, then we ought to be properly introduced first.'

She lifted her chin. 'It ought to be enough that the Queen trusts me.'

'Perhaps it ought to be, but…' He put his wrists together in a gesture that suggested his hands were tied and Mathilde narrowed her gaze, determined to prove that she wasn't as naive as he assumed.

'*I* know who you are.'

'Because I told you.'

'I know who you keep company with, too.'

That wiped the smile off his face. All trace of humour vanished in an instant, replaced by a hawklike intensity. 'Is it common knowledge, then?'

'No.' Her sense of triumph was fleeting. There was a dangerous edge to his voice suddenly that made goose pimples rise on her skin. 'Only a few of the Queen's ladies know. The ones that she trusts.'

'Good.' His expression softened again, though there was still a watchful look in his eyes. 'Then it seems we're both of us conspirators.'

'We are not!' The accusation brought her anger back to the surface. No matter how dangerous he sounded, she wouldn't be accused of treason. 'I want no part in any conspiracy!'

'It might be too late for that. Although if you feel so strongly about it, then it might be wise to leave the Queen's service sooner rather than later. Go back to this home of yours.'

Go back? She felt her lips part in surprise. Even at her most homesick, she'd never seriously considered the possibility. No doubt it was what her father would want her to do under the circumstances, but once there, he'd only find some other way to be rid of her. In another household or a convent perhaps. No, there was no place for her at home any longer, whereas here, she was valued by the Queen of England herself. A wronged queen, according to Lady Cecily and Katharine, who only wanted to reclaim the position that was hers by marriage and in the name of her son, too! How could *that* really be treason? She knew what her father would say, that the King could do no wrong, but Isabella hadn't actually done anything treasonous yet. Maybe she wouldn't. Maybe it was all rumour and speculation. Maybe it would never become a question of sides. Or of treachery…

'There are still ways to return to England if

you want them.' His eyes were roaming over her face, she realised, as if he were trying to read her thoughts.

'No.' She shook her head finally. 'I don't want to leave the Queen.'

'Then you may not be able to avoid conspiracies. The future may be dangerous.'

She rolled her eyes before she could stop herself. He might be right, but she was tired of being spoken to like a child in need of instruction.

His response was to take another step closer, bracing his hands on the wall on either side of her shoulders until she was effectively trapped between them. 'But perhaps you'd like a little danger, lady?'

She swallowed hard, regretting the eye-roll as the hubbub of voices from the hall seemed to fade into silence, as if the world had just contracted to the small space around them. He was too close for comfort now. Too close for decency as well, but there was only stone wall behind her and no way to escape the cage of his arms.

No part of him was touching her, but she could feel the heat of his chest emanating through his tunic and smell the faint whisper of wine on his breath. Her own was coming in short bursts again, too, as though she'd just sucked in all the air from the stairwell and couldn't let it out again, as if she'd forgotten how to function normally, yet the sense of panic was different from before, almost like anticipation. Despite the fact that he was a traitor, her body was tingling in places she'd never conceived of tingles before, as if his fingers were sliding over her bare skin. She had the sudden, startling idea that she might want them to.

She licked her lips, intimidated, excited and curious all at the same time, her body trembling with the wantonness of her own thoughts. 'I should go back before anyone misses me.'

'Yes.' His eyes darkened, the pupils swelling until the blue was barely visible. 'You probably should.'

He should go, too, Henry told himself, his gaze drawn first to the slick of moisture left on her bottom lip by her tongue, then to the tiny flutter of her pulse at the base of her throat. He should have slipped out the moment she'd entered the stairwell, but he'd been caught off guard for once, startled by her sudden appearance just when he'd been thinking about her, as if his desires had actually guided her towards him. Desires a man like him had no business having for any lady.

Despite their meeting in the courtyard that morning, he almost hadn't recognised her when she'd first entered the hall, dressed like a cultivated lady of the court and not an innocent country girl any longer. Part of him had missed the country girl, the other part had found itself admiring the way her kirtle clung to the willowy curves of the body beneath. He'd thought about her surprisingly often over the past few months and now here she was, her *and* her curves, not to mention those luminous, big brown eyes, standing close enough to touch if she let him. *Would* she let him? His fingers were itching to do so, to slide along the ridge of her collarbone and up the narrow column of her throat, although it would undoubtedly be wiser not to. It wouldn't do either of them any good to be seen talking together in private. Reputations were precarious things, for spies as well as for ladies.

'Do you care for the Queen?' It took all his self-control to drop his hands from the wall, wrenching his thoughts back to their conversation instead.

'What?' She blinked, looking glassy-eyed and disorientated for a few seconds. 'Oh...yes. She's been very kind to me.'

'Only because it suits her. They're all the same. Kings, queens, barons, earls. No matter whose side you're on, never trust any of them completely. Loyalty is an admirable quality, but they wouldn't hesitate to throw any of us to the hounds if necessary.'

She glanced past his shoulder towards the doorway, as if she were unnerved by his bluntness. 'You're not a noble, then?'

'Sir Nobody of Nowhere, at your service, my lady.' He smiled and made an exaggerated bow. 'If it makes you feel any better, I don't belong at court either.'

'So we have something in common.' Her brows puckered as if she were regarding him in a new light. 'Why are you telling me this?'

'Because you ought to be warned and I thought that nobody else might have told you.'

'Then why do you serve Mortimer if you think so poorly of him?'

'Because a man needs to belong somewhere if he's to make anything of himself and some masters are better than others.'

'Better than the King?'

'Yes.' He lifted a shoulder, agreeing without hesitation. 'The King is a tyrant. He rules by fear, breaks his own laws and neglects the good of his subjects.'

'Then you're a traitor, too? Like Roger Mortimer?'

'I suppose so. And *you* are Lady Mathilde Gosselin of Rudstone Manor near Scarborough. So now we may consider ourselves introduced.'

She inhaled sharply as if she were alarmed by the sound of her own name. 'I don't consort with traitors.'

'Ah, but you already are.' He leaned forward so that his mouth was only a hair's breadth away from the shell of her ear. 'Stay with the Queen if you wish, but be certain that you know who she really is. Don't give her any more credit than she deserves.'

Her body stiffened, though she didn't move away. 'I trust her.'

'Trust?' He felt a moment of pity. 'Courts are dangerous places for people who *trust*.'

'Then perhaps *you* ought to leave.'

'As you wish.' He took a step backwards, resisting the urge to press his lips against the smooth skin of her neck instead. 'As a matter of fact, I'm leaving in the morning, but I'll be back soon, Lady Mathilde, and I look forward to renewing our acquaintance.' He paused briefly. 'If you're still here, that is.'

Chapter Five

'Hurry!' The page made a beckoning motion. 'They're gathered in the hall.'

'Already?' Henry swore under his breath, striding through the dark corridors of the palace as fast as his bruised and knotted muscles would allow. It felt strange to be back, as if he'd only just left and yet been gone for months, too. The past few weeks seemed to have passed in a blur of travel, from France to the Low Countries to England, then back across the Channel to Hainault again, before a messenger had arrived summoning him urgently to Paris. At this rate, he was going to hear hoof beats in his sleep. 'Has anything happened yet?'

'Not yet, but I heard a rumour that one of the English envoys is planning to make a scene this evening.' The page grinned conspiratorially.

'They say he's going to announce the King's demands in front of the whole court.'

'It's about time. If you discover anything else, you know where to find me.'

Henry handed the boy a coin and then slipped inconspicuously through a side door into the hall, taking a place at the end of one table. Once seated, he glanced around, making sure nobody had noticed his arrival before looking up at the dais where the twelve-year-old Prince Edward sat between his mother and uncle. From a distance, they looked like a pair of guards, keeping the future of England safe between them, though whether as an honoured guest or as a prisoner it was impossible to tell.

He gave a cynical grunt and then turned his attention more enthusiastically towards the Queen's attendants, searching for Lady Mathilde. He was just starting to think that she'd taken his advice and left when he finally found her, seated on one of the higher tables, looking even more like a lady of the court than the last time, dressed in an embroidered brocade gown with her dark hair swept back in a gold crespinette. As he watched, she raised a cup to her lips, though her eyes were moving slowly around the room, he noticed, as if she were searching for someone, too. *Him?* His blood stirred at the idea, though no doubt he was flattering himself. A lady who looked like that might have any number of admirers by now, all of them with better names and prospects than him. Still, he was surprised by *how* pleased he was to see her still there. After five months, she was just as intriguing as ever. Just as distracting, too. Despite the importance of the evening, he couldn't help but wonder how it would feel to take her in his arms, to feel the soft press of her body and the warm touch of her lips against his. If only...

He wrenched his thoughts back to the present as a man approached the dais, dropped down on to one knee and begged leave to speak. He carried a message from the King of England, he said, an important one, bidding the Queen to leave France and come home.

Henry shook his head, smiling at the envoy's naivety. No doubt he'd said the same words in private already, but he'd obviously thought that a public demand would be more effective because he spoke in a loud voice, intended to carry to the far ends of the hall, one that made the hush that followed all the more pronounced. It went on for so long that people began to exchange glances, until finally the Queen got to her feet, lifted her chin and calmly denounced her husband.

'I will not.'

In stark contrast to the envoy, Isabella didn't raise her voice and yet somehow it carried even further, all around the hall and back again, echoing portentously in every ear. Judging by the envoy's stunned expression, the King hadn't given any instructions about what to say in the event of a refusal, as if he'd never even considered the possibility. The King of France, on the other hand, obviously had. The very moment that Isabella stopped speaking, he stood up beside her and pledged his fraternal devotion and support. It was like watching a play, Henry thought, every word and movement carefully choreographed and rehearsed. And just like that, the rebellion had begun. After months of prevarication and stalling, the matter had finally come to a head.

Slowly, he moved away from the table and back towards the door. He'd seen what he'd come to see. In the morning, he would ride back to Hainault and tell Mortimer the time had come, but first he needed some sleep.

He paused in the doorway, unable to resist one last look back over his shoulder, not at the Queen, but at the woman who'd said that she trusted her. Lady Mathilde Gosselin's expression was torn, like a woman trapped in the midst of events she didn't wish to be a part of and with no idea what to do.

He felt a pang in his chest, accompanied by a powerful impulse to stride across the hall and rescue her, to take her by the hand and flee, but it was too late. The Queen had spoken. There was no turning back now.

'W-widow's robes, Your Grace?' Mathilde stuttered, wondering if she'd misheard.

'Yes.' Isabella glanced at her impatiently. 'Were you not listening to me last night?'

'Yes, but I...' She faltered. In all honesty, after the first few sentences, she *hadn't* heard a great deal of the Queen's speech, the words drowned out by the sound of panic ringing in her ears.

'Cecily,' Isabella snapped her fingers. 'Come and help me dress. Kat, take the girl away and explain.'

'I'm sorry.' Mathilde shook her head as Katharine led her into the next chamber. 'I just don't understand—why does she wish to wear widow's robes?'

'To symbolise the rift in her marriage.'

'But for a king who's still alive...isn't that treason?'

'Aye.'

'And *we* dress her. Won't that make us traitors, too?' Her stomach lurched. That would be her father's first thought when he heard about what had happened, she knew, that his own daughter was betraying the King. She'd hardly slept the previous night for worrying about it, torn between her filial duty to him on the one hand and her newfound loyalty to the Queen on the other. No matter which side she chose, she wound up feeling guilty.

'A bad king is a traitor to his own country.' Katharine spoke matter-of-factly. 'Edward is the villain, not us.'

Mathilde turned to look out of the window at the palace gardens, wishing that she could be so certain. Oddly enough, she found herself wanting to speak to Henry Wright about it. Even though she'd told him to leave, she'd still searched the hall for his face every day over the past few weeks, and now that they were on the same side, *sort of*, she had mixed feelings towards him. There was something undeniably appealing about his cynicism and frankness, not to mention his handsome features. Wicked though it was, she also couldn't forget the strange tingling sensation she'd felt the last time they'd met, nor the way her body had reacted to his close proximity. She'd relived the memory several times over in her dreams, going even further, too, imagining what might have happened if she hadn't left the stairwell when she had…

'What's going to happen next?' she asked before her wayward imagination could run away with her.

'An invasion.'

'Of England?'

Katharine gave her a scathing look and she felt her cheeks flush. *Of course* of England, though it was hard to imagine a queen invading her own country; even harder to imagine herself as a part of it.

'Why doesn't the King just agree to her demands?' She tried to ask a more intelligent question.

'Because no man wants to be told what to do by a woman.' Katharine's voice held a bitter edge. 'And she couldn't trust him even if he did. He's made promises before, but Despenser always returns and gets rewarded with more jewels and titles for the privilege. Nobody with sense believes the King's word any more.'

'You mean he lies?'

'Maybe not when he speaks. Maybe he truly believes what he says and then changes his mind the next day, but a king should keep to his vows.

Whatever Isabella does next, he's brought it all on himself. Sometimes force is the only way.'

Mathilde winced, thinking of her home and family. 'When will the invasion be?'

'In the spring, as soon as the weather improves and the Channel crossing is safer.'

'But won't the King be expecting it? Won't he have time to prepare?'

'If he's not, then he's an even greater fool than I thought, but it can't be helped. It's hard to muster an army and plan an invasion in secret.'

'So the Queen's already gathering an army?'

'Honestly, girl!' Katharine shook her head with exasperation. 'What do you think Mortimer is doing in Hainault? From what I've heard, he's already discussing a betrothal between Prince Edward and the Count's daughter Philippa in exchange for soldiers.'

'But I thought the Prince was going to marry the Infanta of Spain?'

'It was suggested, but there was no formal agreement. Now it looks like there won't be.'

Mathilde squeezed her brows together. The world as she knew and understood it seemed to be rearranging itself before her eyes, as if a familiar painting had suddenly sprung to life, revealing deeper, darker depths. Her gaze fell briefly on the river that ran through the centre of the gardens before she jerked her head away, the sight of the water making her shudder.

'What will happen to us if the Queen leads an invasion?' She tried to make it sound like a possibility instead of a certainty.

'Then we'll go with her.'

'With the army?' Mathilde clutched the edges of her mantle tighter at her throat, feeling chilled all of a sudden. As much as she wanted to serve the Queen, she didn't want to be part of an invasion. She especially didn't want to see any fighting, but even *she* knew it would be hard to have a rebellion without any bloodshed.

'We're the Queen's ladies. We go where she goes.'

'What about Prince Edward? Will he come?'

'Aye. She'll keep him tight at her side.'

'It must be hard, having to choose between his parents.'

'Perhaps it would be if he had any choice.'

Mathilde sighed, pressing her forehead against the windowpane and feeling a pang of sympathy for the young Prince. As she stood there, a man appeared on the path below, walking in the direction of the stables. There was something familiar about his gait, she noticed, almost as if she'd made a point of remembering it…

'What do you make of him?'

'Who?' Her heart leapt as she recognised Henry.

'*Who?* Prince Edward. Who else?'

'Oh… I don't know.'

'He has the look of a king, I think, a lot like his grandfather.'

'Mmm…' Mathilde murmured noncommittally, sucking in a breath as Henry turned his head and looked up suddenly as if sensing her scrutiny, his gaze moving along the palace windows before it reached hers and stopped.

'One of Mortimer's men?'

She gave a start as Katharine peered over her shoulder. 'Yes, I think so.'

'On his way to fetch him, no doubt. They'll all be here soon, every exile and enemy the King has ever made. Mark my words, Mortimer will be at the Queen's side within a fortnight.'

Mathilde nodded, fighting the temptation to lift a hand and wave as Henry removed his hat and made a small bow. Had he been at court the whole time, after all? No, she would have caught sight of him somewhere. He must have returned recently and was already leaving again, but if he was going to fetch Mortimer then surely that meant he would be back soon, too? Then she could speak to him properly…

'Don't worry about the future, girl.' Katharine's voice sounded weary all of a sudden. 'Kings and queens make the decisions, not us. We're only their servants.'

'But we serve them…' Mathilde bit down on her bottom lip, ashamed to admit that for a few moments she hadn't been thinking about Isabella or Edward or the future of England at all.

Chapter Six

～～～～

Winter 1325

'My Lord of Wigmore, welcome back to Paris.'

'I'm honoured to be here, Your Grace.'

Henry bent down on one knee as Mortimer made a show of deference to the French King. As displays went, it was a mere token gesture since both men, and most likely the whole court, knew who Mortimer had really come to see. They all knew how quickly he would attempt to excuse himself, too, although on this occasion, Henry found himself in sympathy with his master. Unwise though it undoubtedly was, now he was back in Paris, he couldn't resist the temptation to seek Lady Mathilde out, if only to find out how she was faring.

Fortunately, it wasn't long before the King drew Mortimer aside privately and Henry was able to escape and make his way through the palace corridors towards the Queen's guest chambers. He had absolutely no idea what excuse he might use for going there, but he'd think of something…

'Look out!' He reared backwards abruptly and then broke into a wide grin as a woman came running around a corner, almost bumping into him in her haste. Luck, it seemed, was on his side. 'Well met, Lady Mathilde.'

'Oh!' She stopped, too, her brown eyes widening with recognition. *'You?'*

'Me,' he agreed, for once wishing he hadn't been so quick to react. If he'd only kept walking, she would have charged straight into his arms. 'Henry Wright, remember?'

'I remember.'

'I'm honoured.' He inclined his head. She was dressed fashionably, but more plainly today, he noticed, in a shade of forest green that perfectly complemented the rich chestnut colour of her hair, which was itself twisted into two intricate, face-framing plaits. The expression *on* that face was faintly cautious, but her words were more encouragement than he'd expected.

'I was just…' She glanced past his shoulder and lowered her voice. 'The Queen heard a rumour that Mortimer has arrived.'

'And sent you to find out what the delay was?' He quirked an eyebrow. 'He's still speaking with the King, but he'll be along this way soon, trust me. You could save yourself a journey if you stay here and talk with me a while. If you wish to, that is?'

'All right.' To his surprise, she didn't hesitate, smoothing her hands over the front of her gown and lifting her chin instead. 'As you can see, I haven't left court.'

'I'm glad.' He reached into his tunic and drew out a small wooden trinket box with a pattern of heartsease etched on the top. 'Since it means I can give you this.'

'I'm afraid I can't accept gifts. The Queen wouldn't approve.'

'Then call it a peace offering. An apology for my behaviour the last time we spoke.'

'I still don't think—'

'Just look inside. The contents are what really matters.'

'Oh, very well…' She accepted the box tentatively, opening the lid and then closing it again with a snap. *'Dirt?'*

'Not just any dirt.' He raised a hand at her indignant expression. She looked as if she wanted to hurl the contents in his face. 'It's a gift, truly.

You said that you were homesick so I brought a little bit of England back to Paris for you.'

'You mean this is English soil?' The indignation faded as her lips curved instead. 'Thank you. That's the most thoughtful—wait! Does this mean you've been back to England?'

'Briefly.'

'Oh…' A furrow appeared between her brows as if she were trying to decide whether or not to say something.

'What is it?' he prompted her.

'Are you a spy?'

He almost laughed aloud at the question. It was hardly a wise one under any circumstances, nor likely to get an honest answer, and yet he couldn't resist telling her the truth anyway. 'I suppose you could call me that. It sounds better than traitor.'

'Aren't you afraid of being caught?'

'Sometimes. I find it best not to think about it.'

'I wish I could do that. I seem to be afraid of so many things these days and I can't seem to stop thinking about them.'

'Such as?'

'Well…' She pressed her lips together for several seconds. 'Not so much my own safety, although I do think about that sometimes, but about what will happen if the Queen really invades England, whether my family will be safe, what my father will think of me for being a part of it…'

'You don't think he'll support the rebellion?'

'No.' She shook her head adamantly. 'My father would never turn against the King.'

'Yet you're still determined to stay with the Queen?' He moved closer, breathing in the faint scent of apples as he tipped his head towards hers. 'Some of her other ladies will be returning to England soon.'

'What?' Her mouth fell open in shock. 'You mean, they're abandoning her?'

'Running away might be a better way of putting it. They know they're not welcome in France any longer.'

'But shouldn't we warn the Queen? They could report to the King what's been happening!'

'They won't be telling him anything he doesn't already know. The point is, you could still get out of here and go with them. Your father might be glad of it.'

'Only for the King's sake, not because he wants me back!' She clamped a hand over her mouth suddenly. 'Forgive me. I should not have said that.'

'Say whatever you like, especially about parents. I've said far worse about mine.'

'Really?' She looked interested.

'Many times, but that's not what we're discussing.'

'Mmm.' She started to tap her foot anxiously. 'Do you know what people are saying about the Queen in England? I'd like to know what my father might have heard.'

'They know that she's refusing to go home. It's been almost a year since she left with no sign of return.'

'But are they angry?'

'On the contrary, I'd say that most are sympathetic. The King's recent behaviour hasn't exactly endeared him to the people.'

'So there are no rumours?' She glanced up and down the corridor. 'About Mortimer?'

'So far, only at court.'

'So far...' She seemed to draw in a long breath before shaking her head. 'No, I can't leave. I know that's what my father would want, but he was the one who sent me here, and now that I *am* here...well, I'm the Queen's lady now. That means that my loyalty is to her.'

'No matter what?'

'No matter what.'

'As you wish. As long as you understand

this may be your last chance to leave before the invasion.'

'Is that what you want?' Her gaze narrowed. 'For me to leave?'

'Not at all.'

'Because this is the second time that you've suggested it. Anyone would think you were trying to get rid of me.'

He lifted his eyebrows, surprised to realise she was right. He was acting as if he wanted her to go back to England when in fact the very opposite was true. 'It's not that. It's just that I don't want you to end up feeling trapped.'

'Why do you care?'

'Because I know what it's like.'

'Oh.' Her eyelashes dipped for a moment before she looked up again. 'Is that what you are? Trapped?'

He made a face. 'Spying isn't a profession I would necessarily have chosen, but I'm one of Mortimer's men. Unless I turn mercenary, I don't have a choice about that. So I do what, and go where, I'm told.'

'Did you help him escape from the Tower?'

'You ask a lot of questions, Lady Mathilde.'

'Because I'm trying to work out whether or not I can trust you.'

'Ah. I thought I warned you about trusting people.'

'You did, but I want to make up my own mind.'

He grinned at that. She really *had* changed in the time since they'd last spoken in the stairwell. The wide eyes were less innocent and the country accent less obvious, although there was still an honesty about her that called out to him. But she was asking about whether or not she could trust him, which begged the same question about her. Could *she* really be trusted? Inasmuch as he trusted anyone, which was never completely. He rubbed a hand over his jaw, deciding to find out just how honest she really was... 'What would you give me to answer your questions, lady?'

She swayed backwards, although she didn't look away. 'What is it you want?'

'Only to ask a question of my own. That's fair, isn't it?'

'That depends on the question.'

'It's nothing terrible. Just about who spends time with the Queen when Mortimer isn't here. Whether there's anyone else she takes into her confidence?'

'Why would you ask? Doesn't your master trust her?'

'He's cautious.'

'Then tell him to ask someone else!' She shoved the trinket box hard against his chest. 'I won't spy on the Queen and I won't be bought either. You can keep your gift, Henry Wright.'

'Wait! I'm sorry.' He caught hold of the box before it fell to the floor, surprised by her fierceness. He'd anticipated her refusal, but he hadn't expected her to be quite so angry. 'I shouldn't have asked. I only wanted to know how you'd react.'

'Why?'

'Because spying's a bad habit, I suppose, and because you looked so suspicious that I didn't dare ask for what I really wanted.'

'And what was that?'

He paused as she put her hands on her hips, knowing that he ought not to say the words and then going ahead anyway. 'Just one kiss, lady.'

She drew in a sharp breath, her cheeks reddening before she tossed her head and stormed past him, heading towards the great hall. 'Compliments won't work either. I'm not such a fool as you think I am!'

'I've never thought you were a fool. Wait! I was in the boat that rescued him!' He called the words out more loudly than he'd intended, gratified when she stopped five paces away, half turning her head over one shoulder.

'You were?'

'Yes. There were three of us. We waited for darkness, then made for the walls of the Tower and waited for Mortimer to appear on the roof. Afterwards, we rowed to the south side of the Thames where someone else was waiting with horses. Then we rode straight for the coast.'

'Did the King pursue you?' She stood stock-still as he came to stand behind her.

'He sent a small army, but by the time the alarm was raised, we were long gone.'

'Mortimer must trust you a great deal.'

'He does.'

'The Queen trusts me, too.' She turned around then, her eyes blazing defiance as if there were tiny fires inside them. 'And I won't betray her. Not ever.'

'I wouldn't expect you to. I won't ask such questions again, I promise, but keep this. Please.' He placed the trinket box back in her hands, his fingers pressing lightly against her palms before he let go. 'It would be a shame to waste good dirt.'

'Did you really bring this back from England for me?' There was a catch in her voice this time.

'Yes.'

'Why?'

'Because I like you, Lady Mathilde. I shouldn't, but I do. And for what it's worth, you *can* trust me.' He let his gaze dwell on hers for a long moment, captivated by the swirling depths of her dark eyes. Looking closer, he could see that they weren't a plain brown at all, but a variety of shades, from mahogany to hazel to amber. Given the opportunity, he could have spent hours staring into them, but this wasn't the time or the place. If he wasn't mistaken, there were footsteps approaching, moving quickly, too... He took a step backwards and winked, breaking the atmosphere of tension between them. 'And now you owe me a kiss.'

He didn't wait to see her reaction, disappearing into the shadows just as Mortimer came striding down the corridor.

Chapter Seven

'Have you ever been in love?' Isabella tipped her golden head to one side, gazing at her reflection in a gilt-edged mirror while Mathilde drew an antler comb through the tresses.

'No, Your Grace.' She felt colour rise in her cheeks as an image of Henry's face flashed, unbidden, into her mind, though judging by the Queen's dreamy expression, she wasn't paying any attention to her reaction.

'You know, I fancied myself in love with my husband once. I was only thirteen when I married, all innocent and full of hope for the future. I thought that I was lucky, that it would be easy to love such a man. Edward was so handsome and I knew so little…' Isabella's voice cracked and then hardened. 'I gave him four children and stood by his side when the barons rebelled. I did everything he asked and yet he still never cared about me. Or his people either. I've no choice but to do what I'm doing now. You understand that, don't you, Mathilde?'

'Of course, Your Grace.'

'If this invasion fails, then he'll call me an unnatural wife and lock me away in some remote castle for ever. That's why it *cannot* fail. I have to succeed, to make my husband treat me as I deserve.' She sat upright again, looking pleased by the thought, gesturing towards one of her finest satin gowns as Katharine appeared in the mirror behind them. 'I'll wear the gold tonight. I want to look my best.'

Mathilde pressed her lips together, refusing to wonder why the Queen wished to look her best for a private dinner with Mortimer. For a woman so skilled at dissembling, having played the part of a contented and obedient wife for seventeen years, she seemed to have lost all her acting abilities when it came to him.

It was sinful, but Mathilde couldn't entirely blame her. Mortimer's escape from the Tower lent him an air of mystery and danger and there was something compelling about his arrogance, not to mention his vivid blue eyes and dark good looks, so much like Henry's. It was no wonder that Isabella was besotted with him, she thought, especially when she'd been neglected by her husband for so long. Maybe it wasn't so very wrong to fall in love under such circumstances.

She voiced her thoughts aloud to Katharine and Lady Cecily that evening when they were sitting alone by the fireside.

'I doubt that Mortimer's wife would agree with you.' Katharine gave a derisive snort.

'You don't like him very much, do you?'

'I don't like the influence he has over her. When Isabella wears widow's clothing she gathers support as a wronged wife, a victim of Edward, but the more she favours Mortimer, the more she risks losing all of that. She's discreet enough, but she ought to curb his behaviour. He acts like some kind of consort.'

'Queens do not marry for love,' Cecily commented softly. 'They know better than to expect it either.'

'Then maybe they *ought* to marry for love,' Mathilde argued, feeling rebellious. 'That way, there would be no need to lead invasions against their husbands.'

'The world does not work that way, not for many of us.'

Mathilde blinked, surprised by the note of sadness in Cecily's voice, even more so when

Katharine wrapped an arm around her shoulders, drawing her close. Katharine was a widow of long standing, but Cecily was still married, although she never mentioned her husband. She only ever talked about her children, three boys, one of them grown, the others being raised in separate households. Mathilde knew that she worried about them and yet some instinct told her that, this time at least, her sigh wasn't for them. There was a sense of intimacy about the way she clung to Katharine, too, one that made her feel as though she were intruding upon something private.

A sound of voices interrupted the silence and Cecily lifted her head with a look of alarm, her eyes already red and swollen.

'I'll see what's happening.' Mathilde stood up, relieved by the interruption, then felt her stomach lurch as she went through to the corridor and found Henry talking with one of the guards. She'd hidden his trinket box, with its content of dirt, away in her small chest of belongings, uncertain about whether or not she ought to keep it, but she'd been unable to put his words out of her mind so easily. He *liked* her, but he knew that he shouldn't. What did *that* mean? And what did she feel about him?

She couldn't bring herself to dislike him any

longer, not when he seemed to genuinely want to help her—to help her escape, even—and he *said* that she could trust him, but he was a traitor, whereas she… In all honesty, she wasn't sure what she was. Loyal to the Queen, but not a traitor. Not yet anyway. Even so, she couldn't seem to prevent all of her inner organs from performing somersaults at the sight of him. Did he *still* want a kiss?

'Lady Mathilde?' Unlike their previous meetings, he seemed less than pleased to see her. 'Pardon the intrusion, but I need to speak with Mortimer.'

'He's with the Queen.'

'So I've just heard.' He made a face, reaching into his tunic and drawing out a narrow scroll of parchment. 'In that case, kindly give him this and tell him Dubois is here.'

'Can't it wait?' She made a face of her own, reluctant to disturb the Queen, but he shook his head emphatically.

'It's important. I would not ask otherwise, lady, I promise.'

Mathilde looked from him to the parchment, staring at them both dubiously for a few seconds. 'All right. Wait here.'

'Thank you.' He still sounded tense. 'I appreciate that it might be…awkward.'

She gave him a look that implied she had no idea what he was talking about before rapping gently on the door to the Queen's withdrawing chamber.

'Come in,' Isabella replied almost instantly.

'Your Grace.' Mathilde opened the door and dropped into a curtsy. To her immense relief, the Queen and Mortimer were merely sitting side by side on a settle, both of them looking towards her expectantly.

'Please forgive the interruption, Your Grace, but this just arrived.' She crossed the room and held out the scroll. 'I was told it's important.'

'Let's hope so.' Mortimer plucked the parchment from her fingers, unravelling it and reading the contents swiftly before murmuring a few names to the Queen.

'All of them will join us?' Isabella looked pleased.

'The moment we land.'

'Is it certain? Can they be trusted?'

'Not by the King.' Mortimer laughed at his own joke. 'But they wouldn't risk sending word if they didn't mean it.'

'Your Grace?' Mathilde murmured quietly. 'I was also told that someone else has arrived, a man by the name of Dubois.'

'Excellent.' Isabella smiled. 'Tell him that his

master is occupied, but will speak with him in the morning. Tell him not to go anywhere or speak to anyone else until then.' She reached into a box and extracted a leather pouch. If the sound of clinking was anything to judge by, it contained coins. 'In the meantime, give him this as a token of appreciation from his Queen with her gratitude. Only be sure to give it to him in person, won't you, Mathilde? I know that I can trust you.'

'Yes, Your Grace.'

She curtsied again and went out, closing the door carefully behind her. Henry was waiting exactly where she'd left him, Katharine standing alongside now, too, her sharp eyes looking him up and down appraisingly.

'Is Mortimer coming?' He got straight to the point, seemingly oblivious to Katharine's scrutiny.

'No. The Queen says that he'll speak to Dubois in the morning, but I've to give him this pouch for now.'

'I'll take it.' He reached a hand out, but she drew her own back, tightening her grip on the leather.

'She told me to give it to him in person.'

'No.' His voice was firm. 'Absolutely not.'

'Why not?'

'Because it's not a good idea, believe me.'

'It's what the Queen commands.' She lifted her chin. 'She trusts me to carry out her orders.'

'And *of course* you trust her.'

'Yes!' She bristled at the cynicism in his voice. 'I do.'

'The resemblance is a strong one.' Katharine interrupted suddenly. 'You're very like him.'

'What?' Mathilde twisted towards the other woman in surprise. What did she mean by resemblance? To whom? Henry had told her that he was Sir Nobody of Nowhere and yet if the look on his face was anything to go by, he understood exactly what Katharine meant.

'So people tell me.' His tone was guarded now.

'What do they call you?'

'Henry Wright.'

'Wright. After your mother's family, I suppose?'

'Yes.'

Katharine nodded. 'Very well, Henry Wright, take her and bring her back again soon. I'll hold you accountable for her safety.'

'Then I'll be sure not to fail you, my lady.' He inclined his head with a look of grudging respect before turning around, stalking out of the apartment and away down the gallery.

Mathilde threw Katharine one last questioning look before hurrying after him, almost running to keep up. She wanted to ask who it was he resembled, but judging by his brisk pace and taciturn silence, he wasn't in the mood for talking and, in that case, neither was she. She'd finally decided how she felt about him and she *didn't* like him, not one bit. The moment she got back, she was going to throw his box of dirt out of the window for good.

She was so busy ranting inwardly, and walking so quickly, that she didn't notice when the toe of one of her leather shoes caught on the edge of a flagstone, sending her stumbling forward, face downwards towards the floor. Instinctively, she lifted her hands to break the fall, but a strong arm reached her first, catching her around the waist and lifting her back to her feet and against an equally strong, solid-feeling chest. She gasped, startled as much by the warm pressure of Henry's body against her own as by the unwanted shiver of excitement that raced down her spine and pooled in her abdomen.

'Mathilde,' he murmured her name and she looked up, seeing his gaze soften as it moved over her face, as if there were something there he didn't understand.

'I thought you weren't talking to me?' She

wrenched herself away with a glare, brushing her skirts down in an attempt to hide her confusion. If he thought she was going to forgive him for his earlier rudeness so easily then he could think again.

'It's not you. It's—' he started to answer and then stopped, muttering an oath before curling a hand around her upper arm and drawing her onwards again, his footsteps only marginally slower than before. 'This way. Stay close and say as little as possible.'

Chapter Eight

⧼⧽

As much as she hated to admit it, there was a good chance that Henry had been right, Mathilde realised, entering a long, low-roofed chamber filled with several rows of tables and benches set between rounded, stone pillars. There were no women anywhere, but more than a dozen men, several of whom she recognised. They were Mortimer's retainers, his guards, though most of them wouldn't be of much use tonight, looking glassy-eyed and clutching cups of ale as they turned in her direction with half-curious, half-leering expressions that made her wish the Queen had chosen someone else to deliver the pouch, after all. Now that she *was* there, however, she had no choice but to go forward, putting on a much braver face than she felt.

If Henry sensed her unease then he gave no

sign of it, leading her across the room to where a man with greasy-looking blond hair was sitting alone beside the fireside, nursing a tankard. He didn't appear quite as drunk as the rest, but there was still a smirk on his face that made her uncomfortable. If he was one of Mortimer's men then she ought to be safe, she reassured herself, although somehow his expression made her feel anything but.

'Dubois,' Henry addressed him tersely. 'Mortimer will speak with you in the morning. The Queen sends you a gift in the meantime.'

Mathilde held the pouch out as she felt his shoulder nudge against her arm, dismayed to find that her fingers were trembling.

'From the Queen?' The man pulled the bag from her hand like a hawk falling on its prey, his face lighting up greedily as he tore the leather cord away and peered inside.

'You're not to go anywhere or speak to anyone before morning.' Somehow she forced the words out.

'I've no intention of doing either.' Dubois looked from the pouch to her with a speculative expression. 'Is this all I get? Or do you come with it, sweeting?'

She gasped, indignation warring with fear. Her throat felt dry and sticky at the same time, making it difficult to answer, but fortunately, Henry did it for her, his grip on her arm tightening as he spoke.

'No. We're leaving.'

'So soon?' Dubois laughed. 'Why can't she follow her mistress's example and be kind to us Mortimer men? Especially when the Queen is *so* very grateful.'

Laughter exploded in the room, only gaining in volume as Mathilde looked around, horrified by the insult to her mistress. She opened her lips, determined to say something quelling this time, but Henry wheeled her about before the words could emerge, hauling her back in the direction they'd come.

'Why leave so soon, Wright? Do you want her for yourself?' Another man stepped in front of them, blocking the way, the stench of ale on his breath so overpowering that Mathilde couldn't help but sway backwards.

'Don't be a fool.' Henry shoved him out of the way.

'We won't keep her for long. Then you can have her back. Come on, pretty. You can be *grateful* like the Queen, can't you?' The other man laughed and darted forward again, sliding a finger beneath her chin and tipping it upwards.

'Let me go!' Mathilde twisted her face aside. 'Pig turd!'

'Get out of the way.' Henry's voice was like steel, sharp and inflexible as a sword.

'Or what? What are you going to do about it?'

Henry moved so fast that his hands were wrapped around the man's throat before Mathilde had even noticed they were gone from her arm. She'd seen him look stern and intimidating before, but never angry, and right now he looked ferocious, slamming the other man against a wall so hard that stone dust erupted around them. She inhaled sharply, her heart hammering so violently that she was half-afraid it might burst out of her ribcage. Other men were stirring now, more and more of them getting to their feet, albeit unsteadily. The situation was getting out of hand and she had no idea what to do. She glanced back over her shoulder towards Dubois, but he only looked amused by the scene.

'Let me go!' the man spluttered, his face darkening to an alarming puce colour, but Henry's grip didn't slacken.

'Go!'

It took her a few seconds to comprehend that he was talking to her, his voice still as hard as his expression, though when she did, she went quickly, slamming the door behind her with an ominous thud. Every instinct of self-preservation told her to run, but she couldn't bring herself to abandon him, not when he was still trapped inside, defending her honour. Desperately, she picked up an empty flagon that had been left outside the door, thinking that she could at least smash it over someone's head if necessary, and then stood back, torn by indecision, listening to the sounds of a thud followed by a scuffle, then a yelp and more thuds, all of them accompanied by raised voices, within.

She'd just about decided to go and fetch help when the door opened again and Henry stepped out, closing it calmly behind him. His jaw was set in a grim line, but his look of fury was gone and he seemed unharmed, his hair and tunic barely even ruffled.

'Thirsty?' He looked at her and quirked an eyebrow.

'What?' She gaped at him for a second, too relieved to make sense of the question, before remembering the flagon in her hand and dropping it quickly. 'It was the only weapon I could find.'

'Fortunately, most of them were too drunk to get this far.' He grunted and took hold of her arm again, his grasp like iron. 'Come on.'

'Are you all right?' She looked him up and down as they walked, searching for injuries, unable to believe that he could have escaped the room so unscathed. He looked completely calm, while her own stomach was still churning with nerves.

'Never better.'

'You shouldn't have attacked him.'

'Shouldn't I?' He looked down at her, blue eyes glittering. 'Should I have let him have you, then?'

'Of course not!' She felt nauseated by the thought of the man's hands anywhere near her. 'But you could have been hurt.'

'So could you.'

She shook her head, unwilling to think about what could have happened. 'I don't understand. I thought they were Mortimer's men.'

'They are. Dubois's another of his spies.'

'Like you?'

'Nothing like me!' A muscle bulged in his jaw. 'The Queen should never have sent you there tonight.'

'She sent me under your protection.'

'Did *she* know that?'

Mathilde clamped her mouth shut defensively. No, Isabella hadn't asked who had brought the news of Dubois's arrival. She hadn't known who her protector would be, if any, but then she couldn't have known how Mortimer's men would treat her either. If anyone was to blame, then it was Mortimer.

Henry's lip curled when she didn't answer. 'She didn't, did she? She sent a dove into a den of wolves because she didn't care to ask. I told you before, don't trust her.'

'Should I trust *you* instead, then?' she challenged him and he gave her a look of incredulity mixed with exasperation.

'Do you need any more proof?'

She swallowed, realising the truth of it. No, she didn't need any more proof. Whatever mixed feelings she'd had on that subject had resolved themselves that evening. She didn't want to think about what he'd just saved her from, but traitor or not, she knew that he'd saved her. She knew that she ought to thank him, too, but somehow she found herself arguing instead. 'You insulted me! You called that man a fool for saying you might want me for yourself!'

'*What?*' Henry stopped walking abruptly, pulling her sideways into a window embrasure. 'That's not why I said it.'

Mathilde lifted her head, shivering in a way that had nothing to do with the cold. The nearest torch had gone out so it was darker in this part of the corridor, but she could still see the fierceness of his gaze, his eyes almost scorching her with their heat. They made a stark contrast to his touch, which was tender as he lifted a hand and pressed his palm against the side of her face, cupping her gently from brow to chin. His fingers felt warm, though she was acutely aware of the calloused patches of his skin. For some reason, she wanted to press her cheek closer against them.

'I was trying to get you out of there.' His voice sounded deeper than it had a few moments before. 'That was all I was thinking about.'

'Oh…' A fresh shiver of excitement coursed through her body. After the heightened emotions of the past hour, even the lightest of touches felt dangerously potent. Her very toes felt as if they were curling. 'Then you didn't mean it?'

'Are you asking me if I want you? What do *you* think, Mathilde?' His thumb dipped, tracing the line of her mouth. 'But I've no right to. You're a lady.'

'Only in name. My family are more like farmers.'

'"Pig turd"?' He laughed softly. 'I wondered where that came from.'

'I have three brothers.' She smiled. 'So you see, not much of a lady. I've no fortune at all.'

'It doesn't matter. You're still noble-born and I'm…' He grimaced and then took a step backwards, sliding his hand slowly, seemingly reluctantly, away from her skin. 'Ask your friend. She'll tell you.'

'Why can't *you* tell me?' She put her hand on his arm, closing the distance between them again, surprised by her own boldness, but her cheek felt cold without his fingers.

'Because…' He sucked in a deep breath and then blew it out between his teeth. 'Because I'm not *just* one of Mortimer's men. I'm a Mortimer, too.'

'What?' She drew her brows together, uncomprehending. 'But your name is Wright.'

'Exactly.'

'Oh!' She felt her jaw drop as the truth dawned on her. Apparently, she was blind as well as naive. She'd noticed the resemblance between him and his master the first time they'd met, but she'd never once guessed at the reason, not even when Katharine had asked whether he was named after his mother's family. 'You mean, Mortimer's your father?'

'Or brother or uncle or cousin. I don't know. All I know is that I have Mortimer blood. For all the good that it does me.' A muscle tightened in his jaw, his expression turning bleak for a moment. 'And a bastard does not aim for a lady, no matter how much he likes her, or how much he might want to. It was wrong of me to ever seek you out.'

He reached for her hand as she continued to stare at him in surprise, pressing a kiss slowly and solemnly into the palm before leading her out of the embrasure and on towards the Queen's apartments.

'Goodnight, my lady.' He made a perfunctory bow at the corner of the gallery, out of sight of the guards.

'Wait!' His farewell seemed to jolt her back to herself as she lifted a hand to stay him, sucking in a breath as it brushed inadvertently against his chest. 'I haven't thanked you for what you did back there.' She paused, staring at her splayed fingers where they rested on his tunic, somehow unable to pull them away again. The urge to touch him was too strong to resist. He'd gone very still, but she could feel the heavy pounding of his heartbeat beneath. It struck her as primal somehow, as if their bodies were joined together as one. She licked her lips, feeling the rhythm in the pit of her stomach, beating in echo to her own. 'I'm very grateful.'

'Grateful?' His voice sounded hoarse, the word seeming to hover in the air between them.

'Yes, and...' She peered up through her lashes, a rush of heat making her cheeks bloom and perspiration break out beneath her tunic. 'You said that I owed you a kiss.'

'I shouldn't have.' His brows compressed, though his gaze dropped to her mouth. 'You don't have to thank me, lady.'

'But I want to. You see... I like you, too, Henry Wright, even though I shouldn't.'

She lifted her other hand, sliding it around the nape of his neck and on into the thick, dark curls of his hair, though, to her embarrassment, he *still* didn't move. He seemed completely frozen, so that, for one horrible moment, she thought she'd made a humiliating mistake, before he muttered something unintelligible under his breath and lowered his face towards hers.

Her pulse quickened as she leaned closer towards him. It was a strange, unstoppable impulse, as if her mind were no longer in control of her body. Instead, every part of her seemed to be quivering with anticipation as his hands encircled her waist and then slid lower, over the flare of her hips, drawing her so close that she could feel the whole length of his body against her own.

It was like nothing she'd ever felt before, hard and muscular and dangerously masculine, fitting perfectly against hers. She saw him tilt his head sideways slightly and then felt his mouth brush lightly against her own for one single, heart-stopping moment before a woman came around the corner and they jumped apart guiltily.

Henry lifted a hand to the dagger concealed inside his tunic, his nerves still on edge from the earlier altercation, then dropped it again almost as quickly. The woman coming from the direction of the Queen's rooms was no threat. On the contrary, she looked to be in some kind of danger herself, one hand clasped to her side as if she were in pain.

'Lady Cecily?' Mathilde gasped and rushed forward, taking hold of the woman's arm with a look of concern. 'What's the matter?'

'My lady?' Henry grasped hold of her other elbow. 'Perhaps you should not be out here?'

'I need…some air.' The woman looked up at him, her green gaze misting, before her whole body seemed to sag and her knees gave way beneath her.

'We should get her to bed.' Mathilde tried to turn her around, but the woman dug her heels in with a surprising show of strength.

'Not yet… Over there…' She gestured towards a window seat, gritting her teeth against the pain as they carried her across to it. 'Thank you. Don't worry, this will pass.'

'Has this happened before?' Mathilde exchanged a worried glance with Henry. 'Shall I fetch someone? A healer?'

'No. It won't do any good.'

'Something for the pain, then?' He crouched down on one knee.

'I have this.' The woman pulled a small vial from her sleeve. 'I've already taken a little. It just needs a few moments to work.'

'What about Katharine? Shall I go and fetch her?' Mathilde was already several feet away.

'No!' The woman sat forward again, stretching a hand out in protest though the movement obviously caused even more pain. 'I don't want her to know about this, not yet. Promise me you won't tell her.'

Mathilde hesitated, but the woman's gaze was fixed on hers and she had no choice. 'I promise.'

'Thank you. You're a good girl. I know that you'll take care of her for me…afterwards.'

'Hush. You'll be able to take care of her yourself.'

'No. I've seen healers.' The woman tipped her head back and closed her eyes with a sigh. 'Don't let her grieve too deeply.'

'Cecily…'

'Come away.' Henry jerked his head towards the opposite side of the gallery as the woman let out a faint snore, the lines of tension in her face gradually slackening. 'She's one of the Queen's older attendants, isn't she? I've seen her before.'

'Yes.' Mathilde nodded miserably, her eyes glistening with tears. 'She hasn't been well of late, but we thought she was getting better.'

'Does she have a husband? If she's really so ill, then perhaps you ought to send for him?'

'She does, but...unless she asks, I don't think she would want me to. They're not close.'

'Ah.'

'She and Katharine...' She dipped her gaze. 'They *are* close. It's not...that is, I don't quite understand what it is, but they've both been very kind to me.' She looked up again, her gaze challenging. 'They're good women.'

'I know.'

'You do?' She looked surprised. 'Then you don't think we should judge?'

'Why? Who are we?' He lifted a shoulder. 'Does she have any other family?'

'Three sons, but she won't want them travelling to France at the moment. The King might suspect them of different motives.'

He frowned. Unfortunately, there was probably some truth in that, however unjust it might be.

'She's been so kind to me.' Mathilde sniffed. 'She and Kat and the Queen. I hate to see her like this.'

'I know.' He placed a hand on her shoulder, fighting the urge to go further and wrap both of his arms around her. As much as he wanted to offer comfort, he'd already touched her more than he should have that evening, albeit nowhere near as much as he wanted to. 'If you need any help with Lady Cecily in the future, send a page to find me. If I'm here, I'll do whatever I can.'

'*If* you're here?' Her gaze widened. 'Does that mean you're leaving again?'

'Perhaps. I don't know. I have to go wherever Mortimer sends me. Often without a great deal of warning.'

'I see.' She bit down on her bottom lip for a moment. 'Henry…about what you said earlier… I want you to know that I understand, but I don't care who you are or where you come from. You've behaved like a true knight this evening.'

He swallowed, feeling a pang in his chest and an unfamiliar lump in his throat. The words made him feel better and worse at the same time. A true knight would have a chance of winning a lady, but their respective positions in life made any alliance between them impossible. If this evening had proven anything it was that they belonged in different worlds and his was too dangerous for her. Maybe in the future things would be different, but there was no way to know when or how or even *if* Mortimer would ever reward him for his service.

In the meantime, he had nothing to offer her but hope. And if what she'd told him about her father was true, then even *that* was reduced to a sliver. He was doubly undesirable as a suitor: a bastard *and* a traitor. Even if he was rewarded eventually, there was no hope of a future together and it was selfish of him to dream otherwise. Besides, it was becoming dangerous, the way he felt about her. Liking and attraction were one thing, but he didn't want to fall in love, especially with a woman he could never have. He'd spent most of his life actively avoiding heartache. How foolish would he be to let down his guard and go looking for it now? The safest thing that he could do was say farewell and make certain he was never alone with her again.

'I was honoured to serve, my lady.' He bowed his head though his eyes never left her face. 'But now you should go back to the Queen's rooms. I'll take care of Lady Cecily.'

'Are you sure?' She glanced over her shoulder to where her friend was just stirring again.

'I won't go anywhere until she's recovered, you have my word.'

'Thank you.' She rose up on her tiptoes and pressed a kiss to his cheek, her lips lingering, velvety soft against his skin, so that it took all of his willpower not to turn his head and claim them. For a tantalising moment he imagined doing just that, imagined parting her lips with his own and dipping his tongue inside, tasting and possessing her whole mouth, but it was no use. Even if, by some amazing chance, the Queen didn't forbid a match with a penniless spy, then her father certainly would. There was no possible way it could end well.

He squeezed his fingernails into his palms, stifling the temptation to reach for her again. 'Goodnight, Lady Mathilde.'

Chapter Nine

Spring 1326

'How long have you known?' It was March by the time Katharine asked the question Mathilde had been dreading.

'A few months.' She threw a guilty glance at the bed where Cecily was dozing.

'I've known that something was wrong for a while, but she kept on denying it.' Katharine jumped as a log made a loud snapping sound in the hearth. 'I finally confronted her this afternoon.'

'I'm sorry.'

'Did she ask you not to tell me?'

'Yes. I think she didn't want to upset you.'

'Then you've nothing to apologise for. You were being a good friend. You *are* a good friend.'

Mathilde bent her head, relieved that the truth was finally out in the open, though it didn't make it any easier to bear. 'She says that she's spoken to healers, but maybe the Queen's physician might be able to help?'

'Pah!' Katharine's tone was bitter. 'I'll ask, but the Queen has no ears for any subject but Mortimer.'

Mathilde winced at the words, though she could hardly dispute them either. Isabella had seemed almost wilfully deaf and blind to Cecily's suffering all through the winter, so preoccupied with her own concerns that she'd scarcely even noticed when Lady Berthe and six of the other spies had slipped away one night, fleeing back to England just as Henry had told her they would.

Something seemed to have gone wrong with the Queen's plans, but frustratingly Mathilde had no idea what. All she knew was that the invasion planned for the spring wasn't going to happen and, not wanting to bother an anxious Katharine with questions, there was only one person she could think of to ask about it.

Unfortunately, she'd barely seen Henry, let alone spoken to him for months. He seemed to come and go, sometimes at court, other times absent for weeks at a time, and she caught only occasional glimpses of him even when he *was* there. After what he'd said the last time they'd met, she suspected that he was avoiding her deliberately. He noticed her, she thought, or at least his eyes always seemed to be moving away whenever she glanced in his direction, but he never passed by or visited the Queen's chambers any more.

Instead, he seemed to have been appointed as some kind of companion to the young Prince, spending most of his time in the stable yard and bailey, practising sword skills and jousting. It was probably for the best. In her heart, she knew that he'd only spoken the truth about their respective positions. It didn't matter how much he liked her, or she him, there was no hope of a future together. She ought to forget him, but that was easier said than done, especially when she didn't truly want to.

After a few days of indecision, she decided to take a chance, making a detour to the stables one morning on her way back from the palace kitchens. By good fortune, Henry was the very first person she saw, his black curls gleaming in the morning sunshine as he prepared his horse for what looked like a hunting expedition. Quickly, she hurried towards him and then stopped in the middle of the yard as she realised how unladylike her behaviour might seem to others. She ought not to be there in such a predominantly male domain, and on her own, too, but as she started to turn away Henry looked up, caught her eye and immediately dropped what he was doing to come and speak with her.

'What is it?' He sounded concerned. 'Is Lady Cecily worse?'

'No.' Mathilde looked down at her feet, feeling foolish and tongue-tied all of a sudden. An hour ago, it had seemed a good idea to come and find him, but now she was painfully aware of other eyes watching them. There were two grooms on the other side of the yard and she could hear voices inside the stables. What if gossip about her behaviour reached the Queen?

'Lady Mathilde?' Henry prompted her and she shook her head apologetically.

'It's nothing. I shouldn't have come. I only wanted to ask you a question.'

He didn't answer immediately, his expression oddly torn, as if he didn't know whether to look pleased or to chide her, before he chose the former and smiled. 'Later. I'll find you.'

She gave a quick nod and hurried away, spending the rest of the day in a state of nervous anticipation, though she was kept busy with tasks. With most of the spies gone, there was a lot more work to be shared, and she was already doing most of Katharine and Cecily's, too. All of which meant she had barely any time to herself until the late afternoon when the Queen announced that she had private business to discuss with Mortimer.

The door to the withdrawing chamber had barely closed behind them before a boy appeared in the corridor, studying Mathilde for a few seconds before tipping his head to one side like a bird, jerking his thumb to the left and then running away.

'Kat?' Mathilde felt her heart give a small flutter at the signal. 'I'm going outside.'

'Now?' Katharine glanced pointedly towards the window. 'It's getting dark.'

'I know. I won't be long.' She threw her red mantle around her shoulders. 'I just want to stretch my legs a little.'

'Mmm.' Katharine gave her a suspicious glance, but fortunately didn't protest as Mathilde ran out to the gallery.

'Well met, lady.' Henry was leaning against the wall, arms crossed with one ankle folded casually over the other. In contrast to his usual plain clothes, today he was dressed like a courtier in the latest French fashion, with dark hose and a turquoise-blue doublet overlaid with a contrasting and expensive-looking burgundy mantle. He definitely wasn't trying to blend into the shadows any longer. Sir Nobody of Nowhere he might have called himself, but today he looked like the son of an earl or a baron or even a baron himself. 'That was quick.'

'You timed it well.'

'I made a point of walking here with Mortimer. The Queen shouldn't need you for an hour at least.'

She gave a restrained smile, trying not to show how pleased she was to be in his company again. 'How did the boy know who I was?'

'I described you. I told him to look for the most beautiful woman in the palace.'

'Don't be absurd.'

'It's the truth!' He held an arm out like a seasoned courtier. 'Shall we take a walk?'

Twilight was deepening as they made their way out into the palace gardens and along an avenue of lime trees. Fortunately, the sky was cloudless and the moon full, illuminating the path ahead of them with pale, silvery light. A couple of guards were already walking there, although they stepped aside quickly when they saw Henry. Mathilde didn't like the way that they smirked, as if they thought he'd brought her there for some kind of romantic liaison, although she could hardly complain when she was the one who'd asked for a meeting.

'You're working too hard,' Henry commented when they were finally alone again. 'You ought to be resting.'

She twisted her face towards him in surprise. 'Have you been spying on me now?'

'I don't need to. There are dark circles around your eyes.'

'Everyone's busy. The Queen doesn't have as many ladies these days. As you know.'

'Yes, I did notice.' There was a hint of a smile in his voice. 'So what was it you wanted to ask me?'

'It's about the invasion and whether it's still going ahead?'

'Of course.' It was his turn to look surprised. 'What would make you think otherwise?'

'Just because it's the spring. I thought that something would have happened by now.'

'Ah.' He nodded. 'There have been some delays. It takes time and money to muster an army.'

'Can't the French King help?'

'There's only so much help Isabella can accept from her brother. A French-born queen sending a French army into England would antagonise the barons just when she needs their support.'

'Then what about Hainault? Prince Edward is going to marry Count Guillame's daughter, isn't he?'

'Are you a spy now as well?' He gave her an approving look. 'Yes, the betrothal is almost agreed upon, only with a dowry of ships and soldiers instead of gold.'

'So you're saying this is just a delay, not a change of heart?'

'Exactly. The Queen's course is set. There's no turning back from it now.'

'Oh.'

'You sound disappointed.' She felt rather than saw his eyes turn questioningly towards her.

'I am. I suppose I was hoping you'd say that the King and Queen were engaged in secret peace talks.' She sighed. 'In that case, I'm sorry for coming to the stable yard. I just didn't know who else to ask and…well, I trust you.'

He squeezed her arm, tugging her closer towards him. 'Don't be sorry, I was glad to see you.'

'Really?' She glanced at him dubiously. 'We haven't spoken for a while.'

'I know. It wasn't because I didn't want to. I just thought that it was for the best.'

'Because I'm a lady?'

'Yes. And because it's dangerous to want what you can't have. Some people would say that it's looking for trouble.'

He stopped walking, making a move as if to sit down on the riverbank, but she grabbed at his sleeve.

'Not there!' She tried to keep the burst of panic out of her voice. 'Somewhere else.'

'As you wish.' He gave her a searching look, although thankfully didn't argue, leading her towards the shelter of a giant oak tree instead. 'Is this better?'

'Much,' she agreed readily as he took off his mantle and spread it out on the ground with a flourish.

'My lady?' There was a twinkle in his eye as he gestured for her to sit, but she hesitated none the less, remembering the expressions on the guards' faces when they'd seen them walking alone together. How much worse would they look if they saw them sitting side by side, half-hidden in the shadows?

'They won't disturb us.' Henry seemed to understand her reticence. 'There are some perks to being one of Mortimer's men.'

'Oh… I see.' She perched on the edge of the mantle, pulling her knees up to her chest. It still didn't seem like something she ought to be doing, but she was tired and it was a relief to rest her legs. 'Thank you. It's been a long day.'

'Like I said, you ought to be resting.' He sat down beside her, his expression concerned.

'So should you. It looks like the Prince keeps you busy.'

'Edward rarely sits still for two minutes at a time.' He chuckled. 'He makes me feel old.'

'How old *are* you?' she asked, feigning un-interest by tugging on a blade of grass.

'Two and twenty. So I really have no excuse.'

'No, I suppose not...'

He leaned back against the tree trunk, regarding her through hooded eyes. 'Don't.'

She started, snapping the grass between her fingertips. 'Don't what?'

'Don't wonder about how old Mortimer might be and whether that makes him my father. I told you, I don't know.'

She flushed guiltily, glad of the darkness concealing her cheeks. 'Won't your mother tell you?'

'She can't. She's dead. Or so I heard anyway.'

'Oh.' She blinked at the note of emptiness in his voice. 'I'm sorry.'

'So am I, although to be honest, it doesn't make a huge amount of difference to my life.

I hadn't seen her since I was six years old. I don't even remember what she looked like.' His shrug looked a little too forced. 'I suppose it might have helped if I'd resembled her a little, but I seem to be all Mortimer.'

'So the Mortimer family acknowledge you?'

'They keep me in their service, if that's what you mean. Spying and fighting for them is all that I'm trained for. It's better than nothing, but sometimes I think a trade might have been preferable.'

Mathilde shifted position, tucking her legs up beneath her as she leaned against the trunk beside him. She'd heard cynicism in his voice before, but melancholy was something new. It made her feel closer to him somehow, closer than she'd felt to anyone in a long time.

'Tell me about that home of yours,' he said, folding his arms behind his head and closing his eyes as if he'd just requested a bedtime story. 'The one you were missing so much when we first met. Rudstone Manor, wasn't it?'

'Yes, between Scarborough and York.'

'What was it you missed most about it? Surely not the weather?' His lips quirked. 'I've been to the north of England.'

'No, not the weather, although it's not always bad. You people further south only think so.'

She couldn't help but smile. 'I missed—*miss*—everything about it. The house, for a start. My great-grandfather built it, but new rooms have been added since. There's a hall with a small entrance room at one end and a solar and bed-chamber above. The kitchen's outside on its own and there's a stable and brewhouse and barn, but no wall, just a wooden fence around the build-ings. Then outside there are fields. We grow wheat and barley mostly and keep sheep and a few goats.'

'I'm starting to understand why you miss it.' He gave a faint sigh. 'I'd like something like that for myself one day. A real home. What about your family? Tell me about them.'

'Why?' She leaned closer, able to study his face in more detail now that he had his eyes closed. In the twilight, he looked almost uncan-nily like Mortimer, all except for his curly hair and a jagged white scar on his chin that sug-gested he'd once been cut there. She wondered how... 'Why do you want to know?'

'I suppose I'd like to know what it's like.'

'To have a family?'

'Yes.' His eyes snapped open again suddenly, like blue orbs glowing in the moonlight. 'Are you close?'

'Very.' She shifted backwards again. 'Especially to my sister, Hawise. She's the oldest, but she got married and left home three years ago. My brothers are all younger. Aland, Laurent and Dicun. Aland is the closest to me in age, but I miss them all.' She paused. 'Then there's just my father.'

'What about your mother?'

'She died when I was twelve.'

'I see.' He frowned. 'So if you were the only woman left when your sister married, didn't your father want you to stay and run his household?'

'No, he found someone else for that, a maid.' She pursed her lips briefly before letting the truth out in a rush. 'He wanted to get rid of me. Apart from anything else, I was unnecessary at home, just another mouth to feed. So he sent me to court.'

'Ah.'

'So you see, there was never really any choice about me going back.' She forced a smile. 'Fortunately, I'm not as homesick as I used to be. I belong with the Queen now.'

His frown deepened. 'Just because you can't go home doesn't mean you *have* to stay with her.'

'Doesn't it?'

'No.' He reached a hand out, lacing his fingers slowly through hers. 'There are other possibilities.'

She drew in a breath, though her voice still emerged as a whisper. 'What possibilities?'

Henry kept hold of Mathilde's hand. There was something comforting about the feeling of her slender fingers wrapped inside his. Something that felt right, too, as if some hollow part of him had been filled. She'd looked so anxious that morning in the stable yard that he hadn't been able to resist meeting her, no matter how much his better judgement had argued against it, and, now he was touching her again after three months of only occasional and distant glimpses, he didn't want to let go. But it was folly. He was spinning dreams, wanting to tell her he wouldn't be a spy for ever, that he intended to be a man of fortune and have a home and land of his own one day, a home that he could share, but he couldn't make any promises, not yet… He needed to barricade his heart before he did something foolish.

He rubbed his thumb over the backs of her knuckles, evading her question to make an offer instead. 'You know, if you wish, I could carry a message to your family. I'm travelling to England again soon.'

'You're going back?' She looked alarmed. 'But isn't that dangerous?'

'Only if I get caught.' He smiled. 'Will you worry about me?'

'Of course I will! You look so much like Mortimer!'

He laughed, resisting the impulse to point out that she herself hadn't guessed the relation. 'So do a lot of people. Fortunately black hair and blue eyes aren't yet a crime in Edward's England. Besides, I'll be a long way from London. Most of my work will be in Scotland.'

'Really?' She looked only mildly placated. 'Why there?'

He lifted an eyebrow. 'Are you *certain* that you're not a spy?'

'A spy would think of a cleverer way to ask.'

'Ah, but perhaps that's the truly clever part. Perhaps you disguise yourself as a beautiful young maiden simply to trick me into telling you stories.'

'I'm not beautiful.' Her brow creased as she turned her head away. 'And I don't have any wiles.'

'You're more beautiful than you realise.' He lifted the hand that wasn't already holding hers to her chin, twisting her face back towards him. 'I'm going to Berwick because the Bruce wants to be acknowledged as King of Scotland and Isabella's prepared to agree.'

'You mean that she's going to give up the Crown's claim to Scotland?' Mathilde stared at him in disbelief and he could understand why. The first King Edward had spent twenty years campaigning in the north. The idea of giving back all the territory he'd fought so hard over seemed incredible, but after the disaster of Bannockburn there was little choice. Isabella couldn't fight her husband and defend England's borders at the same time.

'Yes. In return for peace, a promise not to cause trouble when she invades. She's a clever woman, your Queen.'

'*Our* Queen,' she corrected him. 'Do you promise to come back?'

Henry looked down at their hands. They were still twined together. Fanciful as it sounded, he felt as if their minds were joined in some way now, too. 'I promise to do my best, although maybe not to Paris. I don't know how long I'll be away, but I'll find you again, Mathilde, wherever you are.'

'And will you meet with me then or will you still avoid me for being a lady?' Her eyes narrowed slightly.

'I *shouldn't* meet with you. It would be better for you that way.'

'Shouldn't that be my decision?'

'Yes, but—'

'It's not as if we'd be doing anything wrong. Neither of us is married or promised to anyone else.'

'Your father still wouldn't approve.'

'I know.'

'I'm illegitimate.'

'I don't care.'

'There's your reputation to consider.'

'I know that, too. The Queen might not like there to be rumours about one of her ladies, but…I like being with you.'

'I like being with you, too.'

'And it's hardly as bad as invading a country!' She gave a nervous-sounding laugh. 'As long as we're discreet, like the Queen and Mortimer, then nobody else would ever need to know… Would they?'

He glanced back towards the palace. He ought to refuse, to say that he absolutely couldn't meet her again, but the words wouldn't come. And maybe they didn't need to. Maybe after the invasion, Mortimer would reward him sooner rather than later, and then they wouldn't be so far apart in station, after all. Maybe there was a chance…a slim and possibly insane one, but he still grasped at it…

'Then we'll be careful.' He squeezed her hand. 'Mathilde, I can't make any promises, I've nothing to offer you at the moment and I don't know what the future will bring. All I can say with any certainty is that I'll miss you.'

'I have nothing to offer either, but I'll miss you, too.' She smiled and then sobered. 'As for your offer, I thank you, but I've no message for home. I haven't heard anything from my father since I reached Paris and it would be too dangerous. I couldn't trust him not to turn you over to the King's men.'

'As you wish.' He slid his free arm around her waist, drawing her close. 'So here we are, the Queen's lady and the traitor's bastard.'

She laid her head on his shoulder, settling against him. 'You shouldn't call yourself that.'

'It's the truth.'

'But not the whole truth. You're a lot more than that.'

He kissed her. He wasn't aware of moving, or of making any conscious decision to do so. He was only suddenly aware of their lips touching, as if he simply hadn't been able *not* to kiss her any longer.

'Mathilde…' he moaned her name into her

mouth, surprised and pleased when she moaned his back. It felt better than he'd even imagined, as if he'd found the one place in the world he most wanted to be. She'd never been kissed before, that was obvious, but what she lacked in experience, she more than made up for in enthusiasm. He didn't hold back either, deepening the kiss while he lifted her on to his lap, wishing that they were indoors, somewhere more comfortable, and not outside, beneath a tree in the cold evening air. Not that it felt particularly cold at that moment. On the contrary, he felt red-hot, almost drunk with the sweet taste of her mouth, with the way that her hands slid around his neck, too, not to mention the feeling of her breasts rising and falling against his chest. He wanted to kiss her for hours, to touch and caress every part of her, but there was no time and it was too risky. If somebody saw them…

'Tell me to stop.' He broke the kiss with a low growl of frustration, burying his face in her neck.

'What?' She ran her hands over his shoulder blades and down his back, her breath emerging in soft pants that inflamed his senses even further.

'Tell me to stop kissing you.' He couldn't resist trailing his lips across the silken column of her throat, his willpower ebbing away as desire began to overwhelm caution. 'Tell me. *Please.*'

'Stop.' She pulled back, her brown eyes swollen to black as her chest heaved against his, so soft and supple, separated only by her gown and his tunic.

'Forgive me.' He clutched at her waist, his voice still thick with desire as he tried to steady his own breathing. 'I shouldn't have done that.'

'I did it, too. There's nothing to forgive.' She gulped. 'Was it good?'

'It was better than good, but it's not a good idea. Not yet.'

'Then maybe we should call it a farewell kiss.' She slid off his lap, crouching in front of him.

'As horrible as that sounds, it might be for the best.'

'Well, then…' She raised her hands to either side of his face, her gaze intent. 'You'll take care in Scotland?'

'I will, I promise.' He had to clench his fingers to stop himself from reaching for her one last time. 'Trust me, Mathilde.'

'I do.'

'Do you promise to take care, too?'

'Of course. The Queen will take care of me,

but now I'd better go. Katharine will be wondering where I am.'

'Yes.' He watched as she stood up, unable to move at that precise moment. 'Goodbye, Mathilde.'

'Goodbye.' She gave him a single swift nod and then disappeared into the darkness.

Chapter Ten

Summer 1326

'Where have you been?' Katharine came rushing out of the Queen's dressing chamber, a look of panic on her face.

'To the herb garden for some lavender.' Mathilde looked around in alarm. 'What's happened? What's the matter?'

'We're leaving in the morning! Which means we need to pack up everything tonight and I've no idea where to start!'

'Leaving?' Mathilde's heart leapt into her throat. Despite what Henry had said, she'd still harboured a faint hope that the invasion wouldn't happen, but if they were finally leaving then surely that meant they were going back to England and war?

Katharine nodded distractedly. 'King Edward

sent a message demanding she leave France at once and King Charles agreed.'

'So her own brother is sending her away?'

'Only because the timing is so perfect. We're expected in Ponthieu.'

'What's in Ponthieu?'

'Soldiers, mercenaries, money.' Katharine's lips twisted in a grimace. 'Then we'll ride on to Hainault. Mortimer's already there, waiting for her.'

Mathilde's thoughts jumped immediately to Henry. Would he be there, too? There had been no word of him since he'd left for Scotland in March, or at least none that she knew of, but then who would have told her if there *had* been? He was a spy and she had no right to ask. It would have looked suspicious if she had. Instead, she'd been forced to rely on hearsay and whispers and there had been precious little of those. No one had even mentioned his name, as if he'd existed only as a figment of her imagination.

Since that evening beneath the oak tree, she'd found herself thinking about him every day. And night, too. How could she not after the way that he'd kissed her? The way she'd kissed him in return… Maybe she shouldn't have, but just the memory made her lips tremble again. It was impossible to forget the way his heart had felt thumping heavily against her breast, not to mention the feeling of his powerful muscles beneath her fingertips. Even far apart, she felt closer to him than to anyone.

He'd promised to find her when he returned and she believed him, although she knew that he'd been giving her a warning, too, telling her the truth as gently as possible, that he couldn't offer her a future together because he was the illegitimate son of a traitor, not to mention a traitor himself. His only hope of advancement was for the invasion to be successful, but it made her uncomfortable to think of profiting from it. She served the Queen, but she still didn't want to take sides. She only wished there was someone she could talk to about Henry, but she had a strong suspicion that no one else would approve. The Queen's ladies needed to be above reproach, no matter how the Queen herself might behave.

'There's so much to do!' Katharine threw her hands up in despair.

'We'll manage.'

'What about Cecily? How will she cope with the journey?'

The other woman's voice broke and Mathilde reacted instinctively, wrapping her arms around her for comfort. She didn't know whether Katharine would appreciate the gesture or not, but to her surprise she didn't push her away. The older woman only stiffened for a moment before embracing her back, her chest heaving with sobs as her fingernails dug into Mathilde's shoulder blades so sharply they hurt. Mathilde didn't flinch or complain. By now, they both knew that Cecily was dying, although neither of them had said the words out loud. She knew that Katharine was right about the journey, too. Travel would only cause her more suffering.

'Perhaps Cecily ought to stay here?' she suggested tentatively.

'That's what I told her.' Katharine pulled away at last, rubbing the heels of her hands over her wet cheeks. 'I said that I'd stay with her, too, but she won't hear of it.'

'Then perhaps we can shorten the journey. Perhaps the two of you could go straight to Hainault?'

'Do you think the Queen would allow it?' Katharine looked hopeful.

'Possibly.' Mathilde lifted her shoulders, unable to answer more definitely when, in truth, she had no idea how Isabella would react. Since Mortimer's departure from Paris in May, she seemed to have turned into a different woman, becoming increasingly moody and short-tempered. It made a striking contrast to the year before. Back then she'd always been so calm and clear-headed, but now she acted as if he was all that mattered.

'I'll ask.' Katharine nodded decisively. 'For Cecily's sake, I'll do it.'

Katharine spoke with Isabella later that evening. Mathilde could hear their muffled voices through the walls as she closed up the last of the coffers, Katharine's beseeching while Isabella's sounded aggrieved.

'Mathilde!'

She straightened up at the sound of the Queen's call, passing a strained-looking Katharine in the doorway to her bedchamber.

'Yes, Your Grace?'

'Bring me some wine.' Isabella snapped her fingers as she paced up and down, her irritation obvious.

'Of course, Your Grace.' Mathilde poured out a cup of burgundy and then waited to be dismissed as Isabella took it and crossed to the window.

'I suppose you know that Kat and Cecily want to leave me now, too?' Her voice sounded petulant.

'I do not think they *want* to, Your Grace.'

Mathilde felt compelled to defend them. 'But Lady Cecily is very sick. The journey to Ponthieu might be too much for her.'

'Is she really so unwell, then?' Isabella gave her a sharp look.

'Yes, Your Grace. The pain in her stomach seems to grow worse every day.'

'Yet she's well enough to travel to Hainault?'

'No, but she's determined to return to England.'

Isabella's mouth twisted into an uncharacteristic pout. 'Oh, very well, then. Tell them they can go straight to Hainault. Kat's getting too old to be of much use anyway and if Cecily's as bad as you say then I don't want her slowing us down.'

'Yes, Your Grace.' Mathilde bit her tongue against a surge of anger. Isabella spoke as if they were simply encumbrances instead of two women who'd served her loyally for almost twenty years.

'You're not planning to leave me as well, are you?' Isabella's voice wavered.

'Of course not, Your Grace.' Mathilde shook her head, the note of appeal instantly assuaging her anger. Isabella was already weighed down with cares, she reminded herself. It wasn't that she held no affection for Cecily or was heartless. She simply had so many things to worry about. If the invasion went wrong, then the consequences would be terrible. No king would ever forgive such a betrayal. The rest of her life would be spent in a prison. A gilded prison, perhaps, but a prison none the less, with only her women for company. No wonder she was preoccupied and afraid of people deserting her.

'Promise me, Mathilde.' Isabella came towards her, placing a heavily jewelled hand on her shoulder. 'Promise that you won't abandon me for anyone else. I need at least one lady whose loyalty I can trust. You know that I'm only doing this because I don't have a choice, don't you? It's for the good of England, for my son's future, too.'

'I know, Your Grace.'

'Then will you promise to stay with me until all this is over?'

She swallowed, feeling a faint stirring of misgiving. She didn't want to make any promise that might jeopardise a possible future with Henry, however unlikely that might be, but then Isabella wasn't asking for forever, just *until all this was over*. She could promise her that much, surely? And after all the Queen's kindnesses, wasn't it the least she could do?

'Mathilde?'

'I promise, Your Grace.'

'Thank you.' Isabella exhaled visibly, the unnatural brightness of her eyes dimming again. 'When all this is over, I'll make sure you're rewarded. I'll make you a great lady of the court some day.'

Mathilde caught her breath at the words, misgiving turning to hope. If both she and Henry were rewarded for their services, then maybe there was a future for them, after all.

'We'll be back in England before the year is out.' Isabella sounded determined and suddenly Mathilde was, too. 'We will redress the wrongs done to us and show gratitude to those who have served us well, I swear it.'

They hadn't stayed in Ponthieu for long, just enough to secure the Queen's finances before riding on again. Isabella had set a fast pace, making Mathilde doubly glad that Katharine and Cecily hadn't accompanied them. There were still moments when she wondered if she were dreaming, riding at the Queen's side as the most trusted of all her ladies now, so that she couldn't help but think how proud her father would have been under different circumstances.

They arrived in Hainault in September to find Mortimer waiting, along with seven hundred soldiers provided by Count Guillaume and a few hundred more mercenaries, though with so many eyes watching, his reunion with Isabella was restrained. It made a stark contrast to the way they'd behaved in Paris, but at this late stage they couldn't afford for anything to go wrong. They needed to be seen as liberators saving England from a tyrant, not traitors engaged in an adulterous affair.

To Mathilde's dismay, however, there was still no sign of Henry, though she searched every face she could find in the crowd, hoping for a glimpse. It was unnerving to see such an immense army up close, their swords and shields and endless rows of tents making the whole scene look grey. Somehow Mortimer had gathered a fleet, too, almost a hundred ships altogether, but the sight of the Channel itself was terrifying. It had taken nearly all of her courage to cross it the first time and she wasn't sure she had enough left to do it again, especially without knowing what lay ahead. For all anyone knew, the King's army might be waiting to attack the moment they landed.

Her only consolation was that both Katharine and Cecily were also waiting in Hainault to greet them. Cecily looked thinner than ever, but the fact that she was standing unaided seemed to Mathilde a good sign.

'Don't let her fool you,' Kat murmured as they followed Isabella into the royal palace. 'She's pretending. To me, too.'

'But why?' Mathilde felt disappointed but not surprised. 'If she's in pain, then why isn't she resting?'

'Because she's afraid that Isabella won't take her if she knows how sick she truly is.'

'I'm sure the Queen would not abandon her.'

'Are you?' Katharine's jaw tightened. 'So was I, once.'

The morning of their departure dawned bright and golden and tranquil, a perfect day for a voyage. Everyone smiled at each other and declared it a good omen, although if that were true, Mathilde thought, then the heavy rain and winds that buffeted their ships barely an hour out of harbour were surely the opposite.

She was one of only six ladies now. Six ladies and one queen in the midst of an army of men, huddled together in the stale air below deck, speaking little—what was there to say?—as they sailed to invade their own homeland. She couldn't sleep, feeling queasy without actually being sick, chewing on ginger root so ferociously that Kat had to warn her to stop before she broke a tooth, focusing all her energy on *not* thinking about the roar of the water surrounding them. It was relentless, as if she were trapped inside some waking nightmare that refused to end.

They had spent two interminable, gut-wrenching days at sea, being violently tossed about and tormented by the stormy waves, as if the weather itself was on the King's side, until at last Katharine ventured out on to deck and called down that she could see land.

Mathilde rushed up to join her, leaning against the ship's railing and willing them safely into harbour. There was nothing safe about England any more, but the sight of dry land gladdened her heart. Somewhere out there was Henry, too, or at least she hoped so. It made her feel sicker than ever to think about what his continued absence might mean. He'd told her to trust him, but it was getting harder and harder *not* to imagine that something had happened.

At long last they dropped anchor off the Suffolk coast. Thankfully there was no opposing army to greet them, which was a mercy since their ships were scattered and it took an age for their forces to regroup and make camp. The Queen's was one of the last parties ashore and as Mathilde stepped on to the sand she made a private vow never to set foot on a boat ever again. Now that she was home, she intended to stay there, no matter what.

She had fallen asleep the moment she closed her eyes the previous night and didn't stir until Katharine shook her awake at dawn. Together they made the Queen ready to meet with her army commanders, but their conference had barely begun before they were interrupted by the arrival of the Earl of Norfolk, the King's own half-brother, riding into camp under a banner of peace. There was a heavy silence as he walked up to the Queen, bent his knee to the Prince and then put his soldiers at their disposal.

To most eyes, Isabella accepted the offer graciously, but Mathilde, who knew her better, could sense her surprise. She and Mortimer had expected support, but not so soon or from so high-ranking a source, and it wasn't long before other barons followed suit. What started as a trickle swiftly turned into a deluge as they arrived one by one to offer their support and lay their arms at the Queen's feet, swelling her army to twice its size in a matter of days.

* * *

As it turned out, the barons were only the beginning. As the army marched inland, south-ward and westward, from Ipswich to Bury St Edmunds and Cambridge, all of the towns opened their gates and surrendered their keys willingly. The inhabitants looked almost eager to do so, their faces wreathed in happy smiles as if they were truly liberators instead of an in-vading army.

Tentatively, Mathilde started to relax and hope that there wouldn't be any bloodshed or battles, after all. It seemed incredible that an in-vasion could be so easy, but it appeared that ha-tred of Edward's regime ran deeper than anyone had realised. Even so, the truth, when it reached them, was so unbelievable that it took Isabella a few days to accept that it wasn't a trick. There was no opposing army because the King didn't have one. His proclamations and summons and threats had all been conveniently lost or ignored.

'The people prefer the Queen,' Katharine an-nounced, her tone triumphant.

'You mean *no one* will fight for him?' Mathilde was suddenly glad of her family's poverty and obscurity. Even with the best of intentions, her father wouldn't have been able to muster more than a dozen men.

'He's brought it on himself. He and Despenser have been too greedy. They've ruled by fear, stolen all the gold in the land for themselves and broken faith with everyone who might have supported them. No matter what promises they make now, nobody will trust them.'

'So it's over?' Mathilde asked hopefully.

'Not yet. He probably has enough gold to buy an army abroad.'

'So Isabella might still have to fight him?'

'If she doesn't catch him first, yes.'

'And what happens if she *does* catch him?'

The look on Katharine's face made her uncomfortable. 'Then it's up to her conscience to decide what to do.'

Mathilde felt a chill run down her spine, no longer afraid for the Queen, but for her royal husband instead. They were no longer an army so much as a hunting party and their prey was the King. Even worse, from her perspective, there was still no sign of Henry.

Chapter Eleven

Oxford
—autumn 1326

'Take this.'

'Yes, Your Grace.' Mathilde bobbed a curtsy as Isabella handed her a folded-up piece of parchment, sealed with wax. She and Katharine had just finished preparing her for bed in a silk shift and slippers, and after a day's ride they were all equally tired, but it seemed she wasn't going to be dismissed quite yet. She took the note and made her way to the door, not needing to be told who it was for. Isabella and Mortimer were still careful to maintain a discreet distance from each other in public and it meant that she was even more of a go-between than she had been in France.

Katharine gave her a sympathetic look as she

left and made her way down to the great hall.
Mortimer was busy talking with some of the barons and she hesitated on the threshold, remembering what had happened the last time she'd
entered a room full of drunken men. She didn't
want to make the message too conspicuous either so she turned and went outside, on to the
top steps of the keep, thinking that perhaps she
could find a boy to carry the note for her, but
it felt so good to be out in the fresh evening air
that she decided to tarry a little while instead.

Oxford Castle was large, but its bailey was
still crammed full of carts and supplies. The
town around it was packed almost to bursting,
too, with soldiers billeted among the citizens,
so many that she could hear the sound of voices
outside the walls even from where she stood.
She wrapped her arms around her waist and
heaved a sigh, wishing that she'd thought to put
a mantle on as she watched her breath emerge
in curling plumes. It seemed strange to be so
much physically closer in distance to her home
and yet, in other ways, even further away than
she'd been in Paris. Would her father still acknowledge her now, she wondered, if she went
back to Rudstone Manor? Or would he turn her
away for disloyalty?

She was still considering the question when

a lone rider appeared through the archway of the bailey. Judging by the slow gait of the horse and the weary set of the man's shoulders she guessed they must have ridden a long way, although there was something familiar about the rider's posture, too. *Very* familiar. She held her breath as he moved in and out of the shadows, half-afraid to acknowledge the faint spark of hope kindling in her chest until he pulled his hood back to reveal a tangle of curly black hair.

It took her head a few seconds to catch up with her heart, which had already skipped a beat and then leapt with excitement, thumping heavily against her breastbone.

'Henry?' She was so afraid of being mistaken that the word emerged as a hoarse whisper rather than a call, but he lifted his head straight away.

'Henry!' She called his name out again in sheer relief, louder this time, abandoning all sense of discretion as she caught up the ends of her surcoat and hurtled at a dangerous pace down the keep steps.

'Mathilde?' He dismounted and reached her in a matter of strides, hauling her body against his so tightly that she felt her feet lift off the floor.

'Where have you been?' She pressed her face

into his neck, ignoring the surprised stare of the groom who came forward to take charge of his horse. Henry's skin was rough and scratchy with stubble and he smelled as if he'd been travelling for days, but she didn't care. All that mattered was that he was there now and safe in her embrace.

'Everywhere. Or at least that's what it feels like.' He set her feet down on the ground again although he didn't loosen his hold, cradling the back of her head in one hand as a slow smile spread across his features. 'I was right. I did miss you.'

A laugh rose in her throat. She felt reckless with happiness, lifting her hands to his shoulders and giving them a small shake to make sure he was real. He'd lost weight, his body all lean, hard muscle beneath her fingertips, yet he looked even more handsome than she'd remembered.

'I've been so worried about you. I thought...' She stopped mid-sentence. She didn't want to say what she'd thought.

'That the King had thrown me into a dungeon somewhere?' He made a tsking sound. 'I told you to trust me, didn't I?'

'So I did for the first two months, but it hasn't been easy.'

'No…it definitely hasn't.' His eyes darkened as he lowered his head and covered her mouth with his own, kissing her with a fervency that made her feel almost light-headed. She gasped against him, feeling a tingling sensation spread all the way from the top of her head to the tips of her toes.

'I was worried about you, too,' he murmured, his gaze heavy-lidded as he pulled his head back finally.

'You were?'

'More than I should have been.'

'What does *that* mean?'

'It means that I seem to lose all common sense when it comes to you, Mathilde,' he answered, a smile playing about his mouth as he smoothed his hands tenderly across her cheeks, sliding her headdress back and threading his fingers into her hair until her braid started to unravel. 'But I couldn't have hoped for a better welcome.'

'Mmm. That's all right, then.' She tipped her head into the caress, revelling in the way her skin heated wherever he touched her. She thought he was about to kiss her again, but then he looked past her shoulder and frowned. 'We might be seen here. Come with me?'

She nodded and he took hold of one of her hands, leading her away from the keep and to-

wards the stables. She stole a quick glance back
over her shoulder, knowing that she ought to
deliver the Queen's message to Mortimer first,
but unable to resist the temptation of a few moments alone with Henry.

'How's the Prince?' he asked as they went.

'In good health,' she answered cautiously.
Prince Edward was the nominal leader of the
army, although he didn't seem very happy about
it. But then how could anyone be happy, she
thought, when he was being used as a weapon
against his own father? Isabella had made a
point of parading him through all of the towns
they'd passed through, but the experience
seemed to have aged him prematurely. 'He
looks older,' she admitted. 'No longer thirteen,
but there's been no fighting at all. Everywhere
we go it's the same. The people love the Queen.'

'Do you think so?' Henry's voice was laced
with cynicism and she felt her spirits sink with
disappointment. She didn't want reality to intrude upon their reunion just yet and she *definitely* didn't want to argue about Isabella. She
wanted him to kiss her again. Her lips were
still tingling from the first time and, at the very
least, she wanted some more practice.

Fortunately, he seemed to feel the same way
because the moment they reached an empty stall

in the stables, he set one hand about her shoulders and the other about her waist, drawing her towards him as he pressed his lips back to hers. It was a deeper kiss this time, slower and more searching, sending a fresh, even more powerful, cascade of tingles shooting straight to her abdomen. She could feel a pulsing, tugging sensation there, too, something between pain and yearning, as if her body were striving towards some other, new feeling she didn't know how to reach. All of her muscles and nerve endings seemed to be quivering with pent-up desire.

Instinctively, she opened her lips and his tongue slipped inside, stroking against hers in a way that both shocked and excited her at the same time. His hands were moving now, too, she realised, exploring and smoothing and pulling her ever closer into his embrace until she felt dizzy and weightless, as if the world around them was blurring and fading away, making all of the past few months spent waiting and worrying almost worthwhile.

Henry slid his hands lower, over the tantalising contours of Mathilde's bottom and hips, fighting the urge to push her up against the timbered partition of the stall and lift her legs around his waist. He'd thought about her

so many times over the past few months, remembering the heady sensation of her body in
his arms, but the reality was even better than
the memory. She was so soft and responsive,
her breasts moulding against his chest in a way
that made him feel almost unbearably tight with
arousal. He hadn't expected to see her so soon,
or to feel such a strong reaction when he did,
and now, despite all of his good intentions about
caution and secrecy, he hardly seemed able to
contain himself. The sheer force of desire was
alarming.

He knew that he ought to release her before he
got truly carried away…and he would…soon…
any moment now…only she tasted delicious, like
apples and sweetmeats and wine all mixed together, and she was kissing him back with equal
enthusiasm. He felt like a starving man suddenly
offered a mouth-watering feast.

'Henry?' She broke the kiss finally, panting
as she tipped her head back.

'Mmm?' He took advantage of the position
to slide his lips across her jaw, grazing her skin
with his teeth.

'I have to go. I'm supposed to deliver a note
to Mortimer.'

'I'll take it.' He reached into her sleeve,
plucking the parchment from inside while he

dipped his tongue into the hollow at the base of her neck. 'I'll tell him I came across you outside the hall.'

'Yes…good.'

'You've no idea how much I've missed you.' He lifted his head, restraining himself with an effort.

'I think I do.' She smiled. 'But you're here now. That's all I care about.'

'About that…' He cleared his throat awkwardly. 'I have to leave again in the morning.'

'What?' She tried to jerk away, but he was ready for it, tightening his arms around her. 'You only just got here!'

'It won't be for long this time, just a few days hopefully.'

'You haven't even seen Mortimer yet!'

'But I know what his orders will be once I tell him my news. I'm sorry, Mathilde, truly, but it's important. It could mean peace, the end of the war or whatever this is. Wouldn't that be worth it?'

'Is it dangerous?'

'No more than usual.'

'Don't joke about it!' She gave him an angry look and then lifted her mouth back to his, her lips clinging as if she, too, couldn't bear to break away. They came apart only when a horse began to stamp in the neighbouring stall. 'Just be careful. *Again.*' She sighed heavily. 'I feel like we're always saying goodbye.'

He pulled her back against him, resting his cheek on the top of her head. The faint apple scent of her hair struck him as sweet and sharp at the same time, just like their reunion. 'It won't always be like this, I promise. Their business won't always come first. I won't be a spy for ever.'

'I know.' Her voice sounded muffled against his chest. 'This is enough for now.'

'For now. But not for ever.'

Chapter Twelve

Henry was gone by the time Isabella emerged from her rooms the next morning, though Mathilde looked around the hall for him anyway, trying not to appear as dispirited as she felt. She'd barely had a chance to feel happy about seeing him again before he'd broken the news about leaving and, yet again, she had no idea when he'd be back.

She had little time to dwell, however, before there was a fresh commotion as a messenger arrived from London, bringing word that the King had abandoned the city and fled towards Wales with the intention of going abroad and buying an army. After a brief conference with her barons, the Queen decided to follow in pursuit, taking a smaller force of soldiers this time, including Mathilde, though grudgingly allowing Katharine and Cecily to stay behind.

* * *

To Mathilde's great relief, Henry re-joined the Queen's forces on the road. He brought another Henry with him, Baron Lancaster, the most powerful man in the north of England and the King's last remaining hope of an ally. Together, they continued west, where they discovered that Edward and his favourite, Despenser, had tried escaping to Ireland, only to find themselves thwarted by becalming winds in the Bristol Channel, forcing them to flee deeper into Wales instead. Lancaster volunteered to go and find them and Isabella allowed it, although she sent Henry, too. It was a dangerous strategy, given that Lancaster had only recently changed allegiance, but one that paid off.

It was only a few days before their party returned with news that the King and Despenser had been found hiding in a wood and captured, although the treatment they'd each received had been markedly different. The King, who stood above the law, had been taken as an honoured prisoner to Bristol Castle while his favourite had been dragged through the streets of Hereford on a donkey to stand trial. The very idea of it made Mathilde shudder.

'We will go to Hereford at once, in the morning.' Isabella's eyes gleamed with triumph at the news. With the King finally captured, the war, such as it had been, was over.

There was yet another celebratory feast in Bristol Castle that evening. Mathilde wasn't sure how appropriate it was to celebrate the capture of a king and, in any case, she was tired of interminable mealtimes, but Isabella seemed to thrive on them. The Queen looked more animated than ever these days, with Mortimer sitting close at her side, even preparing her plate on occasion. Mathilde wished that *she* could sit beside the man she cared about, too, but as usual he was seated a long way from the dais, out of her eyeline.

It was only after the feast, when some of the tables had been cleared for dancing, that she spied Henry standing alone on one side, staring at her with a hard intensity that made her nerves prickle with unease. He looked almost harrowed, as if he were clenching all of his facial muscles so tightly that the skin across his jaw and cheekbones was being stretched. Even when she looked away she could sense him still staring, until at last she couldn't bear it any longer.

Subtly, she tipped her head to one side and then made her way towards the screen at one end of the room, looking for a quiet alcove where they could talk, though she'd barely taken a few steps beyond it when a hand grabbed her arm, pulling her out of the hall and into the shadows.

'Henry?' she gasped, relieved to recognise his profile, despite its sternness. 'What's the mat—'

She didn't finish the question as his lips descended on hers with a ferocity she'd never felt, or even sensed, in him before. She stiffened, shocked by the onslaught, not knowing how to react as his hands grasped her waist and then slid roughly upwards, over the sides of her breasts, crushing her against him so tightly that she could feel the pounding of his heartbeat through both of their tunics. *That* was fierce, too, as if he'd just run up a mountain, not sat through a feast. She sensed a desperation about him, a raw need behind his kisses, as if he wanted more from her, but it was more than she could give, at that moment anyway.

'Henry!' She pushed hard against his chest. 'Stop!'

'I'm sorry.' He released her at once, almost staggering as he wrenched himself away, his expression even more haggard than before. 'I didn't mean to hurt you.'

'You didn't.' She shook her head quickly to reassure him. 'I was surprised, that's all.'

'I would never hurt you, Mathilde. You know that, don't you?'

'Of course I do, but what's the matter? What's happened?'

'I don't want to burden you. I just—' He twisted his head to one side, the muscles in his neck and jaw all bunching at once. 'We shouldn't even be out here together. It's too risky.'

'But I *want* to be here. To share your burden, too.' She splayed her fingers over his chest, rubbing the place where his heart was still pounding, trying to soothe him. 'Please, Henry. Tell me what's the matter.'

There was a heavy pause before he spoke again, his voice strained-sounding. 'I didn't think that I would feel sorry for him. I didn't expect to feel pity.'

'For the King?'

'Yes. It was no glorious victory. We were like hounds hunting a lame rabbit. There were only half a dozen men with him.' He shook his head and swallowed as if the words were distasteful. 'Just half a dozen out of a whole kingdom.'

'He was a tyrant.' She repeated the words she'd heard so often.

'I know, but still a king. I can't take any satisfaction in seeing any man brought so low.'

'It must have been terrible.' She moved a step closer, stretching up on her toes to press her forehead against his. 'The Queen has no intention of reconciling with him, does she?' She made it sound like a question although they both knew it was not.

'No.'

'Do you think she ever did?'

'Maybe at first.'

'Before Mortimer?'

He rubbed her forehead with his own, seeming to consider. 'I don't know. Even without Mortimer, you can understand why she wouldn't take the risk. King Edward isn't a man to be trusted. If they reconciled, she'd never be safe. He'd find some way to get his revenge.'

'Then she has no choice but to take him prisoner.' The words made her feel better. They were a much better reason for Isabella not to reconcile with her husband than her affair with Mortimer, but it was still hard to see what would happen next. If the King and Queen couldn't be reconciled and a king couldn't stand trial, what *would* happen to him?

'So now we get a new king.' Henry answered

the question before she could ask it. 'Another Edward.'

'The Prince?' She lifted her head, genuinely shocked. 'You mean a new king while the old one still lives?'

'Yes. It's never been done before, but it might be the only way. Isabella can say that her husband abandoned the country when he sailed for Ireland.'

'But he never reached Ireland. He never left the Bristol Channel.'

'He still boarded the ship. That's enough to say he gave up his right to rule.' Henry lifted his shoulders, though there was still a frown in his voice. 'Whatever happens to Edward next will take place in secret, but he'll be persuaded to renounce his kingship somehow. Then Isabella will want to have her son crowned as quickly and publicly as possible. It's the quickest way to make people forget she still has a living husband.'

'What about Despenser?'

Henry tensed. 'He's another matter. People want someone to blame.'

'So he'll stand trial?'

'For what it's worth, although he won't be given any opportunity to speak. The verdict's already decided.'

'What?' She opened her eyes wide. 'But that's not fair.'

'That's war. If the positions were reversed and we were the ones on trial for treason...'

'Then the King and Despenser wouldn't show any more mercy.' She finished the sentence for him. 'That doesn't make it right.'

'I know. A battle would have been more honourable than this.'

'But then more people would have been killed.' She smoothed a hand over his still taut-looking face. 'None of this is your fault. You were only following orders.'

He leaned forward, kissing her tenderly this time, as if he were trying to wipe away the memory of his earlier roughness. 'Thank you for listening.'

'I'm glad that you told me.'

'Mathilde...' He sounded hesitant again, reaching for her hands and folding them tightly between his. 'I need you to promise me something.'

'What?'

'Promise me first.'

'How can I promise if I don't know what it is?'

'Because you need to trust me.'

She pursed her lips before relenting. 'All right, I promise.'

'Good.' A look of relief crossed his face. 'Don't go to Despenser's trial. Find an excuse to stay behind.'

'You mean lie to the Queen? I can't do that!' She wrenched her hands away, surprised that he would even suggest such a thing. 'She needs me to accompany her. We've already left Katharine and Cecily behind in Oxford.'

'Surely she has other ladies?'

'A few, but…'

'Then don't go. You won't want to be there.'

'I'm her lady! She trusts me!'

'She doesn't need you for this. Mathilde, I'm begging you, some sights cannot be forgotten. Pretend to be sick, pretend you've twisted your ankle, do whatever it takes, but don't go to the trial.'

'I'll ask,' she compromised finally. 'The decision will be up to the Queen, but I'll ask.'

He held on to her gaze for a few seconds longer and then sighed. 'She doesn't deserve you.'

Chapter Thirteen

*Palace of Westminster, London
—winter 1326*

'I never thought I'd see London again.' Cecily lay back against her pillow, smiling though her skin was wan and her cheeks far too gaunt. 'It seems like a lifetime since we left.'

'It's very strange to be back.' Mathilde agreed. She hadn't spent long in London before travelling to Paris, but she was glad to be reunited with Cecily and Katharine again, although it was obvious now that Cecily didn't have long. Even Isabella had been forced to acknowledge it, though she'd been subdued ever since Despenser's trial and subsequent execution in Hereford. Mathilde wondered if she was still angry at her for not attending. She'd feigned a severe headache on the day and then given herself a real one by feeling guilty throughout, although the brutal stories she'd heard afterwards had made her glad that she'd agreed to Henry's promise, after all. Isabella herself hadn't said a word about the events, or about anything much, but then she had a great deal to think about, Mathilde told herself, preparing her son's coronation for a start. It was no small task to replace one king with another, especially while the other still lived, albeit now as a prisoner in Kenilworth Castle.

'Do you still see your friend?' Cecily's soft voice intruded on her thoughts suddenly.

'My friend?'

'From Paris. Henry Wright, I think it was, one of Mortimer's men. He told me when I woke that evening.'

'Oh…yes.' She felt a pink flush steal over her cheeks. Cecily had never mentioned the evening when she'd caught her and Henry almost kissing before. 'Sometimes.'

'Peace. I'm not accusing you of anything.' Cecily gave one of her gentle smiles. 'Do the two of you care for each other?'

Mathilde threw a swift look around the room, making sure they were alone before nodding. 'Yes. Very much.'

'Then I'm happy for you. Ah!' A spasm racked the other woman's body as she reached for one of Mathilde's hands. 'Do you think he would help me again?'

'Of course. What is it you need?'

Mathilde paid close attention as Cecily gave her directions and then hastened to do as she asked, sending a page to fetch Henry. He came and agreed to the request at once, leaving court that evening.

Henry returned two days later with her three sons.

They were all like Cecily, with tawny hair and large green eyes that looked sombre as they entered her sick room. The younger two reminded Mathilde of her own brothers, caught in that stage between boyhood and manhood when they weren't sure which they wanted to be, so she stepped outside to give them privacy. If they needed to cry, then she didn't want her presence there to stop them.

Katharine was nowhere to be seen, but Henry was still in the corridor, pacing up and down as he waited to take Cecily's sons home again afterwards.

'They're all together now.' She fell into his arms with relief. 'How was it? Did you have any problems finding them?'

'No. They're all being raised by different

families, but not too far apart. There was only one stumbling block.' He wrapped his arms around her, sounding apologetic. 'I had to go to their father and tell him the reason first. I could hardly take them away from their homes without his permission.'

'Of course. I should have thought of that, but it couldn't be helped.' She attempted a smile and failed miserably. 'Didn't he want to come and see her, too?'

'Apparently not.' He made a face. 'Now I understand why Cecily prefers court. He wasn't a pleasant man. It seems they said their goodbyes a long time ago.'

'Well, at least he didn't stop her sons from saying them, too. Thank you for helping her.'

'She's your friend.' He lifted a hand to brush a strand of hair away from where it had fallen across her nose. 'There isn't much I wouldn't do for you, Mathilde.'

She lifted her face and kissed him gently, too aware of what was happening on the other side of the wall to do any more, then laid her head against his shoulder in silence, waiting. In truth, she didn't know how long they stood there. It could have been minutes or hours before the door opened again and the three young men emerged. The youngest was weeping openly and the eldest, a squire of around her own age, had an arm wrapped around his shoulders. His name was Edmund, if she remembered correctly.

'Does she need anything?' Mathilde stepped forward at once.

'No. She's dozing now.' Edmund let go of his brother and bowed. 'I'm indebted to both of you. For bringing us here and for taking care of her.'

'It was no trouble.' Henry came to stand at her shoulder.

'I'm still grateful.' Edmund's gaze moved between them before settling on her. 'I wish that there was some way for me to repay you.'

'There's no need,' Mathilde protested. 'I love your mother dearly.'

'As she loves you, but it would please me, and her, I think, to give you a gift. Here.' He reached up to his shoulder and unbuckled the circular clasp that held his cloak together. It was wrought gold with a diagonal band across the centre and four small sapphires set at equal points around the edges.

'Oh…no.' She gasped. 'That's far too much.'

'For fulfilling my mother's last wish? I think not. Take it and think of her whenever you wear it. Please?'

'Then I will. For Cecily's sake.' She gazed

admiringly at the clasp as he placed it in the centre of her palm, surprised when his fingers lingered briefly.

'Thank you for everything, Lady Mathilde.'

'It was n—'

'We should go,' Henry interrupted before she could finish the sentence, his tone brusque and his expression hard suddenly, as if he were displeased by the gift. For a fleeting moment she wondered if he were jealous, although the idea seemed ridiculous under the circumstances.

'Very well.' Edmund made another bow. 'In that case, I hope that we meet again under happier circumstances, Lady Mathilde.'

'As do I.' She bade his brothers farewell and then watched as they all walked away, still surprised by Henry's brusqueness, though she didn't have much time to think about it before she heard a thud from inside the room.

'I'll get it!' She hurried forward to pick up the cup that Cecily had knocked into the rushes.

'Thank you. I must have hit it with my arm when I rolled over.' Cecily looked exhausted, but happy. 'Please, thank your friend again for bringing my sons. You'll never know how much this has meant to me.'

'I'll tell him.'

'And forgive me for asking...' Cecily sounded

hesitant. 'But does the Queen know about your attachment to him?'

'No-o.' Mathilde felt a stab of guilt. 'I suppose I ought to have told her, but she's been so busy. And I haven't done anything dishonourable. I would never bring shame on her household.'

'I know that.' Cecily's expression warmed again. 'But has *he* spoken of his intentions?'

'Not directly. We both know that marriage is impossible, for the time being anyway. Neither of us has any money.'

'Then for your sake, I hope that Mortimer rewards him well when all this is over. I wish you both happiness, but in the meantime…' Cecily frowned and beckoned her closer, lowering her voice to an undertone. 'Don't let Isabella find out. There's one rule for her and Mortimer and another for the rest of us, and she doesn't like sharing. If she thinks that your loyalties are divided, then she'll try to separate you from him. Don't give her the chance. Keep your friendship a secret until his prospects improve.'

'If you think that's for the best…' Mathilde nodded uncertainly. She didn't believe that the Queen would ever do anything so malicious, but now wasn't the time to argue. 'Cecily, I've something else to tell you. I'm afraid that Henry had to speak to your husband in order to bring your sons here. It meant telling him about your sickness.'

'So Edmund told me, but it's all right. I would never have expected him to come with them. I have Kat now, even though she's been hiding all day, afraid of meeting my sons, I think.' Cecily paused and then looked up, her eyes wide and pleading. 'I know I should not ask, but...'

'It's all right.' Mathilde smiled reassuringly, already knowing what the other woman wanted to say. 'I'll look after her, I swear it.' She bent and pressed a kiss to her forehead. 'I'll go and fetch her back now.'

It was the last thing she ever did for Cecily. She and Kat held a vigil together that night, sitting on either side of her body. Even Isabella joined them for a few hours. Mathilde didn't turn her head to look, but it sounded as if the Queen were crying.

Isabella told Katharine to take some time away from court to visit her family and Mathilde was glad of it. It was painful to see the tension in her friend's face as she kept her sorrow all to herself, unable to grieve properly among so many people. She suspected that Isabella saw it and sympathised, too, although some of her other ladies were less charitable. Erlinda Hackford, one of the Queen's new attendants, muttered something about Cecily's illness being a punishment and Mathilde found herself throwing a cup of wine over her new silk houpelande in retaliation.

In truth, the action came as an equal surprise to both of them. Staring at the empty cup in her hand, Mathilde could only wonder what had come over her. She'd never done anything so shocking before in her life and of course Erlinda marched straight to the Queen.

'Did you do what she accuses you of?' Isabella arched an eyebrow when Mathilde came to stand in front of her, dismissing the rest of the ladies with a careless wave of her hand.

'Yes, Your Grace.' Mathilde bowed her head, although she couldn't bring herself to say she was sorry. She wasn't. 'Perhaps I should not have done it.'

'Perhaps?' To her surprise, Isabella sounded amused. *'Perhaps* I would have done the same if I'd been there. You were defending your friend. Both of your friends. I cannot punish you for that. Love is love, is it not?'

'Yes, Your Grace.' Mathilde lifted her head in surprise.

'Sometimes it makes us do things we do

not expect, even of ourselves.' Isabella's gaze seemed very pointed all of a sudden. 'Maybe sometimes they're the wrong things. Maybe we have regrets, but often there's no choice. You'll understand that when you fall in love yourself some day.' There was a brief pause. 'Unless you have already?'

'Me, your lady?'

'You're an attractive young lady. You must have admirers. Is there no one you favour? No one you love?'

Mathilde's mouth went dry. She *cared* for Henry, she seemed to spend half of her life worrying about him, she was even prepared to risk the damage to her reputation by meeting him, but love was too strong a word…wasn't it? She hadn't let herself dwell on her feelings too deeply while there was still no hope of a future together, but maybe she could talk to the Queen about them? Surely *she*, of all people, would understand what it was like to care for someone you shouldn't? A Mortimer especially? And maybe Isabella would tell her that it was all right, that Henry's birth didn't matter and their secrecy was all forgiven. Maybe she would even offer to help them…

It was on the tip of Mathilde's tongue to tell her everything, only the memory of Cecily's warning made her hesitate. What if the Queen *didn't* understand or approve? She had the power to ensure they never saw each other again. How could she take the risk?

'I've no dowry, my lady.' She evaded the question instead. 'I cannot afford to fall in love.'

'A practical answer.' Isabella's eyes narrowed slightly before dropping to the gold brooch fastened to her girdle. 'I have not seen this before. A gift?'

'Yes, Your Grace. Lady Cecily's eldest son, Edmund, gave it to me. To remember her by.'

'Edmund… I would like to have met him.'

Mathilde almost laughed out loud with relief. Obviously the Queen had no idea about Henry if she was asking about Edmund. 'He reminded me of her a great deal, Your Grace.'

'Mmm.' Isabella looked thoughtful. 'Well then, you may go. I'm prepared to overlook your behaviour this time, but it must not happen again.'

'It will not, Your Grace, I promise.'

'Then we'll say no more about it. Your loyalty does you credit, Mathilde. I would that all of my ladies were more like you.'

Chapter Fourteen

*London
—spring 1327*

'You need to get out of here.'

Mathilde started at the sound of Henry's voice in her ear. Quickly, she spun around, searching the hall for some indication of danger. 'Why? What's happened?'

'Nothing new, but the Queen and Mortimer will be busy with the council for hours. This is the perfect opportunity for me to show you London.'

'*Show me London?*' she repeated, gaping as if he'd gone mad. 'I can't just leave court!'

'Why not?' He quirked an eyebrow. 'We should make the most of whatever freedom we have. Besides, you deserve some time to yourself. She's had you running around for weeks.'

'And she might need me again today. I ought to be here just in case.'

'Mathilde, how many times have we had a chance to talk properly over the past three months?'

Frowning, she opened her lips and then closed them again. He was right. They'd barely had any opportunities to meet since the coronation in February. Isabella and Mortimer had been appointed co-regents until the new King was old enough to rule by himself and they were busier than ever. Which inevitably meant that she and Henry were, too.

'She has other ladies.' He jerked his head to where Katharine was sitting beside the great fireplace. 'They can attend to her, if necessary.'

'I suppose so…' Mathilde chewed on her bottom lip indecisively. Katharine had returned to court two weeks before, not quite her old self again, but better than when she'd left. 'But I don't want to burden her with anything.'

'She offered.'

'When?'

'A few minutes ago when I suggested you could do with a day of adventure. She said to go and enjoy yourself and that she'd think of an excuse if the Queen called for you.' He raised his hands when she looked at him sceptically. 'Those were her exact words, I swear it.'

'But I can't just go off into the city with you. It wouldn't be seemly.' Despite the primness of the words, Mathilde felt a tide of excitement start to rise up inside her, tempted despite her better judgement. She'd never seen London except from horseback or as part of the Queen's entourage, and the prospect of escaping the court for an afternoon with Henry was both intriguing and exhilarating. If she could only be sure that the Queen wouldn't summon her… As she wavered, Katharine met her eye and gave a small nod.

'Think of it as a day of misrule,' Henry murmured, his hand touching lightly against the small of her back. 'Now, no more excuses. Meet me by the main gate in half an hour and wear something plain.'

He left before she could think of another excuse, not that she tried very hard, throwing Katharine a grateful smile before running up the stairs to her room and rummaging through a coffer for one of her mother's old gowns. Despite their age and ragged appearance she'd been reluctant to leave them behind in France and now it felt good to see them again, as if she were greeting old friends. Hastily, she pulled the scratchy fabric over her head and then draped an old, waist-length grey cloak about her shoulders, drawing the hood up so that nobody would recognise her from a distance.

'You came, then?' Henry was sitting on a barrel outside the gatehouse as she approached, his handsome face breaking into a wide smile at the sight of her.

'You made it sound too exciting to resist.' She grinned back. 'Now I want to see everything.'

'Then everything it is.' He cocked his head, his gaze warming appreciatively. 'You were wearing that dress on the first day we met.'

'Was I?' She glanced down, surprised to realise he was right. 'You have a good memory.'

'I'm a spy. I remember details, especially pretty ones.'

'You told me I looked nervous that day.'

'Nervous *and* pretty.' His gaze flickered past her shoulder towards the keep.

'What is it?' Mathilde glanced around, too.

'Just making sure we're not being watched. Ready?'

'Ready.' She nodded and he took hold of her hand, lacing their fingers together as he led her through the gatehouse and out into the city.

Like Paris, London was huge and sprawling,

with more than a hundred parishes, each one of which sounded as if it were ringing its bells simultaneously. Mathilde had no idea where they were going and, after a few twists and turns along streets that became increasingly narrow and more winding, no idea where they were either. There were houses and shops on either side of them, most at least six floors high and shadowed with balconies or overhangs that turned the world into a series of interconnected tunnels with only thin slivers of sky above. She glanced upwards, looking for a reassuring glimpse of blue, and saw only grey chimney smoke. In such a maze, she knew she was entirely reliant on Henry to help her find her way back again, but the thought didn't bother her. She trusted him. Even Katharine appeared to trust him and her approval was the hardest of anyone's to obtain.

At last, they entered a bustling marketplace and she tensed, feeling as if all her senses were being assaulted at once. The scene was a jumble of noise and colour and smells, with just about every type of shop she could think of— blacksmiths and silversmiths and apothecaries and pelterers and spice traders all working side by side—as well as street vendors carrying trays of pies and bread on wooden trays. The combination of aromas alone was overwhelming, like leather and fish and herbs all rolled together.

Henry must have sensed her unease because he let go of her hand and slipped an arm around her waist, drawing her against him so that the whole sides of their bodies were pressed together. Despite her fear, she felt a frisson of excitement at the contact. She knew that she ought not to allow such liberties, especially in public and broad daylight to boot, but today was different. What had he called it? A day of misrule. They weren't members of the court any more, just two citizens wandering freely about the city. It made a pleasant change to feel so at liberty. And if they chose to walk together so closely, who was going to object? Who was ever going to know?

'We'll be through all this soon.' Henry raised his voice above the hubbub. 'Don't worry.'

'Where are we going?' she shouted back.

'To the *r*—!'

'Pardon?'

'To the *r*—!'

She gave up trying to understand, concentrating instead on not bumping into people and breathing a sigh of relief as they finally turned and made their way down a side street, the sounds and smells and crush of the marketplace gradually receding until they were standing alone on an empty jetty beside the Thames.

'*Oh!*' Instinctively she reeled backwards, a sudden onslaught of panic clawing at her throat. With her eyes cast downwards, she hadn't been aware of the river until that moment.

'Mathilde?' Henry turned towards her in surprise. 'Are you all right?'

'Ye-es.' She dug her fingernails into her palms, trying to distract herself from the fear, but they were standing so close to the edge, the water swirling in tight circles like a bubbling cauldron below her feet, that she had the feeling of being on the edge of a precipice. 'I n-need to get my b-breath back. The market was so crowded.'

'Sorry about that. I'll find us another way back.' He gave her a sympathetic squeeze and then lifted his arm, pointing downriver. 'I just thought you'd like to see the view from here. Impressive, isn't it?'

'View of what?' She followed the direction of his hand and then gasped in amazement, her fear momentarily forgotten. She'd heard tales about London Bridge, but it surpassed anything she'd imagined, spanning the entire width of the river on nineteen vast stone pillars. Then there were the arches—twenty in total—on top of which were built hundreds of timbered houses and shops, each in a different style, with precarious-looking hautpas extending over the sides on massive wooden struts.

'It's incredible.' Even despite the water rushing beneath, she couldn't stop staring. 'I've never seen anything like it. Is it a bridge or a building?'

'Both.'

'Do people live on it?'

'Live, work, bake pies. That's where we're going by the way, to the finest pie shop in the whole of London. England probably.'

'Oh.' She dragged her gaze away from the bridge. The last thing she wanted to do was set foot on such a structure, but Henry looked so pleased with the idea that she couldn't bring herself to say so. 'Are you telling me that we've left the royal court to visit a pie shop?' She swallowed her unease, teasing him instead.

'Would you prefer more partridge?'

'No!' She laughed, shaking her head with mock horror. She was sick to her back teeth with Isabella's favourite delicacy. The court had to eat it almost daily. 'Pie sounds delicious.'

'Then let's go. I'm starving.'

They made their way along the jetty, then up some wooden steps on to the main thoroughfare, dodging their way between riders on horseback and several large carts laden with boxes and barrels. As it turned out, the bridge wasn't half as intimidating as she'd feared. With shops on both sides blocking the view of the water she could almost forget that they were walking above a river, allowing her to relax again. One of Henry's arms was still around her waist and she slid her own out from beneath her cloak to curl around him, too. He darted a quick look sideways, but she only lifted her chin and smiled. It was nice to surprise him for a change.

'How do you know London so well?' she asked, still smiling.

'I stayed in lodgings here while Mortimer was in the Tower. There wasn't much to do except explore the city and wait for instructions.' He turned his head, his mouth brushing lightly against the top of her ear. 'I tried a lot of pie shops, but this is the best.'

She sucked in a breath, the feeling of his lips against her skin making her pulse quicken. It reminded her of the last time they'd kissed in Bristol, months ago now. He was right, it *had* been too long since they'd had more than a few stolen moments together. And it had been much, much too long since he'd kissed her.

'Here we are.'

She sniffed the air appreciatively as he

pointed towards an unobtrusive-looking wooden building, so narrow that it seemed to have been rammed in between two others as an afterthought. The smells emanating from within, however, were mouth-wateringly delicious, making her stomach growl with anticipation. Henry handed a few coins over the counter and an ancient-looking woman passed them a hand-sized pie each. Mathilde nodded her thanks. The pastry was freshly baked and still hot to the touch, making her fingers sizzle.

'Can we sit?' Henry offered the woman a few more coins and she gave a toothless grin, pointing over her shoulder towards the back of the building.

'My thanks. This way.' He jerked his head to Mathilde and they headed past the counter and behind a brightly painted screen to a table set beneath a large, square-shaped window, its shutters folded back to give a spectacular view east over the river.

Mathilde forced herself to keep moving forward, her mind spinning at the thought of eating in such a spot, though it was no hardship to sit when her knees felt so unsteady. The current actually seemed slower here in the middle of the bridge, but the water still looked dark and treacherous, as strong and unstoppable as time itself.

'You don't like the river.' Henry's tone altered as he sat down on the stool opposite. It wasn't accusing, just alert, as if he'd suddenly come to the realisation.

'What?' She lifted her eyes to his with a jolt.

'You didn't want to sit on the riverbank that evening we walked through the gardens in Paris either.'

'No.' She could hardly deny it. 'I didn't.'

'What is it? The water?'

She glanced sideways out of the window and then quickly back again. 'Not the water itself, but areas of water, rivers especially.'

'I should have realised sooner.' He started to get up. 'I'm sorry. We can go somewhere else.'

'No.' She caught at his hand, summoning all her nerve to tug him back down again. 'I appreciate the offer, but if I can brave sailing across the Channel then I can sit on top of a bridge. Maybe it will help me to get past the fear.'

'You don't have to, not on my account.'

'I know, but we're here now.' She lifted her eyebrows. 'You wouldn't stop me from sampling the best pie in London, would you?'

'Hmm.' He looked unconvinced, shifting his stool away from the window so that her gaze was drawn into the shop instead of outwards. 'Sailing back from France must have been quite an ordeal for you.'

'It was.'

'Then I'm sorry I wasn't there to help.' He looked genuinely regretful. 'Have you always felt this way?'

'No-o… Not always.'

'So there's a reason?'

'Yes.' She lowered her gaze, though she could still feel his questioning one on her face. 'It's because of my mother. She drowned when I was twelve.'

'Ah. I'm sorry. We don't have to talk about it if you don't want to.'

She swallowed hard against a tight feeling in her chest. Part of her wanted to change the subject, as she always did when anyone asked about her mother, and yet another, apparently stronger, part of her wanted to talk about it for once, the words already forming on her lips. 'They called it an accident, but it wasn't. My father and I found her and there were stones in the pockets of her gown. I watched him take them out and then he told me never to speak about it to anyone. So I never have, not even to Hawise. Until now.' She lifted her eyes back to his, looking for judgement and not finding any.

'Then I appreciate your telling me.'

She nodded jerkily. 'I've hated areas of water ever since. As for my father…he was never the same afterwards. He hardly ever looked at me again, let alone spoke to me. For the next five years, he acted as if I barely existed. And then he took me to London and left me there. Sometimes, I think it was because I looked like her and he couldn't bear it. Other times, I think he was angry that I saw what she did. But most of all, I think it was because he blamed me.'

'How could he blame you?'

She squeezed her eyes shut for a long moment, considering telling him the whole truth and settling on half instead. 'My mother was always unhappy. Sometimes she would just sit and stare without speaking for hours, like we weren't even there. She didn't like being a mother, I think, and every time she had another baby she got worse. Maybe we drove her to it, my brothers and sister and I. Into a mortal sin.'

'You didn't.'

She blinked at his certainty. 'How do you know?'

'Because you were a child. You can't blame a child for something like that. It wasn't your fault.'

'Thank you.' She felt the tightness start to

ease a little. She'd gone against her father's wishes by telling him about the stones, but she felt relieved rather than guilty, as if she'd been carrying around something equally heavy. Maybe she'd tell him the rest one day, but just talking about what she'd witnessed that terrible morning made her feel lighter already. So much that even the sound of the river beneath the window seemed to recede slightly. 'I think that was why I was so homesick at first. Because deep down I knew that it was for ever, that I would never be able to go back. Only it took me a while to accept it. I think—I know— that my father doesn't want anything more to do with me. I haven't had a word from home since I arrived in Paris. Not a word for almost two years.'

'You could still send a message yourself. My offer stands. Your father can hardly turn me in to the King now.'

'But what would I say? I chose the Queen. I *still* choose the Queen. I doubt that he'll ever forgive me for that, but at least *she* values me. She relies on me, too, *and* she cares about me, more than my real mother ever did.' She bit her tongue. 'I know that I shouldn't say such a thing. My mother's sadness was like a kind of sickness. Some days I hate her for it, other days I pity her, but every day I wish that I'd stopped her.'

'How could you have done that?'

'I don't know. Maybe if I'd spoken to her more, tried harder to make her happy, but after a while, I stopped trying. We all did, but I've always felt guilty, as though I failed her.'

'Sometimes nothing you can do or say to a person makes any difference.'

She lifted her brows, alerted by something in his voice. 'What do you mean?'

'Because I *know*.' He turned his head to look out of the window. 'It's true that I have my mother's family name, but not because her family wanted me. As far as they were concerned, I ruined her life and brought shame on them all. Maybe I did. Obviously she felt the same way because she took me to Ludlow Castle when I was six years old and left me there.'

'You mean she abandoned you?'

'Not quite. She spoke to someone. I don't know what was said, but they took one look at my face, presumably recognised me as a Mortimer by-blow, and that was that. She never even said goodbye. That was the day I learnt never to trust anyone.'

'Henry, that's terrible.' Her heart wrenched at the thought of him as a small boy, abandoned by the one person he ought to have been able to trust the most. No wonder he was so cynical.

'When I think of Lady Cecily and how determined she was to come back to England, to see her sons one last time...' He shook his head. 'I never saw my mother again, but when she left, it was like she took a part of me away with her, too. It took me a long time to feel anything but hollow inside. Even now, there are times...'

'I understand.' She touched his hand when his voice faltered. 'You loved her.'

For almost a full minute she thought that he wasn't going to answer and when he did, his voice sounded different, not like his own. 'Yes. It still wasn't enough.'

'What about Mortimer?'

A muscle twitched in his jaw, subtly but distinctly. 'What about him?'

She followed his gaze out of the window, towards the Tower in the distance. 'You always talk as if you don't care about him, but then why did you help him escape? Why take the risk?'

He shrugged. 'Because sometimes risk is worth the potential reward. And I suppose I didn't want him to be executed. He's never acknowledged me, but he still took me in when he could have left me to fend for myself. It was a debt that needed paying. As for caring, it's not like that. He would never send his legitimate sons to the places he sends me. They were all knighted at the coronation while I got to stand at the back and watch.' His lip curled. 'I don't know whether or not he's my father, but he's all I have, as pitiful as that sounds. And the worst part is that he doesn't see me as anything more than a servant.'

'Then he's a fool.'

A flicker of a smile passed over his face. 'Then it seems we both have less than perfect parents. We both know what it's like to feel unwanted.'

She leaned sideways, forcing herself into his line of vision. 'At least we want each other.'

'Yes.' The flicker spread into a real smile. 'Yes, we do. Now don't let your pie get cold.'

She took a bite reluctantly, then moaned with satisfaction as the juices hit her tongue. Despite the serious subject of their conversation, she felt ravenous all of a sudden. 'Mmm. This is delicious.'

'I told you, the best pie shop in London.'

'Now I believe you.'

He let his gaze linger on her mouth a few moments longer than necessary before pushing his stool back and heading to the counter for two cups of ale. 'You can have another pie if you like?'

'No, thank you.' She was already licking her fingers. Tempting as the idea was, she felt pleasantly satiated and she didn't want to spoil it. 'That was perfect.'

'Good. In that case…' he passed her one cup and lifted the other '…to us.'

'To us,' she repeated, feeling a warm glow in her stomach that had nothing to do with the pie. 'And afternoons of freedom!'

Chapter Fifteen

Henry chewed slowly on his pie, inwardly chiding himself for not having noticed Mathilde's fear of the water sooner. He ought to have realised in Paris, but he'd been so preoccupied with thoughts about kissing her that evening that he'd forgotten all about her sudden panic on the riverbank. If he'd only remembered, it would have stopped him from making such a potentially monumental mistake today. As venues for their afternoon of freedom went, he could hardly have brought her anywhere worse, and yet, despite that, he was glad that they'd come, as though the river itself had somehow drawn them closer together. He felt honoured, too, that she'd trusted him enough to talk about her mother, although he'd been somewhat unnerved by the way she'd spoken about the Queen afterwards, as if she thought of her as some kind of replacement, someone to whom she could prove her worth after what she considered her failure. He understood the impulse, but as mother figures went, Isabella wasn't exactly the safest choice, especially now...

He glanced surreptitiously across the table, seized with a strong urge to protect her. She was already far too dependent on Isabella. If she was right about her father, then she had no home to return to if things went wrong at court, which, thanks to Mortimer and the Queen's increasingly grasping and autocratic behaviour, he was starting to think was a distinct possibility. The great future that everyone had expected and believed in already seemed under threat, just a few months in. He hoped that things would settle down soon, but if there was trouble then Mathilde would be vulnerable... Just the thought of it turned the pie to lead in his stomach.

'Mathilde...' He tossed the last piece of crust out of the window for a passing gull to enjoy, coming to an impulsive decision. A risky one, but one that still, strangely, felt right. 'There was another reason I invited you to come out with me today. I wanted to tell you something.'

'Mmm?' She tilted her head to one side, her expression a hundred times more relaxed than when they'd first sat down. 'It's not that you're leaving again, is it?'

'Ah. Well…'

'Oh.' Her face fell in a way that made him want to leap over the table and gather her in his arms.

'The Scots have begun launching raids into the borders. Mortimer's riding north with an army and I have to go with him.'

'I see.' She gave a sad-sounding sigh. 'I'd hoped that all that was behind us.'

'So did I, but that wasn't what I wanted to tell you either. I have some good news for once. Mortimer's granted me a manor as a reward for my service.'

'Henry, that's wonderful!'

'The property isn't large, but it's a good one. East of Ludlow, towards Worcestershire. It's a start.'

'Just a start?' She laughed. 'How many manors do you want?'

'Several. I want to be a man of fortune, of rank even some day. I want…'

'What?' She prodded when he hesitated.

'A knighthood.' He cleared his throat after the word. 'Although I know that sounds ridiculous.'

'No, it doesn't. If anyone can do it, then it's you.'

'Thank you.' He inclined his head, grateful

to her for not mocking. 'Until then, a manor house east of Ludlow is all I can offer, but it's your home, too, if you want it.'

'What?' Her mouth dropped open. 'What do you mean?'

'You could marry me.'

'Marry?' She looked so stunned that he was half tempted to laugh. 'I don't understand. Are you asking me to marry you?'

'I don't see anyone else here.'

'But I thought it was impossible?'

'It was. *Before*.'

'I've no fortune, no dowry, nothing at all.'

'And I'm a bastard, but at least now I'm a bastard with a house and land of his own.'

'It's just all so sudden. I didn't expect...'

He clamped his brows together. 'Did you think I was only amusing myself with you? That my intentions weren't honourable?'

'Of course not.'

'Then were you amusing yourself with me?'

'No! I just didn't think that marriage was a possibility for me—*us*—not for a long time anyway. I thought that I'd be like Katharine and simply remain in the Queen's service.'

'Is that what you want?' His spirits sank with disappointment. 'Are you so much the Queen's lady?'

'No… I only thought there was no alternative. That's why I promised to—' She bit her lip abruptly, a shadow passing over her face.

'Why you what?'

'It doesn't matter.' She gave her head a small shake as if to push the thought, whatever it was, away. 'The point is, we've never spoken about marriage before.'

'I never had a manor before.'

'We've never even talked about how we feel, not really.'

'Feelings aren't something I'm used to talking about.'

'But don't you think, if we're considering marriage, that we *ought* to discuss them a little?'

'Mathilde…' He took a deep, steadying breath. In all honesty, feelings were the last thing he wanted to discuss. Talking about his mother had stirred up enough of the long-ago heartache he preferred to forget and besides, what he was suggesting at that moment was more of a practical arrangement, for *her* protection and *his* peace of mind… 'Maybe I've been a spy for so long that I'm not very good at showing my emotions any more, but you know that I care for you. I think that you care for me, too, and there's something between us, isn't there? Some connection that makes it impossible for us to stay apart?'

'Yes.' Her lashes dipped. 'I think there is, too.'

'Then let me give you my vow. This isn't how I would have chosen to ask. I wanted to wait until I had more to offer, but I want you to be safe.'

'Why wouldn't I be safe?'

'Because the future might not be as stable or peaceful as we hoped. At least this way, if anything happens to me in Scotland, you'll have somewhere to go. My manor will become yours.'

'Don't talk like that. Nothing's going to happen to you.'

'I hope not, too, but there's no harm in taking precautions.'

'I'm not your responsibility. You don't have to marry me just to protect me. I'll be with the Queen.'

'That's what I'm worried about.'

'Don't!' Her eyes widened with a look of outrage. 'Don't talk about her like that.'

'Mathilde, I hope that I'm wrong, but you have to admit her behaviour since the coronation hasn't been very encouraging. It hasn't endeared her to the barons either. She's claimed so much land that she's almost as rich as the King himself.'

'Some of that was her dowry lands.'

'Exactly. *Some.* And then there's Mortimer. You know he's claimed Chirk for himself now?'

'What's wrong with that?'

'It was his cousin's land. He disinherited his own cousin.' He clenched a fist on the table. 'They're beginning to act as if *they're* the rulers.'

'They're regents.'

'Regents while both the old and new King still live. It's not right. They rule in the new King's name and consult him on nothing.'

'They include him in their councils.'

'Their *official* councils, yes, but most decisions are taken by Isabella and Mortimer alone. There's unrest among the barons already.'

'All of this won't be for ever. The King will be fifteen before long. Soon he'll be able to rule in his own right.'

'Aye, but until then, they won't give up even the tiniest shred of power.'

'But they *will* eventually. The Queen will do the right thing when the time comes, believe me.' She leaned across the table as if she were trying to convince him with her closeness. 'A corrupt king has been deposed and a good king set in his place. Surely the worst is behind us?'

'I hope so.' He rubbed a hand around the back of his neck, wondering how they'd got into an argument about Isabella when he'd been trying to propose. 'But just in case, if we marry before I leave for Scotland then I'll know that you're safe no matter what happens. Please, Mathilde, marry me today.'

'Today?' She laughed as if he were joking. 'That's impossible. I can't marry without the Queen's permission.'

'There's no time for that and this might be the only opportunity we get. It won't even take long. There's a goldsmith at the other end of the bridge and a chapel in the middle. We can buy a ring, say our vows and be back at the castle before it gets dark. As long as we have witnesses here, no one else need ever know.'

'So…' Her expression shifted, her eyes brightening with something like excitement. 'You mean we could get married in secret?'

'Yes.' He sat forward, too, so close that their faces were almost touching. 'We can ask Mortimer and the Queen for their permission when I get back from Scotland. The only way they would ever discover we were already married is if anything happened to me.'

'So we wouldn't ask their permission *until* the fighting was all over, when the country was finally settled?'

'Exactly. Then the only problem would be if they refused.'

'Why would they refuse? You have a manor now.'

'The Queen still might not think I'm good enough for you.'

'Then I'd tell her that you are.' Mathilde waved a hand dismissively. 'She'd listen to me, I know it.'

'Well, then?'

She reached for her plait, her expression thoughtful as she twined it slowly between her fingers. *'Until all this is over...'*

'What?'

'Nothing.' She dropped the plait again. 'So if we *were* to get married today, would we really be married? Would we have to lie together?'

He shifted on his stool, wincing at her choice of words. 'There would be no *have to* anything. It would make the contract more binding since no one could call the marriage into question afterwards, but I would never ask you to do anything you didn't want to.'

'Oh.' She bit down on her lower lip, chewing it in a way that sent a stab of lust straight to his groin.

'Mathilde?' he prompted her after several

seconds without an answer, unable to bear the tension any longer.

'Hmm? Oh...' She released her lip, her cheeks flushing a dusky shade of pink. 'I was just thinking... What if I were to get with child?'

'We'd have to be careful.'

'Do *you* want to lie together?'

He stared back at her, uncertain about what to do with his expression as every nerve in his body cried out an affirmative. 'Isn't it obvious?'

'I don't know. Is it?'

'Mathilde, when we kiss, can't you tell?'

'We haven't kissed for a long time.'

'Oh, hell!' He practically leapt over the table, hoisting her into his arms and kissing her in a way that left, he hoped, no doubt of his desire for her. 'There. Believe me now?'

'I...yes.' Her gaze was slightly unfocused.

'So?'

'So I think I'd like to be married properly, too.'

'In that case—' He smiled and lowered his head again, only to find one of her fingers pressed against his lips.

'Except that you don't trust me.'

'What?'

'You said so earlier, that you don't trust any- one, even though you're always telling me to trust you. That ought to work both ways, don't you think?'

He rubbed a knuckle over the bridge of his nose, feeling as if he were being led into a trap. Caring was risky enough, but trust gave her even more power to hurt him. 'I suppose so.'

'Well then, that's my condition. I'll marry you, *properly*, if you can honestly say that you trust me, too.'

'It's not that I *don't* trust you.'

'Not good enough. You have to say that you do.'

'I'm already offering you my protection.'

'Which I appreciate.'

'Some women would be grateful.'

She pulled away, her eyes flashing. 'I won't marry you out of gratitude.'

'I didn't mean it like that.' He ground the words out. 'I know it's not exactly an honour to marry me. You could do much better.'

'I didn't say that I wanted better. I only want trust.'

'All right. I just need a moment.' He drank up the last of his ale, walking up and down the small room half a dozen times before coming back to sit down again.

'Is it so hard?' She looked almost sympathetic.

'Harder.' He placed both of his hands down

flat on the table, staring intently at the space between them. He already knew the truth, but saying it aloud made it more real somehow. More threatening, too, as if the ground were shifting beneath his feet. 'Lady Mathilde Gosselin, I… trust you.'

'Thank you.' She placed her palms softly over his knuckles. 'In that case, Henry Wright, I would be very happy to marry you.'

Chapter Sixteen

'I can't believe we've only been gone a few hours.' Mathilde turned a smiling face up to Henry, her footsteps slowing as they approached the front gates of Westminster Palace. 'It was certainly an interesting tour of London. I never expected to be married by the time we got back.'

'Me neither.' He drew to a halt, tightening his arm around her shoulders, struck with a sudden, unnerving impulse to turn them both around, walk back in the direction they'd come, and then keep on walking, away from Mortimer and the Queen and the court and all of it. The royal palace they'd spent so long trying to reach now looked ominous and forbidding.

'Really? You didn't plan to ask me to marry you, then?'

'No. Not yet anyway.'

'Oh.' Her expression turned crestfallen. 'I

was hoping that at least one of us had thought things through.'

'I did. I just did it quickly.' He tugged her into the shadows of a house. 'I only wish we had more time together today.'

'So do I. Although I suppose I'd better take my ring off now.'

'Here, let me.' He took hold of her hand, drawing away the gold band he'd placed on her finger just one short hour before. 'It won't be for long. I'll be back in a few months and then we can speak to Mortimer and the Queen and do everything properly.'

'But maybe not too soon?' She looked faintly worried, tucking the band away in the leather pouch at her waist. 'The Queen might still need me for a little while afterwards. Katharine, too. I promised Cecily that I'd take care of her.'

'Then we'll ask when we're both ready.'

'Thank you.' She sounded relieved, standing up on her toes to press a kiss against his cheek. 'Henry…' Her voice faltered as she sank back down again. 'Where will we go, if we want to make our marriage binding before you leave for Scotland? It's not easy to be alone in the palace.'

'True…' He paused, trying not to make it too obvious that he'd already spent some consider-able time pondering the matter and that was even *before* they were married. 'I did have an idea about that. There's an empty room on the floor above the Queen's chambers, at the far end of the gallery. It's a small one, set aside for the servants of guests, but it's standing empty at the moment.' He set his hands about her waist. 'I'll go there tonight. Every night until I have to leave. I know it might not be easy for you to get away, but if you can find a way...'

'I'll find a way.' Her pulse fluttered in her neck as she answered, so delicately that he couldn't resist dipping his head and kissing her there, a wave of heat flooding his body as she made a small, guttural noise in the back of her throat.

'Don't take any risks.' He could hardly believe he was saying the words. 'We still have to be careful.'

'I know, but I'll be there. Only I might have to tell Katharine. I'd like to tell her about us anyway and I know she'll keep it a secret.'

He made a face. 'So now you want me to trust someone else, too?'

'No. Just trust me to trust her.'

'That sounds complicated, but all right. Tell her if you wish.'

'Thank you.'

He kissed her one last time before letting go,

willing his body temperature back to normal and pushing misgivings about the future aside as they turned in the direction of the palace. After all, Mathilde was right, England had a new king, one who would soon be old enough to rule in his own right. Then Isabella and Mortimer would *have* to step aside and there would finally be peace. The future was still bright. He'd just been a spy for too long, seeing dangers where none existed.

None the less, the sooner he got back from Scotland, the better.

'Something's happened.' Mathilde glanced sideways nervously as she and Henry walked back in through the gatehouse. The world outside the castle was still one of sunshine, but once inside, she had the strange impression that the sky was several shades darker, as if grey clouds were massing into a thunderstorm overhead. Most of the stable hands and guards were gathered together in small groups, too, talking in low voices and looking over their shoulders as if they were afraid of being overheard.

'You're right.' Henry nodded, his jaw already set in a hard line. 'Come on.'

They hurried into the hall, across to where Katharine was sitting in the exact same spot where they'd left her several hours before. There was a new alertness about her posture now, however, the hands in her lap white-knuckled with tension.

'What is it?' Mathilde asked at once. 'What's happened?'

'Ah, you're back. Good.' Katharine lowered her voice, beckoning them closer. 'Somebody tried to free the old King.'

'Free him?' Mathilde gasped. 'But I thought he didn't have any supporters?'

'He doesn't. Not enough to retake the country, but still a handful, apparently. They didn't succeed, but it was closer than it ought to have been.'

'I should go to Mortimer.' Henry's tone was grim.

Katharine nodded and pushed herself to her feet. 'We ought to go upstairs and wait for the Queen. You're back just in time.'

'Yes... Of course.' Mathilde caught Henry's eye, saddened that the happiness and excitement of the day had faded so quickly. She had a feeling that he was thinking the same thing, that their wedding day, never mind the prospect of a wedding night, was over.

'How did you enjoy your afternoon?' Katharine took Mathilde's arm as they reached the top of the stairwell. She'd become noticeably more stooped of late and needed help to walk any distance, as if losing Cecily had weakened her. 'Where did the two of you go?'

'To London Bridge. We ate pies.'

'Pies? Next time, bring me one back. That sounds more appetising than partridge.'

'Much better.' Mathilde smiled at the memory, hoping that there *would* be a next time, although it seemed doubtful that she and Henry would have another chance to visit the city before he left for Scotland.

'You have a good man there.'

'I know. You wouldn't have let me go otherwise. I was surprised that you did.'

'Hmph. I probably shouldn't have.' Katharine chuckled. 'But he was good to Cecily and I'll always be grateful to him for that. Besides—' there was a new, pointed note to her voice '—you're a good girl. I know that you won't do anything foolish.'

Mathilde glanced around quickly as they entered the Queen's chamber. The other ladies were working on a large piece of tapestry in one corner, far enough away to be out of earshot, making it impossible for her to contain her excitement any longer. 'We made vows to each other.'

Katharine's eyebrows almost disappeared beneath her headdress. 'You married him?'

'Yes!' Mathilde pressed a hand to her mouth, laughing gleefully behind it. 'Today, on the bridge.'

'Well…' There was a heavy pause. 'Well, then.'

'Do you think it was a mistake?' She pulled her hand away, disappointed by her friend's reaction. The words were neither congratulation nor condemnation.

'No-o.' Katharine made a face as she sat down on the royal day bed. 'It's only marriage itself that I don't like.'

'You were married once, weren't you?'

'A long time ago, but we were ill-matched from the start. He was thirty years older than I was and we had nothing to talk about. No children either. We were miserable together for ten years and then he died. Fortunately, I found Cecily and we were happy. As much as we were allowed to be.'

Mathilde crouched down beside her. 'You know, she was very worried about you, about how upset you'd be afterwards.'

'Pah.' Katharine shook her head although there was a hint of moisture in her eyes. 'It is how it is. I'm an old woman now, but I know I was lucky to love and be loved. That consoles me.' She put a hand on Mathilde's wrist, her grip surprisingly strong. 'Do you love this new husband of yours?'

Mathilde took a deep breath, trying to clear her head and answer honestly. Everything was happening so fast she hardly knew what to make of her feelings. She'd married Henry on instinct, because everything he'd said on the bridge had made sense and because she couldn't imagine wanting to be with another man as much as she wanted to be with him. Was *that* love? She still didn't know. She needed time to think.

'I care for him,' she answered carefully. 'And I know that he cares for me. I think we're well-suited.'

'Then don't worry about looking after me. You should take your chance at happiness. We do not get many in this life.'

'I will, but only once the country is settled. I won't just abandon you.'

Katharine squeezed her wrist and then let go as Isabella swept like a sudden blast of wind into the room, her usually calm features agitated.

'Leave us!' she snapped at the other women. 'Mathilde! Help me undress. This gown is too tight. Hurry!'

'Yes, Your Grace.' Mathilde leapt up at once,

unfastening the ties at the back of the gown as quickly as her fingers could accomplish the task. To her surprise, the Queen was shaking slightly.

'That's better.' Isabella rolled her shoulders, stretching with relief as Mathilde pulled the gown down over her stomach and hips. *'Wine!'* She held a hand out imperiously and Katharine passed her a goblet, though she screwed her mouth up after only a mouthful. 'This tastes sour. Fetch something else.'

'I'll go, my lady,' Mathilde offered.

'No. Kat can do it.'

'Yes, Your Grace.'

Katharine threw Mathilde an eloquent look on her way to the door and she felt her stomach lurch with nerves. With guilt, too. Maybe she *had* acted too impulsively and ought to have waited for the Queen's permission to marry Henry. It had made sense to go ahead at the time, but now it seemed a poor way to repay the Queen's trust in her. Obviously Isabella had something she wished to discuss alone and Mathilde judged by her mood that the conversation didn't bode well. The only thing she could think of was her recent trip into London with Henry, though surely Katharine would have mentioned if her absence had been noticed?

'What are people saying in the hall?' Isabella fixed her with a hard stare. 'What are they saying about my husband?'

'Oh.' She almost sagged with relief. Not about Henry then... 'Just that there was an attempt to free him and it failed.'

'*And?* What do they *think* about it?'

'I'm not certain, Your Grace.' She bit her tongue, unwilling to admit the reason why. She could hardly admit to spending the afternoon away from the palace. 'They're nervous, I think.'

'Why? He has no power any more. He's no longer a king! There's no need to be nervous!' Isabella went very still suddenly. 'What about me? What are they saying about me?' There was a momentary pause. 'And Mortimer?'

'I don't think they would say anything in front of me, Your Grace.'

'No...' Isabella's foot tapped up and down. 'Perhaps not, but if you hear anything, anything at all, you must tell me at once. No matter what it is or who says it, do you understand?'

'Yes, Your Grace.'

'Good.' The Queen lifted a hand to her cheek with a smile. 'Forgive me for being so short before. I should not take my temper out on you. You're one of the few people I can trust, Mathilde. I don't know what I'd do without you.'

'You don't have to, Your Grace.' She bowed her head, feeling a warm sense of satisfaction at the words.

'Ah, there you are.' Isabella's gaze moved past her to Katharine, returning with a fresh jug of wine. 'Come, we need to decide what I'm going to wear tonight.'

Chapter Seventeen

Henry marched up and down the small chamber, glancing at the door every time he went past. Common sense told him that there was little hope, if any, of Mathilde coming that night. The chances of her being able to get away from the Queen's rooms unnoticed were just the same as they'd been the previous night and the one before that, their wedding night, and he was due to ride north in the morning, to help Mortimer muster an army for Scotland. Yet tonight was their last chance to be together and every small noise, every creak of a floorboard and thud of a door elsewhere in the palace, made his heart, not to mention other areas, leap with anticipation. Every minute that passed felt like a slow torture.

He pushed his hands through his hair and groaned aloud in frustration, trying to console himself with the thought that her absence was probably for the best. As much as he wanted to consummate their marriage and make the contract binding—hell, as much as he wanted her for any reason—it was arguably safer not to do so. If he were to get Mathilde with child *before* the Queen gave her permission for their marriage then it would mean her immediate dismissal from court. Not that he could view *that* as an entirely bad thing since it would mean getting her away from Isabella, but for Mathilde's sake, he would do everything in his power to avoid it.

If she came.

He muttered a few choice epithets, none of which made him feel any better, while he started to undress by the light of the solitary candle. If he was going to be disappointed again then he might as well lie down and try to get some rest. He had a long day's ride ahead of him tomorrow. He just hoped that he'd get a chance to say goodbye to his wife before he left.

He kicked off his boots, tossed his tunic and undershirt aside and then froze, crossing the room swiftly at the sound of a faint knock.

'Mathilde?' He flung the door open, hardly daring to believe the evidence of his own eyes. She was dressed in a floor-length woollen cloak, the hood pulled up over her head and with a pair of slippers poking out underneath.

'I couldn't get away before.' She sounded as if she was apologising, which was ridiculous since he didn't think he'd ever been so pleased or grateful to see anyone in his whole entire life. 'I kept trying, but the Queen's been sleeping badly and she calls for us sometimes in the night.'

'It doesn't matter.' He reached for her arm and tugged her inside, throwing a cautious look up and down the gallery before closing the door softly behind them. 'You're here now.'

'I had to come.' She pushed the hood back, revealing a breathtaking mass of silken, chestnut hair falling loose over her shoulders. 'I heard that Mortimer was leaving tomorrow and I couldn't bear the thought of not saying goodbye. I would have climbed out of the window if I'd had to.'

He reached up, pushing his fingertips into the tresses as he cupped her face in his hands. 'I appreciate that, but if it's too much of a risk then—'

'No,' she interrupted him, half closing her eyes as he caressed her. 'I'm not going back yet. I don't care if the Queen misses me. We couldn't have our wedding night, but we can still be together now.'

He felt a sharp stab of desire at the words. After three nights of waiting and wanting, he was tempted to simply lift her on to the bed and throw himself on top of her, but he restrained himself with the knowledge that she was a virgin. She might not know what lying with a man actually meant. She might be horrified when she found out. She might be keen to run away then. In which case, he'd have to embrace her chastely and then find a bucket of extremely cold, preferably frigid, water to pour over his head. Maybe he ought to have brought one just in case...

'Are you certain?' He faltered over the question, trying not to notice the soft rise and fall of her breasts against his chest, bracing himself to hear the answer. 'Did anyone ever tell you what to expect?'

'What do you mean?'

'On your wedding night.'

Her lips formed a distinct O shape before her eyes twinkled and a small, almost mischievous smile spread over her features. 'I grew up on a farm.'

'You mean—'

'I mean...' She took a step back from him,

unravelling the cloak from around her shoulders to reveal a thin, white linen shift. 'I know enough.'

He swallowed, heat prickling over his skin as his throat turned arid. In the flickering candlelight, every curve and contour of her willowy figure was visible, from her round breasts to her small waist and shapely hips. He let his gaze feast on them, his whole body throbbing in response. Just the sight of her flushed skin made him ache to possess her. She was perfect, everything he'd ever desired in a woman since the first time he'd set eyes on her, and only an arm's length away. He wanted to savour every moment, to kiss and touch and memorise every dip and hollow of her body, to make it truly a night to remember during all the long months they'd be forced to spend apart.

She was his, his wife, and they only had one night. He would make it special. And he'd be damned if he didn't make it as good for her as he was absolutely certain it was going to be for him.

Mathilde waited, wondering if she'd done something wrong. Henry's expression looked faintly stunned, as if she'd shocked him by being too brazen. The thought made her temperature soar and her skin turn to what was surely an unnatural shade of red. Nervously, she started to shrug the cloak back over her shoulders, but his hands shot out, catching her by the wrists.

'Don't.' His voice had a husky quality she'd never heard in it before, as if the words were actually scraping against his throat. 'You look beautiful.'

'Oh.' She let the cloak slip from her fingers and into a puddle at her feet, his voice turning her emotions from anxious to strangely powerful. He looked beautiful, too, she thought, letting her gaze dip for a moment, if that was the right word, which it probably wasn't, only handsome didn't seem quite right either. He looked more than that, his bare torso corded and rippling with muscle.

'Come.' He tugged gently on her wrists, drawing her slowly, but steadily, towards the bed.

'Are you sure no one else uses the room?' She gulped as she realised where they were going, feeling as if her heart had just leapt into her throat.

'I checked with the maids, don't worry.'

'The maids? Then they know we're here?'

'They know *I* am, but not who with. It's all

right.' He smiled reassuringly. 'Any good spy makes friends with the maids. They know most of the things that are going on.'

'Oh.' She knitted her brows, not sure how she felt about that.

'You're not jealous, are you?' He sounded faintly amused.

'I think…maybe. Just a little.'

'You shouldn't be.' He turned her so that she was standing with her legs pressed back against the bed. 'I belong to you now. For always.'

Mathilde sucked in a breath, her gaze drawn to the bulging muscles in his arms as he gathered her shift up over her hips and waist and shoulders, then tossed it on to the floor beside her cloak. The words weren't an admission of love exactly, but they were ones of fidelity and affection, sending shivers of desire racing through her body and raising goose pimples on her skin.

'You're cold.' He noticed at once, guiding her on to the mattress and lowering himself beside her. 'I couldn't risk drawing attention by lighting a fire.'

'I'm not cold. I'm just…quivery.'

'*Quivery?*' He lifted an eyebrow. 'That sounds uncomfortable.'

'It's not, not exactly. It's in here.' She placed a hand over her stomach. 'Inside.'

'Ah. In that case, let's see what we can do to ease it…' He bent his head, kissing her knuckles before lifting her fingers one by one and pressing his lips to the place beneath.

She stiffened, hardly daring to breathe as he covered her stomach in slow, tender kisses. *Quivery* no longer seemed like a strong enough word. *Pulsing* seemed more appropriate.

'How's that?' he murmured against her skin.

'Honestly? I think you're making it worse.'

'Do you want me to stop?'

'*Definitely* not.'

She felt rather than heard him chuckle as she arched her back, pushing her body up against his lips. Her breasts felt heavy and aching and she could feel her heartbeat low in her abdomen now, a gradually accelerating rhythm that seemed to fill and vibrate inside her whole being, sending her thoughts spinning into incoherence and making her ache for more. She reached for his head, sliding her hands through his hair and teasing the curls between her fingers. 'I've wanted to do this for a long time.'

'What?'

'Play with your hair.'

He laughed again. 'I wish I'd known. You can play with it whenever you want. In fact, you can play with any part of me whenever you want.'

'Really?' She blinked, not quite sure how to respond. 'Is there anything you want me to do now? Should I kiss you?'

'We'll get to that. First, I want you to be comfortable.'

'I *am* comfortable.'

'*More* comfortable, then. Like this.' He lifted his head briefly to smile at her and then lowered it again, taking one of her breasts into his mouth and gently caressing the nipple. Then he slid downwards again, moving his tongue in small circles while his hands followed behind, tracing similar patterns over her skin. It ought to feel wicked, she thought, but instead it felt right. She cared for him, she trusted him. Most of all, at that moment, she wanted him. As for love…perhaps it *was* love. She couldn't imagine feeling any closer to anyone. She couldn't imagine letting anyone else ever touch her so intimately either.

'You feel so good.' He made a guttural sound as he moved back up the bed again, nuzzling his face against her neck. His eyes were blue, she was sure, but at that moment they looked entirely, intensely black, filled with a look of raw hunger.

'So do you.' She smoothed her hands over his shoulder blades and then around to his chest where she could feel his heartbeat, thrumming hard and fast beneath her fingertips.

'I can't wait much longer...' His voice was even huskier as he nudged her thighs apart, positioning himself between her legs.

'I know.' She raised her lips to whisper in his ear. 'Neither can I.'

'I'll be as gentle as I can, but there might be some pain.'

'It's all right.' She reached for one of his hands, twining their fingers together. 'I trust you.'

They both moaned as he sank into her, breaching her defences and pushing slowly but relentlessly until he was completely sheathed.

'Mathilde?' He held her hand above her head. 'Are you—'

'I just need a moment,' she gasped raggedly, willing her body to relax and adjust.

'Tell me when you're ready.' The words sounded strained. 'I won't move until then.'

'Ye-es.' She closed her eyes, placing her feet flat on the bed and moving her hips gently as she sought for a more comfortable position. Fortunately, the movement itself seemed to ease the soreness, encouraging her to do it again, and then again, until she was writhing beneath him. A spark of pleasure flickered to life in her stomach and grew, coiling outwards. It felt surprisingly, wonderfully, good.

'Wait!' Henry pressed downwards abruptly, pinning her to the bed. 'Are you trying to kill me?'

'What?' She tried to tilt her hips upwards again, but it was like trying to move a mountain. A very hot, solid, heavily muscled mountain. 'Why?'

'I can't be still.' He sounded as if he were clenching his teeth together. 'Not when you're doing that.'

'Oh.' She smiled with understanding and relief. 'Then you should move, too.'

He gave a low groan, not waiting for any further encouragement as he lifted himself on to his arms and thrust inside her with deep, powerful strokes.

'Henry…' She tipped her head back, part-amazed, part-thrilled by the way her body reacted. There was a new feeling of slickness between them now as they pushed and pulled and rocked back and forth, the tension building to a point where she thought that it couldn't—surely it couldn't?—get any stronger. And then her whole body tensed and a wave of sensation rolled over her, a sudden clenching followed by a dizzying, wonderful release. She let out a cry of surprise mingled with pleasure as Henry pushed inside her once last time and then withdrew, spilling his seed on the blanket between them.

The candle was almost burnt to the quick by the time Mathilde awoke, opening her eyes to find herself lying face to face with Henry. One of his arms was draped over her waist, his fingers stroking languorously across the small of her back.

'You fell asleep.' His lips curved as he spoke.

'I didn't mean to, but I couldn't seem to help it.' She glanced at the candle. 'How long has it been?'

'Maybe an hour.'

'An *hour*?' She launched herself upright, putting her hands to her face in horror. 'I ought to go. And *you* ought to be sleeping. You have a long journey tomorrow.'

'I know.' He looked unperturbed, folding one arm behind his head and smiling up at her. 'But I wanted to look at you for a while. I want to remember everything about tonight.' He drew her down into his arms again, holding her close against his chest. 'I don't know how long I'll be gone. Hopefully just a few months, but it depends on the Scots.'

'I'll be waiting.'

'Then wait here a moment.' He kissed the top of her head and then slid out of bed, walking naked across the room and coming back with a bowl of water. 'Here.' He moistened a strip of linen and rubbed it gently between her thighs. 'For your blood.'

'Oh... Thank you.' She smiled, surprised not to feel more self-conscious with him, perhaps because he was so unselfconscious with her. Maybe it was wanton, but just the sight of his bare skin and powerful muscles made her breathing erratic again.

'Are you all right?' His brow furrowed as he put the bowl aside. 'It wasn't too painful?'

'Only at first, but then it was quite...*very*... pleasurable.'

'I'm pleased to hear it...*wife*.' He leaned forward, kissing her tenderly before reaching under the bed and pulling out a piece of folded-up parchment. 'This is for you.'

'What is it?'

'The deeds to my—*our*—new manor. Just in case.' He put a finger to her lips as she started to protest. 'They're safer here in London with you than in an army camp with me. Just think of it as taking care of them for a while.'

'Then I will.' She clasped the parchment to

her chest, feeling her eyes prickle suddenly. 'But that's the *only* reason.'

'Thank you.'

'I should go.' She wriggled upwards, trying not to sniff, the tender look in his eyes almost too much for her.

'Yes.' His voice turned sombre as he reached for her hand, helping her out of the bed and back into her shift.

'Goodbye, Henry.' She turned towards the door, not daring to look at him again in case she started crying in earnest.

'Goodbye.' He seemed to understand, wrapping her cloak lightly around her shoulders. 'Take care of yourself, Mathilde.'

Chapter Eighteen

*North of England
—summer 1327*

Henry sat down at an empty table, reaching for a piece of bread and peering surreptitiously through the open folds of the tent. Mortimer and the King were arguing outside, their raised voices becoming increasingly audible to everyone around them. At this rate, it wouldn't be long before the whole army camp could hear, although perhaps that was the point. Over the past few months, Edward had become increasingly vocal about the *many* ways in which he disagreed with his regent, but he'd never gone as far as to air his grievances outside before, in full view of his guards and soldiers. It was as if he wanted them all to know his position, Henry thought, as if he *wanted* them to take sides, too.

Whatever Mortimer and the Queen might want or believe, it was becoming obvious that the young King wouldn't tolerate being governed for much longer. Fighting the Scots was now more and more a side issue to the real conflict.

'Arguing again, I see.' A man with wheat-coloured hair and a wide, white-toothed smile dipped his head under the tent flap. 'What's that? The second time today?'

'Third.' Henry gave a taciturn nod. Nicholas de la Beuvriere was around his own age and un-relentingly friendly, despite the absence of anything resembling encouragement. Not that Henry disliked him. In truth, he enjoyed his company far more than he did most of the King's hangers-on and companions, only he recognised another spy when he saw one. He had no doubt that Nicholas's light-hearted manner concealed an astute, perceptive and probably calculating mind. The only question was who he was working for.

'It's getting worse.' Nicholas sat down opposite, not waiting for an invitation. 'I wonder if Mortimer's told him about his plans for a peace treaty.'

Henry tore his bread apart, refusing to show any sign of surprise. Mortimer had discussed the possibility of a treaty with only his closest advisors at a private meeting to which Nicholas had definitely *not* been invited. 'And what plans would those be?'

Nicholas grinned, ignoring the question. 'You can understand the King's objections. It must be hard for a grandson of Edward I to accept any defeat, but this is his first military campaign. A treaty would be hard to swallow.'

'I suppose so. *If* that's what they're talking about.'

'For my own part, I wouldn't mind a treaty. I'm sick of waiting around for the Scots to attack us whenever they feel like it. The Bruce is far too clever to be drawn into open battle like Mortimer wants and, in the meantime, tempers get frayed. As we have daily proof.'

'No campaign is easy.'

'A treaty might be the best thing for England, too,' Nicholas persisted, rubbing his chin as if he were simply thinking out loud. 'It's about time we had some peace and prosperity. Though no doubt the Scots are aware of that. Mortimer makes it too obvious that he wants a quick resolution. Anyone would think he was eager to get back to London, though whether out of love or mistrust, who knows?'

'You think he doesn't trust the Queen?' Henry lifted an eyebrow.

'A woman who led an invasion against her

own husband and now usurps her son's power?' Nicholas grinned, as if the words were only spoken in jest. 'Would you?'

'Fortunately, I don't have to decide. Time will tell all, I suppose.'

'If events don't force the issue.' Nicholas held his gaze long enough to imply another layer of meaning, though not long enough for Henry to be certain. He was only left with the strange impression of being tested. 'However, something tells me he's not the only man here whose thoughts revolve around a woman.'

'Meaning?'

'Just that I know the look, my friend, that one where you stare at the horizon with a dreamy expression on your face. You're in love. You have all the symptoms.'

'Do I?' It took an extreme effort of will for Henry not to react. 'You speak as if love's a disease.'

'Perhaps it is, of the mind anyway. It can change people, for certain. And *you* haven't denied it.'

Henry rubbed his hands together, brushing away the last remaining breadcrumbs. *Was* he in love? Barely an hour had passed since his departure from London when he hadn't thought of Mathilde. Not just their one night together, though he'd relived the memory of it often enough, but the way she looked and spoke and smiled and…*everything.* Just picturing her face caused a warm glow in his chest.

Did *that* make it love? Yes, he cared for her. Yes, he wanted to protect her, but surely love was a step too far? And yet…somehow the word persisted in his mind, making him nervous. He'd already admitted to caring for and trusting her. If he was in love with her, too, then he'd put himself in the very position he'd sworn never to be in again. He would have given another person the power to crush all of his hopes and happiness just as his mother had done.

'There goes the King.' Nicholas jerked his head sideways. 'Going to stew in his own tent, I expect. Maybe I'll go and join him soon, let him rant for a while.' His expression was almost *too* nonchalant. 'Perhaps you'd care to join me? The King likes you.'

'I like him.'

'He trusts you, too, even though you're Mortimer's man.'

'And you think he's wrong to do so?'

'I didn't say that, although some people have wondered where your loyalties would lie if it came to a choice between the two of them. You might be a Mortimer, but you're a man with a conscience, too, however much you try to conceal it. You know Edward will make a good king.' Nicholas's gaze seemed very intent suddenly. '*If* he's ever allowed to become one.'

'He will be.' Henry looked away, answering with more certainty than he felt. The words were uncannily similar to the ones he'd said to Mathilde on their wedding day. If he didn't know better, he might have thought Nicholas had been spying on *him*.

'Are you certain?' Nicholas filled two cups of wine and slid one across the table. 'Don't answer now, but if you ever want to discuss the matter further, you know where to find me.'

Henry paused for a moment before accepting the wine. 'I've had enough of intrigue.'

'Indeed?'

'And even if I hadn't, like you said, I'm a Mortimer.'

'Understood. In that case, I wish you well, my friend, and perhaps—'

'Perhaps we've just been discussing the weather?'

'Exactly.' Nicholas chuckled. 'There's certainly enough of it. Can you imagine what the winters must be li—' He stopped talking as Henry clamped a hand over his arm. 'What?'

'Listen!' Henry half stood, alerted by the feeling that something wasn't quite right. It wasn't anything he could put his finger on exactly, just a vague sense that something, somewhere in the camp, wasn't as it should be. The usual, background murmur of voices was missing, replaced by an ominous silence. He clenched his brows and moved towards the tent flap, holding his breath to listen, and that was when he heard it, a low indistinct rumbling building to a roar. The thunder of approaching hooves.

They were under attack. He knew it a few seconds before the screams started.

'We have to protect the King!' Nicholas shouted as they drew their swords and charged outside together, racing across the encampment towards the royal tent.

Henry didn't answer, ducking as an arrow whistled past his head, so close that he felt the air vibrate against his ear. He took a quick look over his shoulder and then threw himself sideways, knocking Nicholas to the ground as he glimpsed a group of riders all drawing back their bows, preparing to fire again.

'What the—' Nicholas froze as a volley sliced viciously over their heads. 'That was too close.'

'Come on.' Henry hoisted him back to his feet, pushing him ahead as they ran to join the circle of guards outside the King's tent. Once there, they turned around, bracing themselves for battle. There was no time to put on any armour, only to grab a shield and hope for the best.

'So you protect your King over Mortimer?' Nicholas threw him an incongruous grin.

'He's my King!'

'Then I have my answer. And I owe you my life.' The other spy lifted his sword as a line of Scottish warriors stampeded towards them. 'Now let me try to repay the favour!'

Chapter Nineteen

Westminster Palace, London
—autumn 1327

'They say Mortimer's approaching London,' Katharine murmured softly as she and Mathilde sat by the fireplace one morning, sheltering from the cold draughts that whistled through the palace corridors like invisible, sharp-beaked birds.

'Already?' Mathilde looked up from the sleeve she was embroidering towards the window, as if she might be able to catch a glimpse of Henry on the road to the capital.

'He—*they*—' Katharine gave her a pointed look '—are back from the borderlands. They should arrive at court before evening.'

'Oh!' She felt her heart leap and then start to race with anticipation. They'd heard varying reports of the English army's progress throughout the summer, but she hadn't dared to hope for their return so soon.

'Something tells me the Queen won't have much need of us tonight,' Katharine continued. 'I doubt that she'll notice if you want to make yourself scarce, too? A headache, perhaps?'

'Thank you.' Mathilde smiled, a warm flush rising in her cheeks. 'I do feel a bit light-headed.'

'Aye, well, we'll see what happens. Sometimes rumours are just rumours.'

Mathilde nodded, trying and failing to concentrate her attention back on the sleeve and then giving up when she had to unpick most of her stitches. It felt like the longest, most interminable day of her life, but thankfully the rumours proved to be true.

Isabella made her way out to the bailey just as daylight was fading, welcoming the King and Mortimer home, though frustratingly, there was no sign of Henry.

'He's not here.' Mathilde caught at Katharine's arm as they stood off to one side.

'Hard to tell with so many men.'

'Not *so* many.' She could feel anticipation turning to panic. 'What if something's happened to him?'

'He's probably just at the back.'

'I'm going to take a look.' She moved discreetly away. 'I won't be long.'

'Lady Mathilde?' A blond-haired soldier appeared out of nowhere before she'd gone more than a few steps, murmuring her name in a low voice.

'Yes?' She blinked in surprise. To her knowledge, she'd never met this man before in her life.

'I thought so.' He made a small bow. 'You're just as beautiful as he said.'

'He?' She did her best to look innocent though her breath stalled at the words.

'Just so, my lady.' The man's gaze turned approving. 'I know nothing about anything either. If I did, however, I would tell you that a certain person has been delayed. A small matter of making a report to the Mayor of London, but he'll be here soon and asks that you meet him tonight in the same place as before.' He leaned closer, looking at a point just past her ear. 'It's still unoccupied. I already checked.'

'Oh. That was…efficient.'

'I rode ahead to make arrangements for the King, but I owed our mutual friend a favour, too.'

'Then I thank you for it, Sir…?'

'No sir, just Nicholas de la Beuvriere. At your

service, my lady. Now, if you'll excuse me.' He made another bow, took a step backwards and was gone as quickly as he'd appeared.

'Not injured, then?' Katharine lifted an eyebrow enquiringly as Mathilde slipped back into place beside her.

'No, not injured.' She smiled with a heady combination of relief and excitement, her thoughts already running to the night ahead.

It was four hours before Mathilde was finally able to leave the Queen's rooms, running up the palace stairwell and falling into Henry's arms the moment he opened the door to the upstairs chamber. 'You're back!'

'I'm back,' he agreed, catching her lips and kissing her until they were both breathless and panting. 'You got my message, then?'

'Yes. Just in time, too. I was so worried when you weren't with the others. I wanted to run up to Mortimer and shake him until he told me where you were.'

'I'd like to have seen that.' He buried his face in her hair and let out a long sigh. 'Although he's in a bad enough mood. Things didn't go so well in Scotland.'

'Tell me later.' She curled her arms around

his neck, pressing her body against his. 'I want to show you how much I've missed you first.'

'Wait… About that.' He put his hands on her hips, holding her slightly away. 'As much as I'd like that, it might not be such a good idea.'

'Why not? I'm your wife.'

'Because we ought to be careful and I don't want to risk getting you with child. We got away with it once, but—'

'Then we'll be careful,' she interrupted, pushing herself forward again and stroking a finger across the back of his neck. 'I've thought about you so often.' She went rigid as a new thought occurred to her. 'Didn't you think of me?'

'Of course I did. I just…' He clenched his jaw, looking as if he were having some kind of inner argument with himself, before bending down and lifting her into his arms. 'Every night.' He carried her towards the bed, dropping her unceremoniously on top of it and then pulling his surcoat and under-tunic over his head in one swift motion. 'I thought of you every night. In my arms, underneath me, on top of me…'

'On top?' She wasn't sure what he meant, but she undressed anyway, quickly unfastening her girdle and wriggling out of her tunic.

'I thought about doing this.' He helped to remove her shift and then rolled down her stockings, his gaze darkening with a look of desire as he climbed on top of her.

'Really?'

'And this...' He slid a hand between them, moving it gently across her stomach and then down between her thighs, making her gasp and squirm with a sudden shock of pleasure. 'I dreamed of touching you here.' Another touch. 'And here.'

'I dreamed of you, too.' She inhaled sharply as his hand moved away and he positioned himself at her entrance, dragging her fingertips down his arms and feeling the muscles of his biceps flex beneath. 'I wanted to remember what it felt like.'

'Like this.' He nudged forward slowly, entering her with a moan.

'Yes...' She sighed with pleasure, coiling her legs around his waist as all her pent-up desire came racing to the surface.

'Mathilde.' He went very still suddenly, bracing himself on his forearms.

'What's the matter?'

'Nothing. You just feel too good. I need a few moments.'

'Or what?' She smiled. 'Show me.'

'Not yet. You first.' He laughed raggedly and wrapped his arms behind her, pulling her on top of him as they rolled over.

'Henry?' She looked down, faintly scandalised by the way her legs were straddling his thighs. 'I don't understand.'

'Sit up and you will.'

'Sit up?' She wriggled upwards, catching her breath at the quivering sensation the movement unleashed. *'Oh.'*

'Oh,' he repeated, grinning wickedly as he stretched his arms behind his head. 'Speaking as a man who's spent the past few months in the saddle, it's your turn to ride.'

'Ride?' She caught her bottom lip between her teeth, narrowing her eyes at his teasing tone, and then started to move, deciding to show him just how good a rider she really was.

'If that was you proving a point then I'm going to have to taunt you more often.' Henry drew in a deep breath and then blew it out again heavily. 'That was…'

'Better than you remembered?' Mathilde laid her chin on his chest, her smile just the tiniest bit smug.

'What I remembered was good. *That* was spectacular. If I'd known it could be like that, I would never have made it to Scotland. I would have deserted somewhere around Cambridge.'

'Then at least I know how to keep you with me next time.' She half closed her eyes as he stroked a hand over her hair, pulling it away from her back to cool her down. Their bodies were still pressed together, still hot and sticky with moisture despite what was undoubtedly cold air around them. He had no idea what the real temperature was, though he probably ought to draw a blanket over them soon to be safe. He didn't want Mathilde falling sick with a chill.

'Can you tell me about it?' she murmured, her voice turning serious. 'Scotland, I mean. Can you tell me what happened?'

'I can.' He heaved a sigh. 'Not that there's much good to tell. It was a shambles. The Scots ran circles around us. They knew the terrain and how to use it to their advantage while our commanders did little but squabble among themselves. Mortimer's agreed to a peace treaty, but it's a heavy blow for England.'

'I don't care. I know I shouldn't say so, but at this moment I wouldn't care if the Bruce had conquered the whole of Northumberland. You're back safely, that's what matters.' She pulled herself into a sitting position, looking him up and

down as if she were making doubly sure that
he was still in one piece. 'Were you in any of
the fighting?'

'Just a few skirmishes.' He shrugged, simultaneously touched and amused by her scrutiny.
'That's all it was in the end, a few skirmishes,
but fierce enough. They almost captured the
King on one occasion.'

'Then surely a peace treaty is the best answer?'

'Not for Edward. He opposed it.' He furrowed his brow as he spoke. *Opposed it* was an
understatement. The King had been livid about
the humiliation being forced on him. There
was little love lost between him and Mortimer
these days and the whole army knew it. More
and more, Henry felt as though his own conscience was being pulled in two directions at
once.

'So Mortimer overruled the King?'

'Mortimer *and* the Queen. No doubt she
wanted Edward back in London where she can
keep an eye on him.'

'He's her son. She has his best interests at
heart.'

'Does she? Or is she keeping him on a leash
instead?'

'Maybe we shouldn't discuss it.' She rubbed

a circular pattern over his chest, her voice tight. 'I haven't seen you for months. I don't want to waste our time together arguing about the Queen.'

'You're right. And about that...our being apart, that is. Now that I'm back, maybe it's time to ask their permission?'

Her eyes shot to his. 'To marry?'

'Yes.'

'But it's so soon.'

'It's what we planned.'

'When we were both ready.'

'Mathilde?' He sat up beside her. 'Is something the matter? Have you changed your mind?'

'No, it's just...' She pursed her lips for a few seconds, looking thoughtful. 'On the other hand, Mortimer's back and there's going to be peace with the Scots now. The invasion's over, isn't it?'

'Ye-es.' He frowned. She sounded as if she were talking more to herself than to him. 'But what does that have to do with our asking permission to marry?'

'It's hard to explain, but it's not as if we even intend to leave court straight away, is it? You still want your knighthood.'

'True.'

'Then the Queen won't think that I'm abandoning her.' Her whole demeanour transformed, her face breaking into a dazzlingly wide smile. 'You're right, it *is* time. Only let me speak with Isabella before you ask Mortimer. I'll ask her permission tomorrow.'

Chapter Twenty

It wasn't that she was afraid to ask, Mathilde told herself, hurrying through the palace on an errand a couple of days later. It was just that the Queen was so distracted, preoccupied with discussions about the peace treaty, making it impossible to find a good moment. It wasn't that she doubted her decision either. In fact, the more she thought about it, the more eager she was to speak with Isabella and ask her permission to marry. She'd felt guilty about keeping her feelings for Henry a secret from the start, but now their relationship could finally be out in the open. And surely there was no reason for Isabella to object since the invasion was over, her own promise was fulfilled and she and Henry weren't even intending to leave court for the foreseeable future. The only real difference it would make was that they would be able to spend every night lying in each other's arms instead of just a few stolen hours when everyone else was asleep...

She was halfway through the great hall when she noticed the hush, accompanied by a new awareness of eyes following her. For a moment she wondered if she'd done something shocking, like forgetting to dress, but the gazes implied more than that. They were judgemental, condemnatory and something else, some other emotion she couldn't quite identify. Whatever it was, it made her flush with guilt even though she had no idea why.

Nervously, she quickened her steps back towards the Queen's apartments. She was almost there, trying to convince herself that she was simply imagining things when Katharine barred the doorway, her face white.

'What's the matter?' Mathilde drew back in alarm.

'There's a messenger come from Berkeley Castle.'

'From the King?' Mathilde corrected herself quickly. 'The old King, I mean.'

'Not from him, about him. You know he was moved there a few months ago.' The skin across Katharine's forehead tightened, the tremor in her voice turning Mathilde's blood to ice.

'He's dead, isn't he?' Her voice sounded odd even to her. Hollow and distant. She knew the words were true even before Katharine's expression confirmed it. 'What happened?'

'Nobody seems to know.'

'The last report said he was in good health.'

'Yes.'

'Maybe it was a sudden illness? A fever?'

'Perhaps.' Katharine looked around and lowered her voice. 'They say there were no marks on his body.'

Mathilde swayed slightly, trying to ignore the implication that marks might have been expected if the former King's death had been the result of foul play. She didn't want to acknowledge the possibility of that. She had to concentrate hard on *not* thinking about who might have benefited. Suspicion was not proof, after all, and she wouldn't condemn anyone without it, especially the Queen. On the other hand...towards Mortimer she felt less charitable. It seemed a coincidence, after all, that he'd recently returned from Scotland—if there was blood on anyone's hands, then she would prefer to see it on his.

'How's the Queen?' She tried to keep her voice calm.

'In shock.'

'Of course.' The words were encouraging. If

Isabella was in shock, then surely that suggested she hadn't been involved in any plot herself?

'What about the King? Has anyone told him yet?'

Katharine looked anxious. 'I don't know. *She* ought to be the one to tell him, if she can bring herself to do it.' She paused long enough to make her next words troubling rather than reassuring. 'She seems genuinely upset.'

Mathilde crossed the corridor to a narrow, glass window overlooking some gardens. Winter was fast approaching and the weather outside had turned noticeably colder over the past few weeks. If she wasn't mistaken, there were even a few flakes of snow twirling and dancing about in the air. No doubt that explained why she was shivering.

'He was a bad king.' Katharine came to stand beside her.

'Yes.'

'He did terrible things. He would have done terrible things to her if she'd failed.'

'Yes.' There was no disputing either of those facts.

'There was more than one rescue attempt. They might never have stopped, not until he was freed. If he'd gathered an army, then it would have meant more bloodshed.'

'Yes…' She turned her face at last when the silence became uncomfortable. 'Everyone was staring at me in the hall.'

'It's because they're in shock, too.'

'They looked accusing.' She finally identified the emotion she hadn't recognised at the time. 'And afraid.'

'Who can blame them? These are dangerous times.'

'But they were supposed to be better ones!' Mathilde said the words angrily. 'That was why she challenged her husband in the first place, wasn't it? To make England a better place, free of corruption and the abuse of power! That was what she said!'

'Hush.' Kat gave her a nudge as a door within the Queen's apartments slammed and Mortimer stormed past, his face like thunder. Mathilde was pleased to see it. If he and the Queen were arguing, then it vindicated Isabella even more.

'Tend to your mistress,' he barked and she curtsied obediently. Katharine, she noticed, did not.

'Your Grace?' Mathilde ventured into the Queen's withdrawing chamber first, half-afraid of what she might find, but Isabella was only sitting, face averted, on her day bed.

'Can I fetch you anything?' she asked as she and Katharine moved closer, slowly and steadily, as if they were approaching a wild animal, but Isabella only shook her head.

'I would never have wished this on him. I admit that I loathed him sometimes. He humiliated me and encouraged others to humiliate me, but I would never have wished for this.'

'Shall I call for your physician, Your Grace?' Mathilde crouched beside her.

'No.' Isabella looked around finally, her blue eyes huge in a face that looked haunted. Her arms were folded around her waist and she was rocking back and forth, as if she couldn't bear to be still. 'I'm not unwell. Only my son…the King…' She stopped rocking abruptly, seeming to come back to herself. 'I must speak to him. Will you bring him to me?'

'Of course, Your Grace. I'll go at once.'

Mathilde made to stand up, but one of Isabella's hands slipped out and fastened around her arm. 'I had nothing to do with this, Mathilde, I promise.'

'I know, Your Grace,' she answered at once, the Queen's obvious shock making her ashamed of her earlier doubts.

'Hurry,' Kat murmured as she brushed past her and out of the Queen's apartments, glad to escape. At this moment there was no sign of her other ladies. They were starting to remind Mathilde of the spies, only it was they who kept their distance this time, as if they, too, were afraid of Isabella.

She hurried through the palace, her eyes fixed straight ahead as if nothing untoward had happened, through the great hall and antechambers and up the staircase that led to the King's apartments. Once there she paused a moment to catch her breath, ignoring the guards' curious expressions as she pressed her hands to her stomach, pushing down a wave of nausea, and then knocked on the door, aware as she did so of several voices inside all falling silent at once.

She lifted her chin, waiting a few seconds before the door opened and she found herself face to face with Henry.

'Oh!' She was so startled that she couldn't think of anything else to say. It was like their very first meeting all over again, as if the past two and a half years had all been a dream, making her feel oddly disorientated. Not that she *ought* to feel surprised, she told herself. The King had always enjoyed his company and yet, at a time like this, she would have expected Henry to be with Mortimer. The fact that he wasn't suggested a deeper friendship

with Edward than she'd realised. Than he'd
told her, too.

'Mathilde?' For once his guard dropped and
he looked almost as surprised to see her. 'What
are you doing here?'

'I...' She had to think hard to remember. 'The
Queen sent me. She asks that the King visit her
immediately. She's very distressed.'

'What is it?' Edward himself called out from
within the room.

'One of the Queen's attendants, Your Grace.'
Henry gave her a nod of encouragement before opening the door wide to reveal three other
men, the King, his secretary and another familiar face, Nicholas de le Beuvriere.

'Your Grace.' She dipped into a curtsy at
once, alarmed by the expression on the young
King's face. He was usually calm and contained
like his mother, but at that moment he looked
angrier even than Mortimer had been, his handsome face mottled with fiery red blotches.

'And what does my *worthy* mother want with
me?'

'I believe that she wishes to speak with you,
my lord.'

'Why?'

She flinched at his scathing tone. The question itself felt like a trick. His anger was enough

to show that he'd already heard the news about his father.

'I'm not certain, Your Grace.' That was partly true, she told herself, keeping her head bent so that he couldn't read her face. She didn't know *exactly* what the Queen wanted to say.

'Are you a liar like she is, then?' She saw his feet advance towards her. 'Would you lie to your King?'

'My lord.' Another pair of feet came between them suddenly. Henry's. 'She's only the messenger.'

Mathilde peeped upwards, afraid that the King might object to such interference, but to her relief he only nodded and then jerked his head at her.

'Go, then.' It was an ungallant gesture, completely unlike him. 'Tell my lady mother that I will visit her shortly.' His mouth twisted into a grim approximation of a smile. 'Tell her that I'll be most interested to hear her explanation.'

'Yes, Your Grace.'

She gave him one last curtsy and then fled, throwing Henry a grateful look as she went.

Chapter Twenty-One

'I couldn't ask her, not after the messenger came with news of her husband.' Mathilde nestled on the bed against Henry, her head tucked into his shoulder while one hand rested on his chest. After the events of the past week, neither of them had wanted to make love. They'd simply lain down together, craving each other's touch for comfort. 'We'll have to wait a while longer.'

Henry swore under his breath. She was right, she could hardly have asked under the circumstances, but if only she'd tried just one day earlier, before the messenger had arrived... Now he had the disconcerting impression that the walls of the palace were closing in around them, compressing the very air. Who knew when they'd get another chance to ask?

'I know.' He kissed the top of her head. 'I'm just glad that you managed to get away tonight.'

'I couldn't before. The Queen needed me. She hardly ate or slept for almost a week. Today's the first day she's faced the court again.' Mathilde's fingers twitched against his chest. 'It's the first time she's seen Mortimer since she received the news, too.'

'Has she been unwell?' He frowned. Sitting at the high table that evening, Isabella had looked as regal and imperturbable as ever, yet harder somehow, too, like a marble statue, pale, beautiful and terrifying in her very stillness.

'Not unwell exactly. Sometimes she paced up and down, sometimes she just sat and stared, but she never seemed content doing either. The physician prescribed a sleeping draught and said that her behaviour was a sign of grief.'

'Or guilt.'

He felt her stiffen and pull slightly away. 'People say Berkeley Castle is in the middle of a swamp. The King might have fallen ill.'

'If he did, then it happened very quickly.'

'Fevers can.'

'Poisons are even quicker.'

'Stop it.' This time she jerked away, sitting upright on the bed, her back very straight. 'She and Mortimer were both here when it happened.'

'That doesn't mean one of them didn't give the order.'

'Or perhaps it was someone else? Someone we haven't thought of? Someone who wanted to ingratiate themselves or claim a reward?'

'How? The old King was well-guarded, especially after the last escape attempt. And even if someone *did* manage to get past the guards, how would they claim a reward? They could hardly come to court and simply announce what they'd done. It would be treason.'

'Then maybe it was someone else who wanted revenge. He had plenty of enemies.'

'That's true.' The idea made him feel slightly better though it still felt like clutching at straws. He didn't want to believe Mortimer capable of such a deed, any more than she wanted to believe it of the Queen, but it was hard to see who else would have benefited.

'She's innocent.' Mathilde's expression was defensive. 'I won't believe otherwise.'

'Maybe she is.' Henry pushed a hand through his hair. 'And maybe Mortimer is, too, but the fact that people are wondering whether they were involved is damning enough. The whole court is buzzing with gossip. *If* it was foul play and whoever did it thought that it would strengthen Isabella and Mortimer's position, then they were wrong. There's even more sympathy for the young King now. It makes me

wonder what would happen if he were to demand Mortimer's removal from court.'

'But he's a regent.' Her eyes widened. 'Surely
the King can't just cast him aside?'

'He might be able to if he has the support of
the barons.'

'Then what would happen to the Queen?'

He didn't answer, knitting his brows instead.
'The worry is that if *we're* thinking all this, then
so is Mortimer.'

'Meaning what?'

He glanced at her stricken face and then sat
up to wrap his arms around her. 'You need to
guard your expression.'

'I'm trying. I'm better than I was.'

'Yes, but it's still obvious what you're thinking.'

'What?'

'That the King might be in danger?'

A shudder ran through her. 'Maybe you only
know that because you were thinking the same
thing, too?'

He clenched his jaw though he didn't deny
it. 'Mathilde, did you tell anyone that I was in
the King's apartments the other day?'

'No.'

'Not even Katharine?'

'No.'

'Good. Don't. It could be misinterpreted.'

'Why?' She twisted her head to look up at him. 'What *were* you doing there?'

'The King summoned me. He wanted to ask me something.'

'What did—'

'No.' He shook his head firmly. 'Trust me, Mathilde, the less you know, the better.'

'Urgh!' She wrenched herself away from him, moving to the other side of the bed with an impatient sigh. 'This is like Paris all over again. I'm not a seventeen-year-old girl any more.'

'I know that, and it's not that I don't want to tell you...' He considered briefly before getting up and going to crouch in front of her. 'What would you say to the idea of *not* asking permission to marry and just leaving court?'

'Just leaving?' She stared at him blankly for a few seconds. 'Together?'

'Yes, although we'd have to be subtle about it. You could say that you're needed back in Rudstone and then come with me instead.'

'To your manor?'

'Exactly. We could go and start a new life together.'

'But what about all the things you said you wanted? What about your knighthood?'

He made a face. 'I'd still like them, but I'm starting to see what ambition and power can do to a man. I don't want that. I don't want to be a part of this court any longer either. I have a certain amount of loyalty to Mortimer, but I have to do what's right and those two things are becoming incompatible.'

'Would he let you go?'

'He can't stop me. I'm a free man. Just like you're a free woman.' He reached up, drawing his thumb across her cheek. 'I could be a farmer instead of a spy. We could have sheep and chickens and grow crops, all of those things you told me about Rudstone. It won't be the same, but we can make it into whatever we want. We can make a new home. Together. So…what do you think?'

'I think…' She hesitated, her expression torn. 'It sounds wonderful.'

'Well, then?'

'But I can't leave just yet. Not while the Queen still needs me.'

'Why? To help ease her guilty conscience?'

'Stop saying that! Stop implying the worst about her!'

'I'm only being a realist.'

'No, you're trying to turn me against her. You're trying to make me choose.'

'Maybe I am.' He stood up angrily. 'Maybe

I'm curious, Mathilde—which one of us *would* you choose, if it really came to it?'

'*You!*' She clenched her fists. 'But when the time is right. You can't ask me to abandon her just when she needs me the most.'

'That's all the time with Isabella!' He rubbed his hands over his forehead in frustration. 'Why are you so blind when it comes to her? You can't honestly tell me you *still* trust her?'

'Yes! And I'm not blind. I know she's not perfect. I just don't believe she's capable of something like this!'

'*She's not your mother!*'

She jerked her head back so fast that it almost bumped against the wall, her face draining of blood in a matter of seconds.

'Mathilde, I'm sorry.' He reached a hand out towards her and then lowered it again as she shrank away. 'I shouldn't have said that.'

'No, you shouldn't have.' She rolled off the bed and on to her feet. 'I know she's not my mother, but I still care. She's been good to me and I need to do the right thing by her. It's the only way I can make amends.'

'What do you mean? Is this because you think you failed your real mother? Because you didn't.'

'Yes, I *did*!' She swung towards him, her eyes

blazing. 'I told you that my mother drowned, but the truth is, I could have stopped it. That night she left, I saw her go. I was only half-awake, but I saw her pull back the curtain between our beds and I knew that it was her. She was always wandering around in the night, like a ghost, and my father would always go after her to bring her back. Only this time, he hadn't woken up and I thought… I thought of getting up and following myself, but then I closed my eyes again, just for a moment, and I must have fallen back to sleep. And then in the morning when I woke and realised that she hadn't come back… I ran outside with my father and that's when we found her in the millpond.' She swallowed visibly. '*That's* why he blamed me. It was because he saw the guilt on my face. He knew what I'd done.'

'Mathilde…'

'*Don't* tell me I was just a child and that it wasn't my fault!' She sounded as if she were speaking from between clenched teeth. 'I was old enough to know that she needed help and I turned away!'

'But you *were* a child and you weren't to know what would happen. How could anyone have known?'

'But if I do it a second time, *deliberately*, how

could I ever live with myself? I want to be your wife, Henry, but I could never be happy if I abandoned the Queen now. I made her a promise.'

He stiffened at the words, struck by a horrible sense of foreboding. 'What kind of a promise?'

'To stay with her until all this is over.'

'This?'

'I don't know. I thought she just meant the invasion. That's why I thought we could ask permission to marry after you came back from Scotland, but now things have changed again and...' She put her head in her hands. 'I don't know what it means exactly. Until there's peace, I suppose.'

He dropped down on to the edge of the bed. 'When did you promise her?'

'Just before we left Paris. It was when Lady Cecily was sick and the Queen was afraid of everyone abandoning her. She asked for my promise and she seemed so alone and vulnerable that I couldn't refuse. And she's *not* what you think! I know that she'll give us her blessing just as soon as the country is settled. Once the treaty with Scotland is signed and there's peace and stability again.'

Henry stared at the opposite wall. He'd known about Mathilde's attachment to the Queen, but this was even worse. Isabella had a hold over her that he hadn't expected, one that she couldn't break without going against her conscience and the memory of her dead mother. She *couldn't* leave yet, which meant that neither could he, because he loved her. He was *in* love with her. He probably had been for the past year, if he'd only allowed himself to admit it. And he couldn't walk away from her, even if it meant torturing his own conscience.

He exhaled heavily, wondering whether saying the words aloud would make any difference. But what if they didn't? What if *I love you* wasn't enough, not compared to her promise to the Queen? What if she turned away, just as his mother had done? He didn't think he could bear that kind of pain again.

'I know I should have told you before we were married...' Mathilde took a tentative step towards him '...but I truly thought it wouldn't be for long. I didn't think—'

She stopped abruptly, furrowing her brow as if she didn't want to put whatever she was thinking into words. *I didn't think the Queen would turn out to be a tyrant,* he finished silently for her.

'I know.' He sighed. 'I just want us to get out of here before it's too late.'

'But if we ask to leave now, then it could

make matters worse, couldn't it?' She perched back beside him, her eyes appealing now. 'It might look as if we suspected the Queen or Mortimer of being involved in the old King's death. Either that or as though *we* were guilty of wrongdoing.'

He swallowed another oath. She was right. Even asking to leave could be dangerous, especially if Mortimer and the Queen were looking for someone to blame...

'All right.' He reached for her hand. 'We go on as before for the time being. We act and behave as if we know nothing and think nothing. I'll wait for you, Mathilde. Only, please, I beg you, don't make me wait too long.'

Chapter Twenty-Two

York
—winter, early 1328

'How does the weather look?' Isabella called out as Mathilde threw back the window shutters and winced in dismay. The morning of the royal wedding was scarcely brighter than the evening that had preceded it, with slate-coloured clouds blocking any attempts at sunshine and threatening snow to come. The King and his new Queen, Philippa of Hainault, had been married by proxy in the autumn and their union was due to be formalised in the still half-built York Minster later that day, but if the sky was any indication, they were going to need several layers of warm cloaks in order not to freeze.

At least it was a joyous occasion for once, Mathilde thought. Perhaps now people would be able to forget the brutal events of the autumn and think more positively about the future again. Edward and his young bride were of a similar age and Philippa's arrival had lightened the sombre atmosphere of the court considerably. Small of stature, with dark hair and twinkling brown eyes, she was blessed with an open manner, a genial nature and a ready smile. The young King already seemed to like her a great deal. As did most people, Mathilde included, although she was careful not to say so in the hearing of the Queen, who seemed determined to maintain a distance from her new daughter-in-law.

She was glad to be back in Yorkshire, too, though it was also hard being so close to Rudstone and yet still too far away to visit, a day's ride at least. She'd briefly considered sending a message to her father, but after almost three years with no word from home, she'd eventually decided that it would be too painful even to try.

Preparing the Queen for the wedding had taken several hours, but the procession that followed was magnificent, with the royal couple riding side by side through the streets of York on magnificently decorated horses, throwing coins into the crowds as they passed. Even a light snowfall couldn't dampen the mood of celebration as hundreds of people came out to watch and cheer on streets decorated with brightly coloured hangings and banners.

Isabella excused herself from the wedding banquet early, but for once she allowed Mathilde to stay behind, taking only a weary-looking Katharine back with her to her rooms.

'Come with me.' Henry came up beside her as soon as they'd gone.

'Where to?' Mathilde smiled eagerly. They were both dressed in blue that day, her in a peacock-coloured kirtle with matching surcoat, him in a paler tabard. It was a shade that perfectly matched his eyes, making them stand out in his sun-bronzed face like gleaming sapphires.

'I can't tell you. It's a surprise.'

'But there's going to be dancing,' she pleaded. 'Can't we just stay for that?'

'What I have planned is better. Trust me, you'll be glad.'

Cautiously, she threw a quick look around and then made up her mind, hurrying out of the hall alongside him and into the bustling town. The atmosphere in the streets was still buoyant and she let herself get swept up in the happy mood, skipping ahead a few steps and then darting down a narrow alleyway away from prying eyes.

'Are you trying to escape from me?' Henry was laughing by the time he caught up with her.

'I just thought we could find somewhere more private.' She leaned back against the timbered wall of a house and gave him a coy look. 'I have a reputation to uphold. The court still thinks I'm a lady of virtue.'

'As you are, most of the time.' He moved closer, his voice husky. 'You have no idea how hard it is to see you every day and not be able to touch you.'

'Yes, I do.'

She gasped with pleasure as their lips met and clung, the two cups of wine she'd drunk at the wedding feast making her feel heady and reckless. Slowly, she slid her arms around his waist, pulling him hard against the cradle of her hips until she could feel his arousal, until there was no space at all between their two bodies.

'Mathilde...' He groaned and lifted her higher against the wall.

'I miss you every day, too,' she murmured the words against his ear. 'I wish...'

'What?' He stopped kissing her neck for a moment to look into her face. 'What do you wish?'

'What you said a few weeks ago, about us leaving and being together.'

'Then we ca—'

'Soon,' she spoke over him. 'I'm certain all of this will be over soon. Once the treaty with the Scots is concluded then there'll be peace and the Queen can begin handing power over to her son. There'll be no reason for her not to.'

'Except power itself.' He rested his forehead against hers briefly and then stepped back, re-adjusting his tunic. 'We can't do this here.'

'I know.' She sucked in a breath unsteadily. He was right. Even if her words hadn't already destroyed the mood, they were in an alleyway in broad daylight and it was far too wanton, no matter how badly she wanted him.

'Come on. Before I forget what I have planned.' He pressed one last kiss to her cheek before taking her hand and drawing her back towards the main street.

'Where are we going?' she asked, trying to distract herself from the hot flush still coursing through her body. *If only* there was somewhere they could go to be alone, but the whole city seemed full to bursting.

'You'll see.' He winked, refusing to say anything else as they walked purposefully away from the centre of the city towards a small but respectable-looking tavern beside the river. According to the sign above the entrance, it was called the Green Dragon, although the reason they'd come was still a mystery.

'We can stay until nightfall. I already arranged it with Katharine. She even convinced the Queen that you deserved some time to enjoy the celebrations.' Henry spoke over his shoulder as he led her into a busy courtyard where several groups of men and a few women were clustered around, drinking ale and toasting the royal marriage.

'That sounds very cunning, but why would we st—' She stopped abruptly, dropping Henry's hand in surprise as she looked up at the balcony and caught sight of her three brothers.

'Aland! Laurent! Dicun!' She gathered up her skirts, racing across the courtyard at the same moment as they came rushing down the steps and flinging herself against each of them in turn.

'Mathilde!' There was a chorus of exclamations and laughter as they embraced her back.

'Is it really you?' She pulled away after a few moments, both overjoyed and bewildered by their presence in York. It had been three years since she'd last seen them and they'd all grown so much. They weren't boys any longer, but young men, albeit just as loud and boisterous as ever. 'What are you doing here? How did you know?'

They all looked towards Henry, grinning at some shared secret.

He shrugged. 'Mortimer had no need of me for a couple of days so I took a ride towards Scarborough.'

'He didn't tell us who he was at first, only that he'd met you in France and that you were in good health,' Laurent interjected. 'Then we talked and he suggested we come and meet you today.'

'You went to Rudstone?' Mathilde gaped at Henry, so touched by the gesture that she had to blink away happy tears. 'Why didn't you tell me?'

'I didn't want to raise your hopes in case my plan didn't work.' He looked faintly embarrassed. 'Fortunately, they were all eager to see their big sister again.'

'And so we are.' Laurent put an arm around her shoulders. 'It's been too long.'

'It has.' She felt as if her face might burst from smiling. 'But what about Father? Is he here, too?'

'Ah…no.' Aland exchanged an eloquent glance with Henry. 'The truth is, we didn't tell him we were coming.'

'We told him that we were going to visit Hawise,' Dicun added gleefully, then sobered at a pointed look from the others. 'Sorry, but you know how he feels about the old King. We knew if we mentioned you…'

'Then he wouldn't have let you come,' she concluded for him. 'He really is angry with me for serving the Queen, then? I was afraid of that.'

'Ye-es,' Aland agreed finally. 'And because you ignored all his messages.'

'What messages?'

'The ones telling you to come home. He actually paid for a messenger to go to Paris and he still sends word with anyone travelling to London. He must have sent at least a dozen.'

'Oh…' She frowned. She could understand messages to Paris going astray, but to London…? One or two, perhaps, but so many seemed unlikely.

'Why *didn't* you come home?' Aland looked at her curiously.

She shook her head, at a loss for how to answer. Even if she *had* received the messages, she couldn't honestly claim they would have made any difference, but the fact that she *hadn't* received them was unsettling. Had they been kept from her? There was only one person she could

think of who could have done such a thing...
She cast a surreptitious glance at Henry and
saw that he thought so, too.

'It wasn't my wish to defy Father,' she answered finally. 'But the Queen is a good mistress. She's been very kind to me, and the old
King—'

'It's all right,' Laurent interrupted. 'We all
know how he raised taxes and broke his word.
Father's the only one who still refuses to listen.
He's angry with everyone these days.' He pat-
ted her arm sympathetically. 'You're better off
where you are.'

'There's somebody else here to see you.'
Dicun grinned, dispelling the newly sombre
mood.

'Who?'

'Who do you think? We went to tell her what
we were up to and she insisted on coming, too.'

'Hawise?' Mathilde spun around eagerly.
'Where?'

'Inside.' Aland grinned. 'I suppose we'll
catch up with you in another few hours, then?'

'If you're lucky.' Mathilde jabbed him in the
ribs and then ducked her head under the low-
beamed doorway of the tavern, letting out a
small scream of excitement at the sight of her
elder sister. She wasn't sure that she could bear

any more happiness. Hawise was sitting in one corner of the room with her husband, John, on one side, a toddler on the other and a small, placid-looking baby in her lap.

'Mathilde!' Hawise handed the baby to her husband and leapt up, her round face beaming. 'Look at you! You're such a fine court lady.'

'Don't be silly.' Mathilde squeezed her tightly, laughing at the idea. She knew that she fitted in at court more these days, but a 'fine court lady' she would never be. 'I'm just the same underneath.'

'I know you are.' Hawise grabbed hold of her arms. 'Now come and meet your nephew and niece.'

'My what?' Mathilde allowed her sister to pull her across the room. 'I had no idea you were even a mother.'

'You didn't receive my messages?' Hawise gave her husband a pointed look. 'You see, I told you she wouldn't have forgotten us.'

John smiled at his wife and Mathilde felt foolish all of a sudden. She'd been self-pitying, assuming that her family had forgotten about her while they'd been thinking the same thing. She ought to have known that they wouldn't, but it still didn't make any sense. Why would the Queen have withheld messages from her sister, too?

'Hello there.' She pushed the question aside to think about later, crouching on her haunches in front of the toddler.

'This is my son, Warin.' Hawise smiled. 'I discovered I was with child just after you left home. Say hello, Warin.'

'Hello.' The boy withdrew his thumb from his mouth long enough to answer.

'And this is my daughter.' Hawise passed the baby over for inspection.

'Well, aren't you lovely?' Mathilde cradled the child in her arms, running a finger lovingly over the tiny cheek. 'I'm Mathilde.'

'So is she.'

'You named her after me?'

'Of course.' The fond look in her sister's eyes made her own swim with tears. 'I've missed you.'

It was the happiest afternoon she'd spent in a long time, Mathilde thought, sitting in the tavern, surrounded by her four siblings. There was so much news to catch up on, so much to explain and so many stories to tell, albeit not all of them good. She learned that her father was well, but that his sight was failing and he was growing increasingly intractable. It made the hope of a reconciliation recede even further away.

'Is it true what they say about the Queen?' Laurent asked. 'That her hair is like spun gold?'

'She's very beautiful.' For once, Mathilde felt uncomfortable talking about Isabella, the thought of her missing letters still playing on her mind.

'Aland wouldn't think so.' Laurent smirked, jerking his head towards another table where their brother was sharing a jug of ale with Henry. 'He thinks Elizabeth Rolfe is the most beautiful woman in the world.'

'Really?' Mathilde lifted her eyebrows to Hawise. 'Is Aland thinking of marriage?'

'Yes. It's a good match and he's right, Elizabeth *is* very pretty, even if she's a little too aware of the fact.' Hawise looked her up and down. 'But you look lovely, too, even more than when you left.' She gave her a subtle nudge in the ribs. 'Your friend thinks so as well. I can tell by the way he looks at you.'

'Oh.' She felt her cheeks darken. 'Do you think so?'

'Definitely. Mathilde…you know I would never accuse you of anything, but who is he to you?'

'Well…' She lowered her voice. 'The truth is, he's not just my friend. He's also my husband.'

'You're married?' Hawise looked startled.

'Yes, but it's a secret. I knew that Father would never give his permission and we had no time to ask for the Queen's, but soon, when things are more settled, we'll be able to do things properly.' She gulped at the look on her sister's face. 'Do you think it was wrong of me?'

'No-o, not necessarily. It just seems strange, that's all.'

'I know, but things have been difficult at court recently and Henry wanted to protect me.'

'What about a dowry?'

'He took me without one.'

'Well then, he has good judgement.' Hawise seemed placated. 'He looks like the kind of man who relies on his own wits, not his wife's fortune. I'm happy for you.'

Mathilde smiled with relief. She was happy for herself. Henry had stayed at a discreet distance while she'd been catching up with her family, as if he didn't want to intrude, although she'd seen him laughing and talking with Laurent and Dicun, too. The sight had convinced her of something she'd already suspected: that she was truly, hopelessly, in love with him.

'Forgive me.' Henry approached the table at that moment, his expression regretful. 'But it's almost time for curfew.'

'Already?' Mathilde felt her spirits sink. She didn't want this time with her family to end so soon. Not for another week at least.

'I'm afraid so.'

'It's been so good to see you.' Hawise's voice sounded tight as Mathilde embraced her one last time.

'It has.' She resisted her own urge to cry. 'I have no idea when I'll see you again.'

'We'll find a way. In the meantime tell your *friend* to take care of you.'

'I don't have to. I already know he will.'

'Thank you for this.' Aland shook Henry's hand as they parted. 'You have our gratitude.'

It was darker than Mathilde had expected when they finally emerged from the tavern, hurrying through the streets to avoid being caught out after curfew.

'Thank you again,' she said to Henry when they reached the hall where the Queen was staying. 'Truly. This has been one of the best afternoons of my life.'

'I'm glad.' He smiled. 'I thought it was important to meet my wife's family.'

'Not all of them. It's as I feared with my father. He really is angry with me for not coming home.'

'I heard. I'm sorry.'

'Aland says that he sent messages, but they never arrived. Do you think…?' She hesitated, wondering whether or not to go on, but needing to know his opinion. 'Is it possible the Queen kept them from me?'

'Who else?'

'Why would she do such a thing?'

'You said that she was afraid of people leaving her. Maybe this was her way of making sure you didn't.'

'But that sounds so underhand…' It didn't make sense either. She'd given the Queen her promise. Surely that ought to have been enough?

'Yes, it does.'

She pressed her lips together, hearing the unspoken accusation as clearly as if he'd shouted it aloud, but still refusing to believe it. She couldn't believe it. The Queen wasn't underhand. *If* she'd withheld her messages, then it would have been for a good reason, because she'd thought they might upset her. And maybe Hawise's had simply gone astray. No, she wouldn't condemn or mistrust her mistress without proof.

She shook her head, pushing her suspicions

aside and wrapping her arms around Henry's neck. 'Let's not talk about it now. I don't want to spoil today. It's been so wonderful.'

'It has.' He placed a hand on either side of her waist, though there was something subdued about him. 'Although I'm afraid it might be our last together for a while.'

'What do you mean? You're coming to Scotland with Mortimer, aren't you?'

'Actually, no. You, Isabella and Mortimer are going to Scotland. I'm not.'

'Oh.' She loosened her hold. His whole manner seemed different suddenly, his face harder than she'd ever seen it before. 'Are you going with the King into Oxfordshire?'

'No. He's going there to spend time with his new bride. Unlike some of us.' His mouth twisted. 'Mortimer has a different task for me. He suspects that Lancaster has been plotting against him and he wants me to find evidence.'

'Oh, no!' she gasped. 'Do you think it's true?'

'I doubt it, not that Mortimer will ever accept that.' He looked around quickly. 'It's one thing to expect me to spy on a corrupt King, another to spy on a man who's simply a rival. As far as I know, Lancaster's guilty of nothing more than being another advisor to the King.

Unfortunately for him, Mortimer doesn't like other advisors.'

'So you think Mortimer's just looking for a reason to oust him?' She clamped her brows together. 'But if that were the case, why did he let him have the position in the first place?'

'Because it would have been dangerous not to at the time, but that was a year ago. Now Mortimer and the Queen have more power between them than anyone else in the kingdom. More than the actual King. *Too* much.' His gaze met hers and darkened. 'You said that you promised to stay with Isabella until all this was over, but what if it's not over in the way you hope? What if she *doesn't* do the right thing and hand power to her son?'

'She will. I know she will. Henry, I—'

'In the meantime, I'm back to being a spy again. I've no choice. Because you won't leave her, will you?'

'Not yet.' She lowered her gaze before the accusation in his. 'I'm sorry. I don't know what else to say.'

'Say goodnight.' He took a step backwards, slipping away from her. 'Goodnight, Mathilde.'

Chapter Twenty-Three

Oxfordshire
—summer 1328

He shouldn't be here, Henry told himself, glancing surreptitiously around the courtyard. If anyone asked, he could think of at least a dozen reasons to explain his presence, but it was still dangerous to risk being seen so far from where he ought to be. If Mortimer found out... He ground his teeth at the thought. There was no *if* about it. Mortimer was bound to find out eventually. His spies were everywhere. He of all people ought to know that, but he'd take his chances and deal with the inevitable when it happened. If there was one thing he'd become good at over the past few years, it was lying with a straight face.

He looked up at the manor where the King

was spending the first few months of his marriage and felt a pang of jealousy, thinking of the home he had hoped—*still hoped*—to share with Mathilde. He'd gone to visit the manor house a few weeks before and been pleasantly surprised. The building itself had been modest, but was well built and well kept, with a sunny courtyard and a small enclosed herb garden that opened up into rolling barley fields and woodlands of oak and birch. The aged steward had taken him all over the estate, giving him a tantalising glimpse of a future that seemed both within touching distance and yet a thousand miles away. He'd been sorely tempted to stay, to put down his bag and send word to Mortimer that he was leaving his service for good, but he hadn't been able to go through with it, knowing he would have gone mad, waiting and hoping for Mathilde to join him, wondering if she was safe with Isabella. Besides, it was a shared dream. If he couldn't live there *with* her, then he wouldn't live there at all.

It was hard enough waiting for news these days. As far as he knew, Mathilde was still in Scotland, serving a queen whose abuse of power she stubbornly refused to acknowledge. Even after she'd learned about Isabella's withholding of her messages, something he'd suspected from the start, she still refused to see it. At least the court would be returning to London soon, but what then? Their situation hadn't changed since York. No matter how much he pleaded, she *still* wouldn't leave the Queen. Which meant more waiting and spying for him, more propping up Mortimer and spying on innocent men who didn't deserve it. Unless he did something about it. Which was why he was there.

'You came.' Nicholas de la Beuvriere greeted him outside the front door, taking his reins as he dismounted.

'You sound surprised.'

'Me? No. Some of the others? Perhaps.' Nicholas grinned. 'But they don't know you like I do.'

'You know me?'

'Better than they do anyway.'

Henry laughed reluctantly. 'Then how do you know I'm not a Mortimer spy?'

'You *are* a Mortimer spy, but I think you've become a reluctant one. I think that you're stuck in his service, supporting a regime you don't believe in, being forced to find evidence against men you have sympathy for. And I think that today you're here as Henry Wright, loyal citizen to the King. How does that sound?'

'Like you think too much.' Henry glanced up at the house again. There was a female face peering from one of the upper windows—the new Queen Philippa, if he wasn't mistaken.

'I have a lot of time to think these days.' Nicholas rolled his eyes. 'The King and Queen are newlyweds. It gives the rest of us plenty of opportunity to wander around the grounds.'

'Ah.' The pang of jealousy felt more like a stab now. 'They're happy together, then?'

'It seems so. Unlike you and your lady, I think?'

Henry gave him a sharp look. 'Meaning?'

'Just that she's a long way away. That can't be easy.'

'No. It isn't.' He rubbed a hand over his chin. 'Maybe you *do* know me a little.'

'I believe that you're a good man who wants to do what's right.'

'And what's right is to depose Mortimer?'

Nicholas lifted his eyebrows. 'You speak plainly.'

'Given the choice, I prefer to. I'm a spy by profession, not inclination. We might as well get straight to the point.'

'Fair enough. Yes. The King thinks that it's time.'

'And you want me to join you because Mortimer trusts me and that could be useful?'

To his credit, Nicholas didn't try to deny it. 'Yes. He needs to be stopped.'

'If it were any other man, I'd agree, but tell me, is it *right* for me to betray my own blood? Someone who might even be my own father?'

'Ah.' Nicholas's shoulders rose and then fell again. 'That I don't know.'

'Neither do I, but whether he's a tyrant or not, I'm the one who has to live with myself afterwards. So...' He clenched his jaw. 'How many men do you have?'

'Just a handful. It's safer that way. It would be impossible to gather an army without Mortimer finding out so we need to capture him instead. On top of which, the King wants as little bloodshed as possible.' Nicholas paused. 'Though of course that makes it all the more dangerous.'

Henry froze, tempted to turn around and leave again, but aware that he couldn't escape a choice for ever. All he knew was that he couldn't carry on as he was any longer, standing back and pretending that his actions didn't have consequences. The choice was no longer between his own blood and a corrupt king. It was between blood and a worthy successor, between tyranny and what was right. Lines were already being drawn. He wished that he could stay on the same side as Mathilde, but she would never see the Queen for who she really was. And maybe that was for the best. He would never risk her safety by involving her in a plot against Mortimer and Isabella. She was far safer *not* knowing, in not being associated with him either. Which meant that *if* he joined the King, then there was only one course of action he could take in regard to her. One that he hadn't yet had the heart to acknowledge.

'Will you come inside?' Nicholas gestured towards the door.

'Yes, but I'm not committing to anything, not yet.'

'I know. You're here as the King's guest, that's all.'

He took a step towards the door, heaving a sigh as he went. 'Do you really think it makes any difference who's on the throne? We already replaced one tyrant with another. Maybe that's just the way of power. Edward might turn out the same way.'

'Perhaps, but at least the authority will be his and not stolen. He's the King by birth and by right.'

'Then why the rush?' Henry frowned, thinking of the words Mathilde had said to him. 'He'll be old enough to rule on his own soon enough.'

'Will he? Tell me honestly, Wright. You know

Isabella and Mortimer as well as anyone. Do you really think they'll surrender power and let him rule on his own without a fight?'

Henry glanced sideways, looking his companion in the eye before shaking his head. 'No. No, they won't.'

'Exactly. And by the time he's old enough, it will be too late to stop them.' Nicholas put a hand on his shoulder. 'Come. Let's get you something to eat and then we can talk some more.'

Chapter Twenty-Four

~~~~~~~~~~~~~~~~~~~~~

Westminster Palace, London
—autumn 1328

'I'm getting too old to travel.' Katharine groaned as she dismounted in the palace courtyard. 'I never want to sit on a horse again.'

'Me neither.' Mathilde agreed wholeheartedly. The journey to Scotland and back had been exhausting, both physically and emotionally. Riding through the borders had been particularly harrowing. There had been signs of destruction and suffering everywhere, the villages all scarred by violence, with houses in desperate need of repair and people in even more desperate need of food. The Scots had paid some reparations for the war, but no matter what anyone claimed, the peace treaty was a crushing humiliation for England. Isabella had agreed to relinquish the

Stone of Scone, captured by the King's grand-father Edward I thirty years before, *and* to give her seven-year-old daughter Joan in marriage to the young Scottish Prince David, both against the wishes of her son.

At least the journey was finally over and they were back in London, Mathilde consoled herself as she followed the Queen through the bailey and into the palace. With any luck, Henry was close by, too. And if he was…she smiled to herself at the thought…it wouldn't be long before he found her again.

She'd barely taken two steps into the hall before *she* found him instead, clamping her lips together to stop herself from exclaiming aloud as her pulse immediately quickened. There he was, standing ready to greet Mortimer, as if she'd willed him into appearing, only somehow it was a different version of Henry from the one she remembered. As she looked, he caught her gaze and bent his head slightly, but his features looked all wrong. His eyes were ringed with shadows and he looked leaner and harder some-how, as if all the planes of his face had become more pronounced, his cheekbones standing out like blades sharpened on a whetstone.

Anxiety gripped at her throat. Had he been sick? But, no, it was different from that, as if there were some invisible wall standing between them. Part of her wanted to run to him, to smooth her fingers over the line of his jaw and make it soft again, yet another part felt compelled to keep her distance.

The remainder of the day was unbearable. Mathilde caught several further glimpses of Henry talking with Mortimer, but as far as she could tell he never as much as glanced in her direction again and concern about what might have happened to him tore her nerves to shreds. By the time evening came, she didn't even wait for the Queen's other ladies to fall asleep, saying that she was going for a walk and then heading straight to their usual meeting place.

It was empty.

Henry paused outside the door to the guest chamber, summoning the courage to go in. After one quick nod of acknowledgement, he'd spent most of the day trying *not* to look at Mathilde, not to think about what he had to do either, though he'd been aware of her every time they'd been in the same room, aware of the concerned look in those big brown eyes, too. His heart had ached at the sight, as if a fist had reached inside his chest and squeezed tight, but it was no use postponing the inevitable. He *had* to speak with her, had to do the right thing no matter how painful. The time when they might have run away together was past and, with it, all of his hopes for a happy and peaceful future. He'd committed to a new course, one he needed to travel alone for her own safety.

If it succeeded, then hopefully one day she would understand and forgive him, whereas if it failed, well, better that she thought the worst of him. Maybe then whatever happened wouldn't hurt her too much. The situation was ironic in a bleak kind of way. Ever since his mother had left, he'd been afraid of being abandoned by someone he cared about and now he was the one doing the abandoning. Hard though it was to believe, the feeling was even worse.

'Henry!' Mathilde flew across the room before he was even over the threshold, flinging her arms around his waist and pressing her face to his chest. 'I was starting to think you weren't coming.'

'I'm sorry.' He gathered her against him, unable to resist holding her one last time.

'I've been so worried.' She tipped her head back, her eyes travelling anxiously over his face. 'Have you been sick? You don't look well.'

He gave a ragged laugh. He'd caught a

glimpse of his own reflection that morning and *not well* was an understatement. 'Have I lost your favour then, lady?'

'What?' She blinked, her expression hurt. 'No, of course not. Never.'

'Forgive me. That was unfair. I'm tired, that's all.'

'Then come to bed.' She smiled, but he didn't respond, reaching for her wrists and peeling them away from his waist instead.

'I cannot. Mathilde, we need to talk. Seriously. I need to know whether you've told anyone about us.'

'That we're married? Only Katharine and my sister, Hawise.'

'And nobody else knows that we're close?'

'No-o.'

'Good.' He let out a sigh of relief.

'Why do you ask?' Her voice sounded more guarded now. 'Henry, what's wrong?'

'It's not so much wrong as…' He took a deep breath. 'I just think it would be better if we didn't see each other any more.'

'What?' She sounded confused, as if he'd just made a joke she didn't understand. 'What do you mean? I'm your wife.'

'Only two other people know that. And Nicholas knows that we meet, but that's all. So as long as they all keep it a secret, nobody else need ever find out.'

'Henry...' Her eyes clouded, as if the spark in them had gone out. 'Why are you saying this?'

'Because it's becoming too dangerous. Meeting was risky enough at the start, but who knows who's watching us now? There are spies everywhere.'

'Then we'll be even more careful.'

'It's impossible. If the Queen found out that you were here, with me—'

'Then I'll tell her that we're already married. I thought about it a lot while we were in Scotland and as long as I stay at court while she needs me, why shouldn't we be married? She might be angry that I didn't ask her permission before, but she can't actually annul the wedding. Or better still, I could ask her permission now. And you could ask Mortimer. Then it could all be out in the open finally.'

'No!' He said the word more forcefully than he meant to. 'We can't do that.'

'Why not?'

'Because it's too late.' He cleared his throat, dredging up the words he needed to say, his feelings teetering on the edge of desperation now. 'The truth is, I've had time to think as well and I've had enough. I asked you to choose and you chose the Queen.'

Her lips seemed to go very pale, moving soundlessly for a few moments until she found her voice again. 'But I explained why.'

'It doesn't matter. We should never have married. It was a mistake.'

'You said…'

'I never said that I loved you.' The words sounded harsher than he'd intended, but he needed to make her believe them, needed her to leave with a convincingly broken heart.

'That wasn't what I was going to say.' Her own voice sounded very small. 'You said that you'd wait for me.'

'I know.' He clenched his jaw. 'But I gave up.'

'So you don't want to see me any more? You expect me to just forget that you're my husband?' She lifted her chin, bringing her gaze level with his. 'Is there someone else?'

'No. It's nothing like that, I swear it.'

'Then I don't understand. Why did you even marry me in the first place?'

'Because you're a lady.' He hated himself for the words, hated the way they made her flinch, too. 'It seemed a good step up for a man like me.'

'I see.' She held on to his gaze for the space of several painful heartbeats, her expression anguished, before it seemed to harden before his very eyes. 'I still have the deeds to your manor.'

'Keep them.'

'No.'

'Please. Just for the time being. Until...' He couldn't think of any way to end the sentence, only shaking his head.

'Very well.' There was a heavy silence. 'Is that all you wanted to say?'

'Yes.' He turned back towards the door and then paused. 'Trust me, Mathilde, it's better this way.'

'*Trust* you?'

He winced at the scepticism in her voice. 'Just remember, if you ever need help, if you're ever in trouble, you can come to me.'

'Just not as my husband.'

'No, not as that, but as a friend. Or if anything happens to me, go to the King. He'll take care of you.'

'Why?' Her gaze flickered suspiciously. 'Why would anything happen to you?'

'No reason, just if.'

She jerked her chin up again. 'Then I thank you for your concern, but the Queen will take care of me. I don't need the King. Or you. Not any more.'

Chapter Twenty-Five

$\sim\!\!\sim\!\!\sim\!\!\sim\!\!\sim$

Wigmore Castle, Herefordshire
—summer 1329

Mathilde lifted a hand to her face, discreetly attempting to stifle a yawn as she sat on a bench in the royal box, preparing herself for yet another day, the third in a row, of jousting. Or rather watching the jousting while trying her hardest to look interested and applauding, which was all she was generally called upon to do. Admittedly, the grand tournament was very impressive. Mortimer's castle of Wigmore had been transformed into an Arthurian scene to celebrate the upcoming marriage of his daughter, the outer walls draped in brightly coloured banners and surrounded by more tents than she could count, but it was hard to summon much enthusiasm for another six hours of riders parading, charging and then coming to be praised by the Queen. Every noble family in England seemed to have been invited, which was probably the case. Mortimer and the Queen were holding their favourite kind of court, one worthy of Camelot in which they were supreme, dressed in matching golden robes as King Arthur and Queen Guinevere.

'Isn't it thrilling?' Felicia Pemberton, the newest lady of the Queen's household, came to sit down beside her, brimming with excitement. She was young, only fifteen years old, and pretty as a kitten, with honey-gold hair and large grey eyes that seemed permanently amazed by everything she saw. No doubt that was the way *she'd* looked four years ago, Mathilde thought, before life at court had jaded her.

'Do you think so?' Katharine, on her other side, leaned forward with a grimace. 'I understand that men need to practise for war, but why they think *we* want to watch it, I'll never understand. We'll be trapped here all day. *Again*. Endless hours watching men charge at each other like fools, as if we've nothing better to do.'

'Oh…' Felicia looked crestfallen. 'But they're so brave.' She turned to Mathilde for confirmation. 'Aren't they?'

'They are.' Mathilde came to her rescue. 'And it certainly all looks very fine.'

'I just hope that nobody gets hurt.' Felicia's small brow wrinkled. 'I can't bear the sight of blood.'

'Sweet Mercy.' Katharine got to her feet abruptly. 'It's no good. I can't stay here.'

'What's the matter?' Mathilde looked up at her in concern. 'Your knee?'

'It's too stiff to sit.' Katharine hobbled forward to where the Queen was sitting, murmuring a few words in her ear before turning around with a wink.

'Come with me.' She held an arm out. 'Help an old woman.'

'Is your knee really so bad?' Mathilde murmured as they walked slowly away from the royal tent, the sound of thundering hooves echoing behind them.

'No more than usual,' Katharine chuckled. 'But it's bad enough watching men compare the size of their lances without that girl talking nonsense.'

'She's very nice really.'

'Yes, she probably is,' Katharine conceded. 'I'm just a grumpy old woman, but I can't bear to watch Mortimer swanning around either. He acts as if *he's* the monarch here. Did you see him eat from the King's plate last night?'

'Yes.' Mathilde furrowed her brow. The sight had caused a stir all through the court, though nobody had dared to make any objection. She'd kept her eyes on her own plate afterwards, reluctant to acknowledge the look of smug satisfaction on the Queen's face.

'And do you notice that *he's* Arthur while Edward is only Sir Lionel?' Katharine shook her head despairingly. 'Whoever heard of Sir Lionel anyway?'

'He was a cousin of Sir Lancelot's.'

'A cousin? Pah! I hear that Mortimer's even had a round table built for the occasion. A table where all men are equal, including himself and the King. The man's as subtle as a rock.' She sighed. 'But there it is. There's nothing we can do about it, except pretend to have sore knees and go for a nap.' She gave Mathilde a nudge. 'I thought you might be glad to escape for a while, too.'

'I am, thank you.'

'You haven't been yourself since we came back from Scotland.'

'Haven't I?'

'No, and you haven't left our rooms at night

or been near Henry Wright for a long while either. Have the two of you fallen out?'

'Something like that.' Mathilde half turned her head away. It had been months since Henry had told her their marriage was over, months in which every glimpse of him had left her feeling utterly wretched and the pain showed no sign of abating. As much as she tried not to think about him any more, it was impossible not to, yet she couldn't speak of him either. She hadn't even been able to bring herself to tell Katharine what had happened, as if saying the words out loud would make their separation more horribly real than it already was.

'Ah. Well, you don't have to tell me anything, but when you're ready—who's that?'

'Mmm?' Mathilde looked around as Katharine gestured ahead with her other hand. A man was walking towards them, dressed in armour as if he were about to take part in the tournament, though his head was uncovered, revealing a swathe of dark auburn hair, glistening with copper lights in the sunshine.

'Oh.' She stopped walking. 'Oh, no.'

'What?' Katharine gave her a sharp look. 'Why *Oh, no*?'

'Because it's Edmund, Cecily's son.' She lowered her voice to a whisper as he came closer. 'Her eldest.'

'Lady Mathilde?' He hailed her from a few feet away. 'What good fortune to meet you again.'

'Indeed.' She bowed her head, unable to curtsy with Katharine's hand gripping so tightly on to her arm. 'It's good to see you again.'

'Excuse me.' Katharine mumbled. 'I need to go and lie down.'

'Yes, of course.' She let her go with a reassuring smile. 'I'll follow shortly.'

'Is your friend unwell?' Edmund looked concerned as Katharine hurried away. 'Does she need any help?'

'She has trouble with her knee sometimes, but she'll be all right, I'm sure.' She forced a smile to change the subject. 'Are you taking part in the tournament?'

'Yes. Very soon, in fact, but I saw you and…' he cleared his throat, his expression suddenly bashful '…I thought perhaps you might grant me the honour of carrying your favour?'

'My—oh!' She felt heat spread across her cheeks in surprise. No man had ever asked for her favour in a tournament before. She might have been flattered if she hadn't felt so guilty, as if she were betraying her marriage vows and misleading Edmund, too. She didn't want to mislead him. Under other circumstances, she might have found him quite attractive, but there was only one man she would ever look at in that way.

'Unless you've already given it to another?' His skin was looking flushed, too, she noticed, the tips of his ears almost matching the shade of his hair.

'No, I just didn't expect… Here.' She reached into her purse and drew out a small linen handkerchief. 'Will this be sufficient?'

'Perfectly.' He gave a relieved-looking smile and bowed. 'I'm truly honoured, my lady. And you still wear my mother's brooch, I see?'

'Oh, yes. I miss Lady Cecily a great deal. We all do.'

'So do I and my brothers. Even though we didn't see her often during those last years. It's not—Lady Mathilde?' He frowned as she gasped suddenly. 'Is something the matter?'

'No.' She swallowed, quickly turning her eyes away from the sight of Henry standing outside one of the tournament tents, staring in their direction. Like Edmund, he was dressed in armour, though without any helmet, giving her a clear view of his scowling face. 'But I should go. I wish you luck today.'

'Thank you.' Edmund reached for her hand before she could move away, pressing a kiss against the backs of her knuckles. 'I only hope that I win for your sake.'

'Mathilde?' Henry saw her start and then stiffen as he called out her name. He'd had to run to catch up with her before she reached the royal tent, resisting the urge to throw a fist into the face of Edmund d'Abernon on the way, and now his insides were churning with guilt and jealousy.

'Yes?' She turned around promptly enough, though her expression was guarded. 'What is it?'

'We need to talk.'

'I'm in a hurry.'

'It's important.' He took a step closer when she opened her mouth to protest. 'Please, Mathilde.'

'Very well, then.' She straightened her spine and folded her hands in front of her as if she wanted to create a barrier between them, the reluctant look on her face making his gut clench. 'I'm listening.'

'Not here. Somewhere more private.'

'No!' Her eyes flashed with anger and something like panic. 'Whatever it is, you can tell me now. Quickly, too. Katharine needs me and the Queen's expecting me back.'

'And we can't disappoint Isabella, can we?' He instantly regretted the sarcasm as her lips pursed.

'If it's about Queen Philippa expecting a baby, then she's already heard the news.'

'It's not about that.' He shook his head, tempted to add something about Philippa's pregnancy meaning that Isabella couldn't prevent her coronation for much longer and then thinking better of it.

'Then what is it?' She was beginning to sound impatient.

'It's about your father.'

'Oh!' She swayed slightly, lifting a hand to her chest as if to brace herself. 'What about him?'

'I received a message from your brother this morning. After what we discovered in York I thought that it might be wiser for him to send messages straight to me, though of course, that was before...' He let his voice trail away and cleared his throat. 'I'm afraid the news isn't good. He says that your father collapsed and died suddenly two weeks ago.'

'No...' Her face crumpled as if she were holding back a cry.

'It was peaceful. He wasn't in any pain.'

'No…'

'Mathilde…' He started to lift a hand, aching to wrap his arms around her, then stopped himself. He daren't take the risk. If he took her in his arms, he wouldn't want to let go again and if they were seen together… He curled his fingers into fists. It wasn't his place to offer her comfort any more.

'I haven't seen him in four years.' Her voice shook with anguish. 'But I still thought that we might be reconciled one day. I thought that maybe there was a chance I could explain everything to him and that he would understand why I didn't come home. I hoped for it.' She tipped her head back, blinking rapidly. 'He died thinking badly of me.'

'He shouldn't have.'

'But he must have done!' Her voice broke.

'You only did what you thought was right.'

She narrowed her eyes, their expression bitter. 'You say that now, but you thought I was wrong, too. You tried to dissuade me against serving Isabella from the start.'

He bent his head, unable to deny it. 'Do you wish me to send a message back to your brother?'

'No, I'll do it myself.'

'As you wish. I'm sorry, Mathilde. If there's anything else I can do—'

'There isn't.' She spun on her heel and walked away, leaving him standing alone, listening to the distant sound of cheering from the tournament field, reminding himself that letting her go was for the best.

Mathilde rushed into the Queen's private tent, dropping on to one of the couches and curling her knees up to her chest, hugging them tight as she lay with her face to the cushions, willing the world to stop for a few hours and leave her alone with her grief.

It was too late. That one thought dominated her whole mind. She'd left it too late to reconcile with her father and now he was gone there was no way to put things right between them, no way to explain her loyalty to the Queen. And Henry had been the one to tell her... A sob tore from her throat. For a moment, when he'd called out her name, her foolish heart had given a small leap of excitement, as it always had in the past. She'd forced it down quickly, but just standing in front of him had caused a physical ache. And then when he'd given her the news... the sympathy on his face had made her even more miserable. Pathetically, she'd wanted him to touch her, to hold her close and tell her that everything would be all right. Now she felt as though nothing would be ever again.

'What's happened?' She felt Katharine come to sit on the couch beside her.

'It's my father. I just got word…he's dead.'

Katharine's hand slid up to her shoulder. 'I'm sorry.'

'It happened two weeks ago. He's been gone all this time and I never knew.' She heaved herself upright, still hugging her knees. 'He didn't approve of me serving the Queen. Back in Paris, when it became obvious that she was defying the King, he sent messages telling me to leave her service and come home, but I never got them. It wouldn't have made any difference, but I found out in York that other messages had gone astray, too.'

'Ah. Isabella.' Katharine looked unperturbed.

'You *knew*?' Mathilde opened her eyes wide.

'No, but it doesn't surprise me.'

'How could she? It was *my* decision to make. She had no right to do it for me!'

'She's the Queen.'

'Yes, but I thought she was a good one!'

'Hush.' Katharine lifted a finger to her lips. 'You're upset. Don't say anything foolish.'

Mathilde gritted her teeth, the discomfort she'd felt in York growing stronger. What if she'd been wrong about Isabella? What if Henry had been right all along and she was not—had never been—the woman she'd thought? What if she'd only seen the mother figure she'd wanted to see? Then she would have given up Henry *and* her father, throwing away any chance of reconciliation, not to mention of love and happiness, all because of a promise to a woman who wasn't worth it. And now…she pressed her face into her hands, a cold lump forming in her chest…now she was trapped as the Queen's lady for ever.

Chapter Twenty-Six

Nottingham Castle
—autumn 1330

'I've to go and fetch the King. Mortimer wants to speak with him,' Katharine grumbled, hobbling out of the Queen's withdrawing chamber with a hand pressed to the small of her back. 'You know, there was a time when Isabella took account of my age.'

'She wants you to go now?' Mathilde looked up in surprise. 'Isn't it too late? He might have retired for the night already.'

'No doubt they've thought of a few more questions.'

'*More?* They've already spent the whole day interrogating his friends. Is that why they called Parliament here? So that they could interview everyone? Or do they really think something's wrong this time?'

'Who knows? Mortimer sees plots and conspiracy everywhere and Isabella's become almost as bad. They're like a pair of angry bees, flying about looking for someone to sting.' Katharine threw a cautious look over her shoulder. 'I remember before you came to court five years ago, before we left for France. The old King was just the same and look how that turned out.'

'Mmm…' Mathilde pursed her lips uncomfortably. 'Well, surely you can at least send a page to fetch the King instead?'

'They won't trust one.'

'Then let me go. You sit down and rest.'

'Thank you.' Katharine eased herself into a chair with a sigh. 'I admit, I was hoping you'd say that.'

Mathilde left the room with a hollow feeling in the pit of her stomach. Katharine was right. Isabella and Mortimer had become more and more paranoid and demanding over the past few months, each of them seeming to spur the other on. All the good will they'd earned by deposing the old tyrant King had drained gradually but inexorably away, like a pot with a hole in its base, leaving behind nothing but resentment and fear. It was becoming harder and harder to defend the Queen's behaviour, even to herself.

The castle seemed oddly quiet that evening as she made her way towards the King's rooms. Surprisingly so given that Mortimer had recently doubled the size of the garrison. For once, there had been no guards outside the Queen's rooms as she'd left and now, even more surprisingly, there were none outside the King's. No one answered her knock either. Perturbed, she threw a quick look up and down the corridor and then put her eye to the crack between the door and its frame, but as far as she could see, the apartment was completely empty, as if the occupants had all gone for a walk or some fresh air, unlikely as that seemed in the dark.

Frowning, she started back towards the Queen's rooms and then slowed her steps to a stop. If she returned alone, then Isabella and Mortimer would want to know why and she had no good answer to give them. All she had was a feeling, a prickling sensation running up and down her spine that told her something wasn't right. In which case, maybe it wouldn't hurt to take a look around first…

She changed direction, making her way down one of the spiral stairwells that led to the great hall. There was a faint murmur of voices below and she peered cautiously around the corner, all of her nerves on alert, then clapped a hand over her mouth, stifling a cry of horror at the sight that greeted her. The King was standing on one side of the fireplace with his secretary and two guards, next to a gaping black hole in the wall, some kind of secret entranceway by the look of it, from which were emerging a small group of men, each of them carrying weapons and wearing the same grim, determined expression. She counted each of them in turn. Six in total, including Henry.

Her heart seemed to slam to a halt and then start pounding rapidly again, so hard that she could feel it like a fist beating against her ribcage. Her thoughts seemed to be spinning, too, faster and faster, like a whirlwind inside her head, scrambling to make sense of the sight, although there was only one, inescapable conclusion. Isabella and Mortimer had been right. There *was* a plot and, if the expressions on the men's faces were anything to judge by, it wasn't simply to free the King from their control. It was to overthrow them, too, but what was Henry doing there? He was a Mortimer! How could he be plotting to overthrow his own blood?

Panicking, she turned and fled back up the

stairwell and along the palace corridors, cold
sweat pouring down her back. There were no
guards to be seen anywhere, as if the plot were
already far more advanced than she'd realised.
It seemed that the keep had already been captured, or perhaps bribed, into silence. Which
meant that only Mortimer and the Queen were
left.

She hurtled through the door to the Queen's
rooms, sagging back against it with a hand to
her chest. Between her thumping heartbeat and
a new, high-pitched keening sound in her ears,
she could hardly stand upright without support.
She wanted to go somewhere and hide, but her
duty was clear. She *had* to warn the Queen.
She had to go and save her before the King and
his accomplices arrived. And she had to do it
right now.

Now. She repeated the word to herself, but her
legs seemed unable to move as a series of other,
panicked thoughts raced through her mind. If
she raised the alarm now, then Mortimer would
have time to barricade the Queen's rooms and
summon more guards from the bailey. There
would be a fight and bloodshed. Henry could
be hurt or worse and if he was captured then he
would be executed for certain. No matter what
had happened between them, how could she

risk that? And what if he was doing the right thing for the country? She put her hands to her head as all the thoughts and suspicions and niggling worries she'd tried so hard to keep out of her mind for the past year seemed to converge all at once. If she warned the Queen, then she might destroy more than Henry. She might destroy any hope of the new King being able to sit on his own throne…

'Mathilde?' Katharine's voice made her jump. 'What on earth's the matter? You look like you've seen a ghost. Where's the King?'

'He's… I…' she stuttered and then leapt forward, seized with a new sense of urgency. If there was one thing she *was* certain about, it was that she had to get Katharine away before anything happened. Despite all her acerbic comments about Isabella, the old woman was still loyal enough to put herself in the way of a sword for her, if necessary. 'I felt unwell. Dizzy. Would you mind going to fetch the King, after all?'

'You do look pale.' Katharine eyed her with concern. 'Perhaps you ought to go and lie down.'

'Thank you. I'm sorry to…' She bit her tongue. 'I'm sorry.'

'Pah. I won't be long.'

Mathilde sank down on to the settle with relief, trying to calm down and gather her wits as Katharine disappeared through the doorway. She was horribly aware of precious seconds passing by, but no matter which way she looked at it, she could save only one person she cared about. The choice was stark: Isabella or Henry, doing something or doing nothing.

She didn't move.

'Mathilde?'

She tensed, seeing the door open again and Henry step inside. Judging by appearances, he was alone.

'Mathilde?' He repeated her name softly, but she still didn't answer. She didn't nod or blink or twitch as much as a muscle, simply watching as he moved closer.

'Is the Queen in there?' He gestured towards the withdrawing chamber. 'With Mortimer?'

She gritted her teeth, still refusing to answer. She could have said yes to both of those questions, but he'd find out the truth soon enough. As much as she didn't want him to get hurt, she wasn't going to help either.

'Mathilde, I know what you think of me.' His tone was anguished. 'But I beg you to do one thing for me and stay where you are. No matter what happens in the next few minutes, don't move.'

Slowly, she twisted her face away. She was

aware of other people entering the room now, but she couldn't bear to watch. Instead, she stared into the fire, watching a log wrinkle and turn white in the flames.

There was an almost unbearably long moment of silence, followed by a loud scraping sound as the door to the Queen's bedchamber was flung open suddenly. Then there were several noises at once: raised voices, oaths, trampling feet and the shriek of metal against metal. She heard Mortimer call out for help, then a thud and a scream. Isabella's scream.

She put her hands over her ears, wincing as the sound seemed to fill her whole head. It was strange how something so momentous could have happened so quickly. An hour ago she'd been sat in this very same spot, innocently reading a book. Now, out of the corner of her eye, she could see Mortimer being half dragged across the floor, bleeding, but not dead.

'Mathilde?' She felt Henry's hand on her shoulder and stiffened. 'The Queen…'

She looked around dully, past him towards the open doorway. There was no sign of Isabella, just a wailing sound from within the chamber. He was suggesting that she go inside now, she realised, to go and comfort her mistress, as if that was still her place, as if she hadn't just betrayed her.

'What are you going to do with her?' She forced the words through numb lips.

'Nothing. She's the King's mother. She can stay here under guard.'

'I see.' She stood up, feeling as though she were facing a stranger. Feeling like one herself. 'Then you can go. Your work here is done.'

For a moment he looked on the verge of saying something else before changing his mind, bowing his head and following after the rest of his companions.

'What's happened?' Katharine passed him in the doorway, her face aghast. 'They have Mortimer!'

'Yes.' Mathilde met her gaze evenly. 'It's over.'

'What? *Isabella!*' The older woman rushed forward, faster than she'd ever seen her move before, charging past her into the withdrawing chamber.

Mathilde followed slowly behind. There were only a few signs of a struggle—an overturned chair, a sword mark on the bedpost, a slashed curtain—and the former Queen Consort of England on her knees in the middle of the floor, weeping into her hands as Katharine rocked her back and forth like a child. Mathilde wanted to join them, to offer some kind of solace, but how could she? She was partly responsible.

She shut the door against the rebels who were now stationed outside. The least she could do was give the Queen some privacy.

It was almost dawn by the time Isabella fell into a fitful sleep and Mathilde and Katharine were able to talk.

'Were you a part of it?' The older woman confronted her at once. 'Did you know what was going to happen?'

'Not until last night. When I went to get the King...' She swallowed and then looked her friend square in the eye. 'I saw them preparing to come here.'

'Then you sent me away?'

'Yes. I didn't want you to get hurt.'

'And the Queen?'

'I didn't want her to be hurt either.'

'You had time to warn her.'

'Yes, but...I didn't.'

She braced herself, expecting Katharine to either denounce or strike her, but to her surprise, she only closed her eyes, looking tired and sad and very old suddenly.

'Your *husband* was with them.'

'I know.'

Katharine sighed and rubbed a hand over her face. Her skin was speckled with brown spots and her fingers were trembling slightly. 'If you want to go to him, you should do it now while she's sleeping.'

'I don't want to.' Mathilde shook her head. It was true. At that moment she didn't want to see Henry ever again. She didn't even want to think about him. She felt like Isabella. Betrayed.

Chapter Twenty-Seven

Westminster Palace, London
—winter 1330

Mortimer's trial was held in London. It was brief, a formality like Despenser's had been, with the verdict already decided at the start. Isabella didn't ask when and where the sentence was carried out and Mathilde didn't tell her, but somehow she still seemed to know, spending the day sitting by her window and doing nothing. It was even worse than the death of her husband. She seemed deaf and mute with grief.

The King came to visit her two mornings afterwards, but Isabella barely looked up and he left again quickly. Henry was with him, but Mathilde pretended to be just as impervious as the Queen. She was still reeling in shock from what had happened. She didn't even know which of them she was angrier with, him or herself, just that she couldn't bear to be near him.

Henry was also the one who brought news of the Queen's fate a week later. Isabella was lying down on her bed, but Mathilde and Katharine were sitting outside her bedchamber, waiting in case she called for them.

'Henry Wright.' Katharine acknowledged his approach with a scowl. 'Or must I call you my lord now?'

'What?' Mathilde looked between them, startled out of her angry silence.

'Didn't you hear?' Katharine's tone was openly resentful. 'It's going to be *Sir* Henry Wright from now on.'

Henry's jaw tightened though his expression remained impassive. 'Call me what you wish, but the King has been generous enough to offer me that title, yes.'

'For your *loyal* service?'

'For liberating him from a tyrant.'

'And did he offer it before or after you agreed to help him?' Katharine narrowed her eyes accusingly. 'What is it you want now, *my lord*?'

Henry's shoulders stiffened. 'The King suggests that his mother remove to Castle Rising in Norfolk. She can go as soon as the weather improves.'

'Then we'd better start packing.'

'Before that, however, I'd like a private word with my wife.'

Wife. Mathilde gave a small start at the word. It was the first time she'd ever heard him use it around anyone else. The first time he'd claimed her publicly, now it was too late.

'Would you?' Katharine's eyes flashed. 'Well, that would depend on whether or not she wants to talk to you.'

'It's all right.' Mathilde stood up decisively. 'I'll speak with him.'

'As you wish, but I'll be here if you need me.'

'I suppose I deserved that,' Henry murmured when they were out of earshot, standing in one of the window bays.

'Yes, you did.' She gave him a quick look up and down. His expression was tense and there were new frown lines ingrained in his forehead and between his eyes, ones that hadn't been there the last time they'd spoken, as if the past year had taken a heavy toll on him, but she was still too angry to feel anything like pity.

'I came because you deserve an explanation for what happened.'

She folded her arms. She already knew the

explanation—*her* side of it anyway. That was as much as she needed to know, but she supposed she might as well hear the rest. 'Go on.'

'The King had been looking for a way to depose Mortimer for a while, but until Nottingham, there were no opportunities to get close enough. He was always so well-guarded. He was getting more and more suspicious, too. It was only a matter of time before we were discovered. Fortunately, for us, it turned out there was an old tunnel through the rock beneath the castle. A secret one, used for escaping in times of trouble. Some of the townspeople told us about it.'

'They just *told* you?' She lifted her eyebrows sceptically. 'You make it sound easy.'

'It was. Mortimer had a lot of enemies. They were more than happy to betray him.'

'Were *you*? Happy, I mean? I remember you once told me you owed him a debt.'

'One I repaid when I helped him escape from the Tower.' A muscle tightened in his jaw. 'But, no, I wasn't happy about it. Nothing about this has made me happy. I didn't *want* to betray him, Mathilde, but I had to. He was trying to usurp the King.'

'It wasn't like that.'

'It was exactly like that! Maybe you didn't

see it because the Queen didn't let you see, but innocent people were suffering. *Again!* I couldn't just sit by and watch and let them get away with it. And Isabella was no innocent victim in all this either. She became a tyrant with an even worse tyrant at her side. It was wrong.'

'Mortimer was still your blood!' She glared. 'Or is that the real reason you did this? Because he was your blood and he never acknowledged you? Was it some kind of revenge?'

His chin jerked as if she'd just struck him. 'Do you really think so little of me?'

She opened her mouth to say yes and then closed it again. Whatever else she might accuse him of, she knew that he would never have acted out of spite.

'You still betrayed him.'

'I know that!' He lifted a hand and pushed it through his hair, his eyes wild looking. 'But I couldn't carry on serving him no matter who he was to me.' A look of pain crossed his face. 'I hated myself for what I did. I always will, but when there's a choice between tyranny and doing what's right, then there *is* no choice!'

'So that's why you resented my loyalty to the Queen so much? Because you thought I was choosing the wrong path?'

'No, I never resented you. Even when I was

angry, I understood why you felt so attached to her.' He moved closer. 'But I had to end our marriage, at least for a while. It was for your own safety.'

'What?' She felt her lips part. 'But you said…'

'I know. I didn't mean any of the things I said. I didn't want to say them, but this was something I had to do alone. If anything had gone wrong, then I didn't want you to be implicated and if they'd found out that we had any kind of association… It would have been dangerous for us to keep on seeing each other.'

'So all of those things you said about our marriage being a mistake and being tired of waiting for me…?'

'All lies. I would have waited for you for ever, but I had to protect you. That was more important than any of this.' His blue eyes glittered with intensity. 'You've no idea how good it feels to be able to tell you the truth now, Mathilde. I never stopped caring about you, not for one single moment.'

'Wait…' She shook her head. 'I don't understand. You broke my heart and now you're saying it was all for my own good?'

'Yes.' He reached for her wrists, clasping them in his hands. 'It broke my heart to say them, too, but it's over now. There's no need for secrecy any more.'

She stared at him blankly, looking back over the past year with new eyes. *Could* he be telling the truth? He looked sincere. He sounded it, too, but how could it be over? She felt as though her emotions were being wrenched in several different directions all at once. She felt relieved, amazed, happy and utterly miserable at the same time. Most of all, she felt sick, as if her body couldn't physically cope with so many conflicting feelings at once. Henry sounded as if he just expected her to forget the heartache of the past year, all of the nights she'd lain awake reliving the pain of his words, not to mention the gut-twisting agony of rejection. Even if it *had* all been a pretence for him, the pain *she'd* felt had been real.

She twisted her arms away, breaking the connection between them. 'If that's true, why didn't you just tell me you were involved in a plot? You said that you trusted me. I would have understood that we couldn't see each other.'

'How could I have told you? I knew how you felt about Isabella. How could I have asked you to betray her by keeping that kind of a secret? Mathilde…' He looked hurt when she flinched. 'It wasn't that I didn't trust you, I promise, but

I knew that it would have torn you apart to choose. If there had been any other way then I would have taken it, but there wasn't. I didn't want you to have to make the same choice I did. This way the burden was—*is*—all on my head, not yours. You're innocent in all of this.'

Innocent... She almost laughed out loud at the irony. She could understand his argument. She could even feel a vague sense of gratitude for it, but a shared burden might have been easier to bear. It wasn't his fault that she'd discovered the plot early, but she still had and she'd had to face it alone, believing he didn't care. He might not have asked her to betray the Queen, but it was still what she'd done in the end. Whether or not it had been the right thing to do, she'd chosen *him* and in so doing, she'd failed her second mother just like she'd failed her first. Only this time, she'd done it with her eyes open.

She let her shoulders sag, feeling as if a heavy blanket of guilt were being draped around them, dampening any joy she might have felt at his words, demanding that she make amends for her failure all over again.

'Mathilde, I love you. I always will.' Henry reached a hand out, his voice wavering. 'Please. Tell me it's not too late for us?'

* * *

Henry watched, heart sinking as Mathilde took a step backwards, her gaze fathomless. After years of telling her that she needed to learn to guard her expression, today she finally managed it, just when he wanted to know her thoughts the most.

'What will happen to Isabella now?' Her voice was completely flat, without any inflection at all.

'Isabella?' He swallowed an oath. Even now, even after he'd just told her he loved her, all she could think of was her royal mistress, as if *they* were already a lost cause. 'I told you, the King suggests that she move to Castle Rising.'

'Suggests?'

'*Strongly* suggests.'

'Will she be free to come and go?'

'Only with his permission.'

'Then it would be more honest to call her a prisoner, wouldn't it? Will she be kept as safe as the old King?'

'Edward would never cause any harm to his mother.'

'No.' Her gaze dipped. 'I suppose I know that.'

'Mathilde…' He cleared his throat, trying to find the words to get through to her. 'I know that I hurt you. I know that this past year has been terrible. It has for me, too. Every time I saw you, it felt like a dagger twisting in here...' He placed a fist over his chest. 'But we can still put things right between us. We can be together properly now.'

'Together?' She repeated the word as if she didn't understand it.

'Yes. There's no need to hide our marriage any longer. I'll tell the King about us and we can live as man and wife from now on.'

She lifted an eyebrow, her gaze questioning for a moment, before she opened her lips and began to laugh.

'What is it?' He put his hands on her shoulders, holding her steady as she swayed from side to side. 'Why are you laughing?'

'Because of you!' She sobered again suddenly, staring straight at him instead, her eyes bright with tears. 'Do you think it's so easy? Do you think we can just go back to the way we were?'

'Yes! No. I don't know. When I joined the conspirators, I didn't know whether or not I'd even survive. The odds were against us. I didn't let myself think any further ahead, but I hoped that if I explained to you...'

'That I'd understand and forgive you?' Her

eyes flashed again and then softened, as if all her anger were slowly draining away. 'I do understand. About Mortimer anyway. As for the rest…how could we ever be happy now? It would all be at Isabella's expense.'

'Not everything is about her!' He tightened his grip on her shoulders. 'Do you imagine that she would think twice? If it came to a choice between *her* happiness and yours, whose do you think she would choose?'

'It doesn't matter. Everyone else will abandon her now.'

'She still won't be alone! The King will appoint people to take care of her. She'll have Katharine, too.'

'Katharine needs looking after herself.'

'Neither of them is your responsibility!'

'I know, but I owe her this.'

'So you'll bury yourself in the middle of nowhere with a woman who's never deserved one ounce of the loyalty you've shown her? What if I forbid it? You're my wife!'

'Forbid?' One corner of her mouth lifted in a cynical smile. 'I thought you were against tyranny?'

'Mathilde…' He could hear the desperation in his voice now. 'Just give me—*us*—another chance and I promise I'll spend the rest of my days proving how sorry I am and how much I love you. I've never said those words to anyone before, but I mean them with every part of me. I love you. Please, I beg you, don't go. You've already given her five years of your life. You don't have to give her the rest, too.'

'I have to go.' Her gaze didn't as much as waver. 'You were right when you said that our marriage was a mistake. Goodbye, Henry.'

She turned her back, leaving him feeling as though the old hollow wound in his chest had just reopened. He'd been rejected all over again by the one person in the world he truly loved. Only this time it was all his fault.

Chapter Twenty-Eight

Westminster Palace, London
—spring 1331

'Madam?' The page in the doorway sounded nervous. 'Your escort is ready.'

'Good.' Isabella swept regally to her feet. No matter how notorious her name had become throughout England, Mathilde thought with a flicker of admiration, her mistress never behaved as anything less than a queen. Powerless she might be these days, but her pride was indomitable. 'Then it's time for us to be leaving. Kat? Mathilde? Felicia?' Isabella lifted a hand, beckoning for the three of them to join her. 'Come.'

Mathilde readjusted her headdress, looking around the chamber one last time before following Isabella out of the door. They had a five-day

journey ahead, but she felt exhausted already.
She usually did these days. She couldn't even remember the last time she'd had a decent night's
sleep. All through the winter, she'd tossed and
turned, dreaming strange dreams about being
buried alive and thinking about Henry. Not just
thinking, but feeling, too. So many feelings that
she didn't think she had the heart or strength for
any more. They hadn't spoken since he'd come
to explain what had happened in Nottingham
and she'd sent him away on the few occasions
when he'd tried to visit Isabella's apartments,
yet he seemed to have occupied her thoughts
every moment of every day since.

'You should stay,' Katharine murmured as
they walked along the gallery. 'Stay here with
your husband.'

'What?' Mathilde twisted sideways in surprise, lowering her voice quickly as Felicia gave
them a quizzical look. 'You can't mean that! I
thought you were angry at him?'

'I am.' Somehow Katharine managed to nod
and shake her head at the same time. '*And* I'm
not. I understand why he did what he did, even
if I can't quite bring myself to forgive him for
it.' She slowed her steps so that they dropped
back behind the others. 'But I *can* forgive you.
More than that, I want you to be happy. There's

no need for you to lock yourself away with us. You still care for him, don't you?'

'That's not…' Mathilde couldn't bring herself to say otherwise. 'Yes.'

'Then stay. Live your life.'

'How? How can *I* forgive him? I know that sounds hypocritical considering what I did, but he forced me to choose. Even unintentionally, he forced me to betray Isabella. How can I forgive either of us?' She drew in a deep breath. 'I owe it to the Queen to stay and make up for what I did.'

'If you're certain…?'

'I am, but…' She paused and then rushed on. 'Kat, what would you have done? If you'd been in my position, I mean?'

'I don't know.' Katharine lowered her head as she hobbled forward again. 'I've thought about that and, truth be told, I've no idea.'

They left the palace and went out into the bailey, through a crowd of eerily silent onlookers. Mathilde left Katharine in the care of a groom before mounting her own horse beside Isabella's, concentrating on keeping her eyes down and her face forward. She didn't want to look around and see who was there in case Henry was among them. She knew that she ought to go and say goodbye, that despite everything, she owed him better than to leave without as much as a word, but she couldn't bear the thought. She felt weary and heartsore, as if she were holding herself together with the last few shreds of her willpower. If she had to say goodbye aloud, then she was afraid that her broken heart would splinter into a million tiny pieces. She would write to him, she told herself, once they arrived at Castle Rising, not that she had any idea what she might say.

Beside her, Isabella looked as stately and magnificent as ever. Perhaps some time away from court would be good for her, Mathilde thought. As far as she knew, Norfolk had no associations with Mortimer and the change of scene might give her a chance to grieve and recover. Perhaps it would be good for both of them.

'Lady Mother.' The King emerged from a doorway at that moment, dressed in a green velvet jacket with golden embroidery to match his crown.

The crowd dropped to their knees as he advanced towards them, kissing his mother's hand with every display of respect while Isabella inclined her head graciously. Mathilde was glad of it. Relieved, too, that he'd come to bid her farewell properly and not simply sent her away in disgrace. Perhaps Henry had been right and Edward would make a good king, after all. After twenty years of unrest, it was about time the country had one of those.

'Lady Mathilde?' The King's eyes fell on her. 'I did not expect to see you travelling today.'

'Your Grace.' She dropped her gaze, wondering what Henry had told him. Did the King know they were married? 'I serve my lady.'

'And we are grateful for it.' He paused for a long moment. 'Just know that you will always be welcome at court if you choose to return.'

'Thank you, Your Grace.' She kept her head bent to hide the glimmer of tears in her eyes. It would be mortifying enough to cry in front of the King, but once she started, she didn't know whether she'd be able to stop.

Mercifully, he waved a hand and the procession started forward almost instantly, heading towards the great gates with a loud creaking of wheels. Mathilde let out the breath she hadn't known she'd been holding and then immediately caught it again, stifling a cry of dismay as Henry rode past her to join the guards at the front. For a horrified moment, she thought that he was about to stop the whole procession, but he only fell in alongside them, a part of their escort, it seemed—a fact that made her want to weep even more. Their situation was unbearable enough, but now the journey was only going to prolong the agony.

The road into Norfolk was a long and tedious one, but they rode quickly. There was no feasting as honoured guests on the journey this time, not for a queen in disgrace, although they stopped at regular intervals to rest and eat and stretch. Henry didn't approach her, but Mathilde was aware of his presence at every moment, more aware than she was of herself. She didn't even realise that she was hungry one day until a boy offered her some bread, although she still refused. Her throat felt so tight, she doubted she'd be able to swallow a mouthful if she tried.

'Isn't he handsome?' Lady Felicia commented one afternoon, riding beside her along a causeway through the rust-coloured Fens. It was the fifth day of their journey and a light drizzle had started to fall, but they were finally, thankfully, within reach of their destination.

'Who?' Mathilde didn't lift her eyes from the ground.

'Our escort, Henry Wright.'

'Oh.' There was a wistful note in the girl's voice and Mathilde felt an irrational stab of jealousy. 'I suppose so, although it's *Sir* Henry Wright now, I believe.'

'No, it's not. Didn't you hear?' Felicia leaned sideways, eager to share some gossip. 'He refused a knighthood.'

'What?' Mathilde felt her heart start to thud heavily against her breastbone. 'What do you mean, he refused?'

'They say that he told the King he didn't want any reward for his service. Can you believe it? He risked execution to help him take the throne and then turned down a reward.'

Mathilde nodded slowly, though her pulse still seemed to be accelerating. Yes, she *could* believe it from a man who'd done the right thing reluctantly and felt guilty about it... 'Did he ask for anything else instead?'

'Not that I know of, although I heard he refused a wife, too.'

'What?' Mathilde swivelled around so fast she almost fell off her horse.

'The King offered him an heiress.' Felicia spoke matter-of-factly. 'He had his pick, they say, but he just said no. He could have been *Sir* Henry, with a large estate and a rich wife, but he turned it all down.'

'How strange.' Mathilde tugged her headdress forward to hide her face. 'Did he explain why?'

'I don't know. Nobody does, except the King.' Felicia sighed. 'But I'm sure his reasons were noble. They say he's of low birth, but there's something inherently noble about him, don't you thi—oh!' she interrupted herself to exclaim. 'There it is!'

There it was. Mathilde lifted her head to see Castle Rising looming like a dark square on the horizon ahead of them. Surrounded by an expanse of flat, inhospitable-looking marshland, it was a fortress in more ways than one, its stone walls tall and bleak and forbidding. She gulped and looked up at the sky, searching for a single ray of heart-warming sunshine, but the clouds were completely grey, as miserable as the vista before them.

'Do you think they're coming to welcome us?' Lady Felicia gestured ahead, along what appeared to be the only road leading in and out of the castle, at a group of horses and riders heading in their direction.

'Something like that,' Mathilde murmured, drawing rein as Henry raised a hand and their whole procession came to a halt, waiting in silence for the riders to reach them.

'Madam, I am Sir Simon Courbet.' The man at the head of the riders stopped just in front of them, making a low bow from his saddle to Isabella. He had a kindly face, Mathilde noticed, though his expression was uncompromising. 'The King has asked me to make you welcome here at Castle Rising. I am your obedient servant.'

'Sir Simon,' Isabella acknowledged him haughtily, as if the words were only her due, forcing his men to part before her as she spurred her horse forward again. 'You may show us the way.'

Mathilde flicked on her own reins, but a hand grasped hold of her bridle suddenly, holding her back.

'Lady Mathilde.' After a quick murmured exchange with Courbet, Henry turned to face her. 'Would you remain behind for a few minutes?'

'I... As you wish.' She lifted her chin to conceal a tremor of panic.

'Thank you.' He inclined his head, waiting until the entire baggage train had rolled past before moving his horse alongside hers, turned in the opposite direction so that they were sitting face to face.

Mathilde waited, feeling as if her chest were being squeezed tight by invisible bands. There were only the two of them now, alone on a causeway in the middle of a wild and boggy marshland, surrounded by reeds and buffeted by bitter winds, with only a few cranes and wildfowl and probably some otters and fish for company.

'This is as far as I go,' Henry spoke quietly.

'Oh.' She felt her eyes widen. She ought to feel relieved, she told herself, but instead she felt as if one of the gusts of winds had just knocked her sideways. 'You're not coming into the castle?'

'No. I wanted to make certain you arrived safely, but the King wants me to return to London as soon as possible. The rest of the escort will make their way back tomorrow.'

'Is it safe, riding alone?'

He smiled grimly. 'We'll see.'

'Oh.' She didn't know what else to say. He really was just as handsome as Lady Felicia had said, even more so than when they'd first met, his features almost uncannily like Mortimer's now, although she didn't want to dwell on that fact. He wasn't Mortimer. He was Henry. Her husband, the man she loved despite everything they'd both done…the man she wanted, but couldn't quite bring herself to forgive. The breeze blew some hair across her face, lashing her cheeks and blinding her momentarily. She was glad of it.

'If there's anything you need, you only have to send word.' His pale gaze was piercing, a perfect match with the wintry sky behind him.

'Thank you.' She drew the hair out of her face. 'I heard that you refused a knighthood?'

'Yes.'

'I thought it was what you always wanted?'

'It was.' His expression was inscrutable. 'But not any more. Not like that.'

'And a rich wife?'

'I already have a wife.'

'Yes. I'm sorry.'

'For what?'

'For holding you back. If it wasn't for me, you could marry an heiress.'

'Is that what you think?' His features turned almost fierce. 'I married *you*, Mathilde. I would marry you again tomorrow. Even if I were free, no heiress in the world could change the way I feel about you. I've wanted you from the very first moment I saw you.' He held her gaze for a long moment. 'But you haven't changed your mind about us, have you?'

She swallowed, listening to the sound of her own heartbeat in her head. Yes, she wanted to say. Yes, she *had* changed her mind, but the words refused to come. *No* words would come. She couldn't say what she wanted to say and she couldn't bid him goodbye here any more than she'd been able to in London.

'Say something, Mathilde!'

'I don't want to argue!' She wrenched the words from her throat. 'I don't want to leave it like this.'

'To leave it…' He repeated the words with a short laugh. 'How should we leave it then?'

'Henry, please…' She reached a hand out, but he was already picking up his reins, preparing to move past her.

'What is this?' Isabella's voice interrupted them.

Mathilde froze. She'd been so engrossed in her conversation with Henry that she hadn't noticed the Queen riding back to join them, Katharine and Courbet behind her.

'Mathilde, what is he saying to you?'

'That's between us.' Henry's face hardened.

'*You* dare to speak to me?' Isabella's voice was more like a snarl.

'I'm one of your escorts.'

'You're keeping my lady from her duties.'

'Her duties are what she wishes them to be. She's a *free* woman.'

'And you're a viper! Mortimer raised you. He gave you a place in his service. A home. A purpose. And you betrayed him!'

'Yes.' Henry didn't try to defend himself. 'I did.'

'Snake!' Isabella's regal mask was utterly

gone, replaced with a look of pure, unadulterated fury. 'You may have found favour with my son now, but I know what you really are, Henry Wright. Naught but a bastard. A worthless, treacherous bastard. Mortimer never cared a damn for you. Do you know what he called you? A mistake. A useful mistake. How I wish he'd left you to starve in the streets!'

'Your Grace!' Mathilde pushed her horse between them, feeling the insult to Henry like a physical shock, as if the Queen had just slapped *her* hard across the face. She was aware of her cheeks blazing, of something shifting in her mind, too... She caught her breath as a single ray of sunlight broke through the clouds suddenly, allowing her to see clearly at last.

'Mathilde!' Henry and Isabella both said her name at once, one voice questioning, the other accusing. Two voices, each belonging to someone she cared about, each representing a different possible future.

'He's not worthless.' Somehow she managed to speak calmly despite the tumult of emotions raging inside her.

'You're defending him?' Isabella's eyes narrowed to slits, as if a new suspicion were just dawning on her. 'Who is he to you?'

Mathilde tipped her head back, tempted to

laugh at the question. She'd spent years worrying that Isabella might guess the nature of her relationship with Henry, but now it seemed that she'd never even noticed they were acquainted, too obsessed with her own concerns to care.

'He's not worthless,' she said again. 'He's a good man.'

'He betrayed Mortimer!'

'Mortimer betrayed the King!'

Isabella gave a sharp hiss, jolting backwards in her saddle, anger and shock warring on her face now. 'You were one of them, too! You were one of the conspirators. *You* betrayed me?'

'No!' Henry spoke before she could. 'She had no part in it.'

'Yes, I did,' Mathilde contradicted him.

'What?' He turned to look at her, his expression part-hope, part-bewilderment. 'What are you talking about?'

'I was sent to fetch the King that evening, but when I got to his rooms, he wasn't there. So I went to look around and I saw you all emerging from the tunnel. I could have raised the alarm, but I didn't. I chose to do nothing.'

He looked stunned. 'You really did that?'

'Yes. Deep down, I think I already knew that it was the right thing to do, but at the time all I could think of was you.' She lifted her shoulders. 'You asked me once who I would choose if it came to it, you or the Queen. Well, it *did* come to it and I chose you.'

'I don't know what to say.' He shook his head, as if he couldn't believe the evidence of his own ears. 'Why didn't you tell me this before?'

'Because when you came to me afterwards, I was still in shock. I couldn't bear to admit what I'd done. Even though I knew you were right about Mortimer, I felt so guilty. And...' She took a deep, shuddering breath. 'I felt as if you'd betrayed me by making me choose.'

'I never wanted that. No matter what I said, I never wanted you to be in that position. Mathilde, I'm so sorry.'

'I know. So am I.' She gave him a reassuring look. 'It wasn't fair of me to blame you when I'd already put you in that position myself. You wanted to leave court after you came back from Scotland, but you stayed for me. You spied on men you didn't want to for me, because I refused to see the truth. I was the one who forced you into a choice first.'

'Then you forgive me?'

'Yes, if you can forgive me, too.'

'You betrayed me!' Isabella's cry cut through the air, high-pitched and hysterical. 'After you promised me your loyalty!'

'I know, but you betrayed me, as well.' Mathilde met her gaze, unflinching. 'When you asked for my promise, you said that you had no choice about what you were doing, that it was for the good of England, but things changed. Once you made your son King, you *had* a choice. You could have chosen peace and reconciliation, but you chose Mortimer and power and yourself instead. So now I choose myself, too.

'I've spent ten years trying to make amends for a mistake I made. I thought that serving you was my chance to put things right. I let down my father, I made excuses and turned a blind eye to things that I shouldn't have, but I was wrong. You and my mother were never the same. She was a victim, *you* weren't, and I won't spend the rest of my life punishing myself for something that had to be done. You're the one who ought to be making amends.' She saw Katharine's nod of approval out of the corner of her eye. 'I said I wouldn't leave you until all this was over. Well, it's over. Now I'm leaving with my husband.'

'Husband?'

'Yes, we were married in secret four years ago.'

'Mathilde?' Henry's voice had a catch in it. 'Does this mean…?'

'It means that I love you.' She smiled properly for the first time in a year. 'I think I've loved you ever since that night we sat under an oak tree in Paris and I promise to stay with *you* for as long as you need me.'

'For ever.' He didn't hesitate. 'I'll need you for ever.'

'Good.' She wheeled her horse about, turning away from the Queen and Castle Rising, back in the direction of London and the future. 'Because from now on, it's going to be just the two of us and we'll make our choices together.'

Epilogue

Herefordshire
—summer 1331

'**W**ait!' Henry pulled on his reins, drawing them both to a halt in the middle of a muddy track. He and Mathilde had been riding in companionable silence through the woods for the past half hour, but if memory served, the road, such as it was, gave way to farmland just around the next corner. Lush open fields, rolling hillocks, not to mention a shallow valley with a river and watermill next to a small hamlet and stone manor house...*their* manor house. 'We need to get down.'

'What?' Mathilde looked around in alarm. 'What's the matter?'

'Nothing.' He swung his leg over his saddle

and dismounted. 'I just thought we could walk the rest of the way.'

'Oh!' Her face lit up with a look of excitement. 'Does this mean we're almost there?'

'Almost home, you mean? Yes, we'll be warming our feet before our very own hearth within the hour.'

'That sounds blissful.'

'And in another *two* hours…' He grinned, waiting until she jumped down before sliding his arms around her waist. 'We should probably test our new bed out as soon as possible.'

'Not before I've explored our new house, thank you very much.' She gave him an arch look and then relented, pressing her body against his. 'Although I suppose we could visit the bedchamber first.'

'Good. It's been too long since I showed you how much I love you.'

'It's been two nights.'

'Exactly. Staying in inns is all very well, but I've missed having you to myself.'

'Then I'm all yours, in another two hours, that is.' She wrapped her arms around his neck, resting her head on his shoulder. 'Henry, are you sure about this? The King was prepared to offer you a lot more than a manor to remain at court. Even Queen Philippa wanted you to stay. She asked me to persuade you.'

'Really?'

'Yes. She said it was a shame we had to leave when you'd make such a handsome knight. Not as handsome as her husband, obviously, but still not bad for an Englishman.' Mathilde laughed. 'Those were her exact words. She's completely besotted with the King.'

'And he with her.'

'Good. I always thought that kings and queens should be allowed to marry for love.'

'Everyone should. Although, of course, *they're* still newlyweds, not an old married couple like us.' He lifted an eyebrow. 'Not that I'm *not* still besotted with you.'

'And I with you.' She lifted a hand to his cheek. 'Which is why I need to be completely sure this is what you really want.'

'It is. I've had my fill of politics and intrigue. I was prepared to stay at court a bit longer to help the King while he needed me, but I'm a farmer now, or I soon will be, with your help. As for our new home…' A torn expression crossed his face. 'I know it was given to me by Mortimer, but that was back when I thought there was still hope for him. There was a time when he did the right things for the right reasons.'

'Power has a way of changing people. Maybe most men would have done the same.'

He squeezed her tighter. 'Maybe. But I couldn't accept all those things the King offered me, not knowing the cost.'

'I understand.'

'Just as long as this is what *you* want, too. We're going to have to get used to a less lavish lifestyle. No more twenty-course dinners and definitely no more partridge.'

'Oh, dear.' She heaved an exaggerated sigh. 'No more jugglers and acrobats and entertainments either.'

'Well, I don't know about that. We'll just have to make our own entertainment.' He raised his eyebrows. 'I'm actually looking forward to that part.'

'We might be too busy working. Gathering crops and tending to the animals.'

'Really? What kind of animals? Pigs as well as horses?'

'Of course. And chickens and goats and sheep. Maybe a few geese.'

'It sounds like we're going to be very busy.'

'Are you afraid of honest, hard work?'

'Well, when you put it like that…' He grinned. 'But I'll get used to it. Now close your eyes.'

She gave him a sceptical look. 'Walking

around woodland with my eyes closed doesn't sound like a very sensible idea.'

'I'll look after you.'

'All right, but if I walk into a tree then you'll be sleeping by yourself for the next month.'

'Understood. This way...' He caught hold of her hand, leading them both a little further along the track. 'Just a few more steps and... there it is.' He glanced sideways when there was no response. 'You can open your eyes now.'

'Oh.' Mathilde blinked a few times. *'Oh!'*

'Well? What do you think of the view?'

'Henry...' Her mouth fell open. 'It's beautiful.'

'It's not bad, is it?' He smiled, his chest filling with warmth as they looked out over the sungilded fields, over gold stalks of swaying barley and a brightly coloured meadow of wildflowers by the riverbank, all pinks and purples and blues, like tiny banners waving to greet them.

'If I'd known it was like this, then I would have encouraged you to leave court sooner!'

'Now she tells me.' He gave her an incredulous look. 'We've waited a long time for this, haven't we?'

'Six years.' She turned her face towards him, her big brown eyes more luminous than ever.

'Six years and one month, actually. We've come a long way since Paris.'

'Then what are we waiting for?'

'Just one more thing.' He took her cheeks in his hands and kissed her, slowly and tenderly, letting the warm glow in his chest spread outwards until it enveloped his whole being. 'Have I told you how much you mean to me?'

'Repeatedly!' She laughed. 'You've shown me a few times, too.'

'As long as you don't forget.'

'How could I, when you mean the world to me, too?'

'No more regrets?'

'No more regrets.'

They didn't look back, walking hand in hand into the future.

* * * * *

Historical Note

I've wanted to write this book for several years—ever since I discovered that there's a secret tunnel in the sandstone beneath Nottingham Castle. However, because it's based around the actual events of the period 1325–1331, with a supporting cast of real historical characters, I knew that I needed to be extra-responsible with my research.

I've come back and forth to the story, fitting it in between several other projects, but the main thing I want to stress is that it definitely *isn't* a biography.

Writing about Queen Isabella was a particular problem, because so much we *think* we know about her life comes from biased sources. In the years after her death, she became known as the She-Wolf of France, with 'unrelenting fangs,' according to Thomas Gray's poem *The Bard*

(1757), and was a hated, even feared example of a manipulative and destructive woman, but the truth, according to modern-day biographers, was a lot more complex.

She was probably greedy, with a strong sense of entitlement, and self-interested, but she was also clever, cunning and, at the start of her rebellion against Edward II, had popular support, seeming to be acting in the interests of her son. If it hadn't been for her adulterous affair with Mortimer, she might have been remembered as a good regent and a devoted mother.

I also want to be clear that I'm not accusing her of anything more than infatuation and self-aggrandisement. Although several historians have suggested that she was complicit in the alleged murder of Edward II—and it's possible that she considered this as a means of suppressing another rebellion—other biographers, such as Alison Weir, believe that the chain of events points more clearly at Roger Mortimer, *if* a murder actually took place. In a bizarre twist, there's actually evidence to suggest that Edward escaped his prison and fled to Europe, where he lived out the remainder of his life as a hermit.

In other words, although they were both ruthless and corrupt, I don't want to condemn

Isabella and Mortimer as any worse than they actually were.

There's a lot of history that I've left out, such as Edward's relationship with Hugh le Despenser, which I've touched on only briefly. My original draft included a scene in Hereford at the time of le Despenser's execution, but the whole event was so bloodthirsty, with such horrific homophobic undertones, that it didn't seem suitable for a romance novel and I didn't want to risk trivialising something so barbaric.

The whole political situation during this period was also a lot more complicated than I've described, but I've kept as true to the actual events and timeline as possible—the one notable exception being Isabella's journey to Castle Rising. She didn't actually move to Norfolk until two years after Mortimer's death, but I couldn't resist a scene on the causeway.

If you're interested in reading more about the bits I've left out, I highly recommend Alison Weir's biography *Isabella: She-Wolf of France, Queen of England* and Helen Castor's *She-Wolves: The Women Who Ruled England Before Elizabeth* for more details. Both were a huge help to me.

As for what happened next… Edward III proved to be one of the more successful medieval monarchs, ruling for fifty years, gaining fame for his victories at Crécy and Poitiers and establishing The Most Noble Order of the Garter—an order of chivalry that still exists today. Isabella, meanwhile, survived into her mid-sixties and was eventually allowed to return to court to visit her family, becoming particularly close to her grandson, the Black Prince. When she died, Edward II's heart—or what was believed to be his heart—was interred with her.

Finally, I want to mention the original London Bridge, the longest inhabited bridge ever built in Europe and an important focus for medieval tourism. It took thirty-three years to build, being completed in 1209, and remained in use for six hundred and twenty-two years afterwards, until it was eventually deconstructed and replaced in 1831.

Fortunately, there's a four-metre-long replica in the Church of St Magnus the Martyr on the north side of the new bridge, which shows just how incredible and inspiring this feat of engineering was.

MILLS & BOON

Coming next month

THE HIGHLANDER'S INCONVENIENT BRIDE
Terri Brisbin

'When is Sheena expected to arrive?'

He thought he had time to truly accustom himself to marrying the one woman he could not abide. He thought he could ease into the decision and ready himself to be, at the least, tolerant of her. From the broad smile that spread over his father's face, Robbie knew that his hopes in this were for naught.

'On the morrow. A messenger arrived with word of her approach.'

Time was up for him and any thoughts he had of avoiding this. He knew his duty to his clan.

Robbie nodded to his parents and walked away. So many thoughts and questions filled his mind that he simply left the keep and headed to the yard next to the stables. The last time he'd seen Sheena she was training her father's newest colt. Unmindful of the danger, she had mounted the horse before it would tolerate a saddle or bridle of any kind and she rode the almost wild horse through the village and back to the keep, with her hair flowing out behind her, loose and wild, making her look like some heathen goddess of old. Incandescent with joy, she faltered when their gazes met and he saw her eyes were filled with only loathing.

And, as in every moment he'd ever shared with her

or any time he watched her, she never did as she'd been told to do. She broke her father's rules, damn the consequences. She disregarded her mother's lessons on correct behaviour and her warnings about a proper upbringing for a young woman who would be a wife to and mother of chieftains or their sons.

Soon, too soon, she would ride into Achnacarry and become his problem. She would need to grow up and change to be the wife of the future chieftain. She would need to become a mature woman who understood her place and fulfilled her duties. She could no longer be the hoyden who ran wild and followed her own path.

Surely, Sheena MacLerie would try to obey her father and mother by carrying out her duties.

Yet, even as he hoped, he knew differently for he'd seen the true Sheena MacLerie and understood what was headed in their direction. She was ill prepared for the role of being a laird's wife. Robbie knew all that and more to a certainty and his stomach roiled in anticipation of her arrival.

On the morrow.

Continue reading
THE HIGHLANDER'S INCONVENIENT BRIDE
Terri Brisbin

Available next month
www.millsandboon.co.uk

COMING SOON!